The Baywood Tales

Dr. James Kennedy

authorHOUSE®

AuthorHouse™
1663 Liberty Drive
Bloomington, IN 47403
www.authorhouse.com
Phone: 1-800-839-8640

Published by AuthorHouse 7/9/2012

ISBN: 978-1-4772-1119-9 (sc)
ISBN: 978-1-4772-1118-2 (hc)
ISBN: 978-1-4772-1117-5 (e)

Library of Congress Control Number: 2012909397

For Diane, Scott, Michelle, Kristina and JP

Table of Contents

The Dog Without a Leash

It was clear to Jimmy Spivac that his dog Kino preferred the soft moist grass beneath his feet to the harsh dry pavement of the roadway. It was no wonder to Jimmy, either, that Kino resisted the leash; it was altogether unnecessary anyway as the last thing on earth Kino was going to do was to leave the side of Jimmy Spivac. As a matter of fact, when out for a walk, Jimmy brought the leash along with him to satisfy a neighborhood code about dogs and leashes. He stopped using it years ago.

Kino was always an outdoor dog, and on cold winter nights, it was by force that Jimmy had to go to his yard and physically carry the sixty pound pure-white purebred inside his house, and once inside, Kino slept with his nose at the doorsill sniffing the wintry outdoor air. During the rest of the year, weather permitting, Kino preferred to be outdoors beneath the maples in his backyard or in the screen room where the fresh scents and sounds of all that was natural to him could be heard and experienced apart from the clutter of things manufactured by man. Consequently, Kino never sat on couches or beds; he never ransacked a kitchen trash pail or chewed up a shoe; he never accidentally spilled an indoor plant or sat begging at the dinner table for tidbits. These things never happened because Kino would not remain inside the house. Kino was an outdoor dog.

There were other curious things to mention about Kino. Kino was not an old dog, having only four years beneath his paws, and it was obvious to everyone that he was the most satisfied dog on earth. Jack London reminded us that all dogs retain inside themselves the capability to heed the call of the wild, but Kino seemed to understand the rules of civilized society perfectly. In fact, to the careful observer, it was true that Kino never barked at strangers; he never jumped up on visitors and he always politely

1

submitted to the groping hands of children who wished to pet his ears. Kino could sit patiently for hours, and Jimmy Spivac might whisper once for Kino and his alert companion was already at his side, good-naturedly waiting. Kino could read Jimmy's intentions on the spot and he was always attentive. When a friend or a neighbor who worshiped their dogs sometimes recounted anecdotes of their struggle to rid their beloved pets of undesirable habits, Jimmy had to remain silent. Apparently, Kino was *born* well-behaved, conciliatory, and with a disposition to be happy. And as for that, people might have said the same thing about Jimmy Spivac, as he, too, was good-natured and well-received by everyone. As for Jimmy and Kino together, they had a relationship that was self-evident, and anyone with an interest to notice, would recognize an unassailable bond that is the archetypal story of a man and his dog.

One night at the annual meeting of the residents of Baywood, the beautiful and spacious waterfront community where Jimmy and Kino took up residence, neighbors were discussing projects necessary to keep the environment as bucolic as possible; the boardwalk needed some repairs; some of the teenaged kids *outside* the neighborhood were racing their cars at night and the Pennington family lost their mailbox to vandals. Janet Briggs, a friendly lover of all things canine, sauntered casually over to where Jimmy was chewing on a pretzel. She took a keen interest in the neighborhood, and she had noticed over time that Jimmy walked his dog *unleashed* each day without incident.

"How on earth do you manage to keep your dog so close at hand?" she asked, after some small talk about things in general. "It amazes me when I see you walking together. If my dog Jude wants to chase a squirrel, it takes all the strength I have to hold her in place."

Jude was a beautiful purebred Golden Retriever, and her escapades in the neighborhood were legendary. On a good day, one could not witness a more resplendent coat as the one worn by Jude, nor fathom a Golden with a more regal pose. She was purchased from a renowned breeder several states away, and her lineage was impressive. On occasion, though, Jude could be spotted shaking free the salt water from the marsh, having chased a duck into flight, and her demeanor was all frolic and sport. Jude liked to remind everyone that she was not simply a show dog; she was an impressive swimmer and athlete as well, even if her coat did become as tangled as a janitor's wet mop.

Before Jimmy could respond to Janet's question about Kino, Ginny and Roy Raynor, coffee and biscuits in hand, sauntered over to join the banter, and when they heard the topic was dogs, they had plenty to relate to since they had reared three champion Labradors.

The conversation began with commentary upon the various characteristics of the breeds, citing the Golden Retriever's predilection to the water, for example; shifted to remarks about the individual personalities of their family pets; and ultimately turned into a mild debate about which factors contributed the most to a dog's general disposition. Roy posited the idea that genetics was the key, and that one needed to do considerable research on each specific breeder. Ginny and Janet agreed, but they wanted to emphasize that the home environment should not be underestimated; no one provided a more loving den for their purebreds than these two caregivers. Finally, the ball came around to Jimmy Spivac, who politely listened all the while, and his neighbors' faces were attuned and eager to hear his views, and Janet once again asked about Kino. Jimmy didn't have a strong opinion one way or the other, genuinely believing, as did his neighbors, that both the environment and genetics weighed heavily when determining a dog's temperament. More specifically, however, it became evident to Jimmy that he was expected to tell the narrative that was Kino's story, and to speak directly of his companion's pedigree and how it was that Kino came to Baywood.

"I paid nothing for Kino," Jimmy began, and his neighbors' brows lifted in disbelief. "He was a gift, and concerning our friendly debate about disposition, I think I have to side with the home environment as the key. At least that has been my experience with Kino."

The ladies were delighted, and Roy was too, but they wanted to hear the rest without a detail unspoken. They settled in for more, and Jimmy decided to tell the whole story.

"About five years ago, just before I moved into Baywood, I completed a lengthy business commitment and finally I had some real time for myself, several months in fact, to vacation. For years I wanted to visit the national parks, and to visit with friends in California, so I rented a van and set out on a road trip. I visited Juniper Springs and the Florida Keys first, made my way southwest to the unforgettable Chisos Mountains of Texas, and then headed to the Grand Canyon. Desirous of some human interaction I guess, I pulled next into Las Vegas and stayed a few days playing Black Jack and Keno."

"Keno?" Ginny asked politely, with a smile. "Is that where you got the name?"

"Well, not exactly," Jimmy replied, "although the word was with me all the while."

Roy looked askance at his wife, and so, too, did Janet, implying that she needn't have interrupted. "Please, continue," he said, before sipping his coffee.

"Upon leaving Las Vegas, I was driving for hours through the God-forsaken flatlands of Nevada, drenched in mid-day sunlight, in the middle of the desert's most barren landscape. I was alone on the road and I was thinking that this isolation was why travelers were warned to check their vehicles before passing through there, when, to my amazement, there appeared before me, puzzling yet unmistakable, a single, solitary stop sign. What's more, tacked lazily onto the stop sign post, there dangled a fence picket with the words, 'Dogs for Sale,' and the picket itself pointed the way. I looked north, south, east and west and there wasn't a thing in sight, but I made a spontaneous decision to obey that picket and see what fate lay in store for me.

"A few miles down the road, a virtual oasis sprang before me, and when I pulled into the drive, a cacophony of sound blasted hysterically as would a mad symphony. I was stunned! Here existed a self-sufficient game farm, encompassing perhaps ten acres or so, surviving alone without a neighbor for miles. Remarkably, thriving upon this ranch, there dwelled as many varied animals as anyone could imagine. Peacocks strutted in front of the van, dozens of dogs bellowed my arrival at their absolute highest decibels, a goat or two strayed nearby, and there were horses and sheep, and I think, a llama. Overhead, hawks and crows and desert sparrows darted wildly, doing their part to add to the chaos. In the middle of this asylum, and amidst the bedlam my arrival had created, a neglected cottage sat empty, and upon its weary façade, another fence picket was tacked precipitously beside the open door. Upon it, someone had scribbled the word 'Office.'

"It was the moment I exited the van that paralysis once again took hold of me, but this time, it was by the thick stench of the farm itself, the likes of which cannot be overstated. The din generated by the startled animals subsided rather quickly, leaving only the odor and the barking of dogs, and once revived, I poked my head inside the empty shanty and called out. No one answered. I remember thinking how much soot had settled upon the worn-out tables and frayed chairs, and how odd it was that there was no actual front door to the lodging. I called out again more resolute this time, and from behind me, I heard a booming response: 'Over here! How can I help you?'

"That's how I met Granger, a stubbly southwest breeder of champion German Shepherds. I explained to him that I might be interested in a puppy, and he wasted no time. Settling the yowling shepherds of his domain with a wave of his arm, he brought me to a fenced pen about thirty feet by thirty, and inside, there were six or seven of the most magnificent puppies. They stood alert at our presence and they were beautiful. These were athletic dogs, and if ever prizes were to be won by canines, I was among the medalists. Vigorous and perfect in every detail, these champions were for sale.

"Granger entered the pen and lifted the six-week old puppies and each melted with compliance. He inspected them topsy-turvy at his discretion, and each one patiently acquiesced. Some pups were dark with mixed tans, two were pure white and two were predominately black, but all possessed dark skin features about the nose, ears and eyelids. They were trophy dogs and Granger knew it.

"Inexplicably, I was feeling ambivalent suddenly, and injudiciously, I decided to forget the whole idea. I excused myself and thanked Granger when I explained awkwardly that I had changed my mind. I was about to pull away when Granger intervened: 'I want to show you something before you go,' he insisted, and in a moment, we were back at the pen.

"Unnoticed before, in the corner of the active enclosure, there was a feeding dock, perhaps two feet high, with a sloping wooden ramp designed for the toddling pups to climb for water and food. Granger walked directly to where the ramp touched the ground, and with one hand groping, he pulled from the recess created there a white lump of diseased fur. In his open palm, he presented to me the runt of the litter, shivering and near death. It appeared as a tumor; its distorted form filthy and ravaged with wounds, and from its eye and left ear, blood-gorged ticks sucked at the last remnants of life.

"'The litter has chewed this one pretty bad,' Granger explained, 'ripping it in their teeth as a rag, gashing at it as an old piece of leather. Poor thing has howled the death cry for weeks, keeping me awake at night.' Granger placed the dying puppy in my hand, and he squeezed free the ticks barehanded as effortlessly as picking berries. 'Come inside. I'll set you with a pad, water dish and some food. You would be doing me a favor; the litter would have this one dead within a few more nights.'

"Back inside the shanty and once again surrounded by all things dusty, I accepted the gift and prepared to leave the farm. Granger scribbled his address on a pad and stuffed the note into my shirt pocket. 'He may live or he may not,' he said, 'but promise me you will write to me in one year and let me know.' I agreed.

"The day had waned into night and that first evening passed without incident. By mid-morning the next day, travelling toward California's Lake Arrowhead, the afflicted puppy's condition turned critical; he had stopped breathing. Heartbroken, I placed my cheek upon the lifeless creature and sighed. However, at this close proximity, I realized that I was mistaken. The diaphragm was moving. So weak and lifeless was this pitiable creature, I was certain he had died. I was wrong; he was breathing ever so faintly.

"After that initial scare, I was convinced we were going to make it. I decided on the name Kino because it referenced a game of luck when gambling in Vegas, but also, because Kino was the name of the unlucky protagonist of Steinbeck's novella, *The Pearl*. I kept a vigilant eye upon Kino, and before long, he gained enough strength to stand, and then to wobble about the van, and then to explore the forest floor at Lake Arrowhead. He was doing quite well overall and each morning brought renewed vigor.

"The second scare came a few days later. Eating healthier portions and becoming more agile, Kino had a solid bowel movement, and from a respectful distance, I saw that something was wrong. The stool was completely white. Hastily, I stuck my head to within inches of it and I was shocked; long strands of squirming white worms writhed as thin snakes from within the movement. I had never seen anything like this before. Kino was sick internally, and he needed a vet immediately.

I wasn't giving up on Kino, so I raced like an ambulance driver into town and the first outpost I came to was a general store that sold everything from gunpowder to shoe laces. With Kino inside the van, I flew to the counter and collared the proprietor: 'My dog is really sick and I need a vet right away. His stool is filled with worms! I think he is going to die.'

I focused on the shopkeeper's face for the first time about then, and his concern turned to a wry smile. 'You're not from around here, are you?' he asked. He coughed and stood up, clamored to a wooden shelf and removed a small square box. 'Give him these pills and follow the label instructions. He will be fine in a couple of days. Your dog's got worms. Ha! Ha!'

"The label read 'Worm Away' and I was flabbergasted. How was I to know that worms in dogs were as ordinary as a common cold? He was right. Kino was fine soon thereafter. In fact, before long, Kino resembled his siblings in the litter, and his pure white coat sheened and his muscular frame developed. Given this second chance, Kino not only survived, he flourished, for his genetics were those of a champion breed."

At this point in the narrative, Jimmy Spivac noticed that another neighbor, Don Lober, was listening from behind his left shoulder. The Lober family included an eight year old Yorkshire named *Maggie* that was frequently at the veterinarian; it was common knowledge that over ten thousand dollars in medical expenses had been assumed to maintain her health. Don Lober held a coffee cake to his chin, and he swallowed before speaking.

"Keep going," he mumbled through the crumbs. "What happened next?"

Ginny, Roy, and Janet were still listening intently to Jimmy's lengthy narrative. All three leaned forward when Roy offered his opinion for consideration:

"You seem to be supporting the idea that a dog's genetics, given a healthy environment of course, will ultimately determine disposition and temperament," Roy pointed out. "Today, thanks to a strong constitution, Kino has recovered completely."

"Not completely," Jimmy continued. "Physically, it is true, Kino's form is perfect. But as we continued to travel through the national parks, Kino became extraordinarily possessive of me. At Sequoya, I could not walk without his ribs brushing against my legs; at Yellowstone, Kino rested at night beside me; at Banff, he followed my every move."

Janet spoke next: "He was so grateful...he became devoted to you... you were his savior...you rescued him from his torturous past. That is why you don't need a leash."

"I was thinking that as well," Jimmy resumed, "until something happened in a state park in Colorado. I was on the road for some time, enjoying the parks, and Kino was a fine companion and a beautiful specimen, over thirty pounds by then, and many families were outdoors enjoying the parks with their pets as well. On one occasion, a small mixed-breed, perhaps ten pounds in weight, approached Kino with a robust bark. Kino behaved as in a nightmare; he leapt to my chest in terror, and he was attempting to find refuge within my shirt. Panicked beyond all reasonable threat, Kino feared for his life. I recall wrenching him from my ribcage with great effort, and yelling at him: 'You are a German Shepherd for God's sake! That dog is no threat to you! It is no bigger than a Miniature Poodle!' Finally, Kino calmed down, but he whimpered uncontrollably until the bewildered family took their friendly little dog away."

The neighbors at the Baywood meeting were preparing to leave for their homes, so Jimmy Spivac wrapped things up straight away. Janet, Ginny, Roy and Don held for the conclusion.

"Four years have passed since those early experiences and Kino has improved greatly. His temperament is calm and deferential, and his devotion to me is without question. Travelling with Kino for months in the national parks has left within him an indelible love for the outdoors. Yet, it is undeniable; those first six weeks as the runt of the litter in that ruthless dog pen had distorted his temperament and disposition. He was the victim of pitiless brutality, and because he will be forever affected, it is unlikely he will ever realize his full potential. Janet, you asked me how on earth I manage to keep my dog so close at hand. I think that Kino is walking on a leash after all, albeit an invisible one. When we are out together, it is true; he does not stray from my side. But it is not because of my training; though I wish it were so. Kino does not need a leash because of his tormented past; he will not wander because he is *afraid* to encounter another dog."

The Incident at Cupsogue

A young man and a young woman were sitting at the edge of the seashore facing the pacific blue horizon. They had risen early and they had the beach quite to themselves. The sunrise was just two hours old, and along the water's edge, it was very peaceful and quiet; the plovers hardly raced at all and seemed disappointed; the terns were hushed and were solemn with waiting; the gulls had difficulty determining the direction of the wind; even the cormorants gave up their swim and lolled lazily about the surface of the sleepy tide. It would have been impossible for the morning to be more tranquil.

Their youngest child, wearing only an oversized tee-shirt, was playing quietly beside them digging tunnels in the sand with a seashell. Her movements were barely perceptible. Behind them, quite a distance away along the dune line, were their two older children, and they were anything but quiet. The excited children were tossing themselves from the top of the steepest dune, the one they had determined the best for tumbling, and they were rolling hysterically down the sand-slide they had formed. Sometimes they stood or kneeled upon their bogie boards, sliding and grasping the safety chord with one hand like a bronco-busting cowhand in the saddle; other times they flipped themselves recklessly headlong like cliff divers with absolute abandonment of all things restrained. Sand covered their bodies like sugar, and they exalted in it and in their freedom, and when they were completely coated, they dashed away to the ocean to be cleansed, only to race back again to their exhilarating ride. It was great fun for them, and their joy and their happiness was as pure and as perfect as the morning itself.

After an indeterminate span of silent serenity, the young man gave out a sigh and whispered to his wife beside him.

"Suppose for a moment," he began, "that a depressed woman made her way along the beach here at Cupsogue, and this woman was troubled because she had suffered terribly from circumstances laden with insurmountable sorrow. Let's assume that her childhood was filled with neglect and abuse and her torment had been endured for many years, and that a more immediate tragedy had broken her spirit completely. Alone and deadened by despair, the woman walked very slowly and her lips trembled because her misery had shaken her to the core; she felt forsaken because no one cared for her, and as for that, she no longer believed in herself or in her future. Upon her face anyone would witness all things disturbing, worrisome and mournful, for an overwhelming sadness had invaded her soul."

The young man paused in the telling of the narrative for he knew he might not be encouraged to continue. He also recognized that he may well have overstated the situation. He enjoyed airing out all of the prattle he could muster, and sometimes it annoyed everyone. He waited patiently.

"Yes, get on with it," responded the woman.

She was accustomed to these hypotheticals, and on occasion, she enjoyed listening to her husband invent them. Thus far, this was not likely to be one of those occasions. Quickly she glanced about her, checked that the children did not wander toward the dangerous crags of the rock jetty, sipped some water, and settled again. The family still had the beach quite to themselves.

He smiled broadly at her willingness to play along for a while.

"But here is the point. Let's say our suffering woman sat down at the shoreline and she began to weep. Overwhelmed with grief, she embraced defeat and she became aware that her resolve to continue on with her life was weakening and she realized that her perspective had shifted; she was considering the surrender of her life to the ocean. Her sadness welled from deep within her bosom, and at last, with her head buried in her hands, she moved her lips in a prayer and she asked for some sign of hope. The outpouring of her tears was a purging of her afflicted soul, and having dispensed with all reserve, she prayed, "Dear God!" for a sign that she should go on living. When she could cry no more, she lifted her face from her hands, and upon opening her eyes, she saw there directly before her, as near as can be, a magnificent sea bird. Startled, she *thought* instantly that here was *the sign*, but at that precise moment, while considering this portentous bird, something else occurred. Above her in the summer sky, unbeknownst to her before, the sun emerged from behind a solitary cloud and sunlight splashed brilliantly upon her face. And then, as if fatefully commanded from above, a warm breeze had arisen and it soothed her skin, and she had to wonder, *she had to wonder*, for it did occur to her *all at once* that she was receiving that very message of hope for which she had moments before so desperately prayed!"

The young woman considered the matter for the briefest of moments.

"No!" she said. "It was a coincidence. God does not send sea gulls to the shore, nor control the clouds and the winds. He does not instigate earthquakes, nor assuage them, and He does not sanction wars in His name. It was a coincidence and that is all."

Having established that point, she addressed another aspect of the narrative that bothered her from the start, and it was clear that she intended to take the ball for a moment.

"I reject your premise at any rate. The idea that she would drown herself is preposterous, and as for seeking solace from her grief, it is unlikely she would wander here. I suppose it is possible, but everyone must deal with unhappiness, and most unhappy people seek distraction instead...within our cities, our museums, our music halls...our literature. We revel in our own ingenious creations...our science and mathematics, our theater, sports and commerce...and from these activities we gain purpose and feel worth. Ask your children, should their mood be despondent, if they would prefer to hike through some hidden chasm in the Painted Desert, or would they choose, instead, a day at Disney World."

"Who is that man?" asked their youngest child, suddenly pointing.

The parents craned their necks at once. An unsettling intruder was entering upon the scene, and his destination was discomforting, as well was his appearance. He was heading straight toward the children along the dunes.

He was a bearded, heavy-set man in his twenties, wearing oversized water shoes, khaki-colored bathing shorts, a hooded sweatshirt with a back-pack about his shoulders, and he carried a piece of driftwood as a walking stick. His appearance was rather like that of a mountain man, and because it was evident that he intended to interact with the children in some way, the adults and children stood alert and frozen to their previous occupations.

It wasn't his appearance alone that was startling; it was his gait. The stranger took long and determined strides, huge, awkward steps that seemed out of sorts, even though everyone appears rather odd when walking hurriedly in thick sand. He happened upon the children very quickly, for they had been absorbed in their activities, and they were concerned. They looked to their parents' locale and were satisfied; their father was speedily on the move, having closed half the distance to the interloper already, and he was clearly aware of the situation. There was no real danger as yet, and when the man seemingly passed by without incident, the children resumed playing, though cautiously and without mirth, and their father relaxed his stride a bit and protectively observed. A most remarkable thing happened next.

It was true that the man passed by the children without incident; but curiously, he stopped walking suddenly in front of a massive pile of seaweed near the dunes. Quickly he removed his pack and he scurried comically like a sand crab into the sea grass. He gathered with both arms a most prodigious amount of the stuff, such that he could barely see where he was going, and he waddled back toward the children, and in particular, to the chute in the sand that was the slide where they had been playing. The children stepped aside and they watched him as he went about the task at hand. He let go the bundle and spread it as best he could about the trough, and then hurried for more. He waved to the kids and to their father as well, and he smiled and then laughed, and he waddled some more as he carried the sea-weed once again to the slide, never minding the tiny shrimp and sand fleas that danced about his gruff countenance. And then he spoke:

"The wet grass is best for sliding," he said, by way of explanation. "You have to put a whole lot of it down for it to really get going. It helps if you take some sea water in a pail and dump it all around."

Without hesitation, he went back a third time for more sea-weed, and while he labored to cover the slide, he resumed speaking:

"Really…I wish I could stay for a ride…but I better not anymore…I'm not a kid anyhow, I guess…Ha! Ha! That's what Mr. Donnelly says to me…'Craig, you're not a kid anymore,' he says… I don't have to work at my job today. I have a job at the game farm, and I just bought a new cell-phone, and boy are they a lot of money. I get paid on Fridays."

As he was finishing up his task, he returned to his back-pack and slid it on. Everyone was confused, but soon it was clear enough. Here was a very friendly man…an honest and simple man…who knew about slides at the beach.

"Well goodbye!" he declared, with a friendly gesture. "I must get going. I am walking all the way to the jetty and back. I am walking and swimming. I love to swim...and I am a very good swimmer...the wet seaweed makes it go faster."

And with that said, he walked down the beach. The children gathered around their father, who was no longer confused. He recognized the special needs of this man, and he knew the man was well-intentioned and kind. He reassured his children and he returned to his place at the shoreline. The kids scooted back to the dune, for they were anxious to set the grassy slide to the test. They resumed with intensity their frolic and gaiety.

"Who was that man?" his wife wanted to know. "Is everything all right?"

The young man took his seat beside her once again.

"I don't know... but I think he's all right. His name is Craig, and I think he may be adult autistic...he is high-functioning and he has some issues...he said he worked at the game farm, and he was friendly enough... even childlike. He reminded me of Collin."

Everyone knew someone who suffered with autism, and Collin was that person for this family. For years, autism was associated with children only, but more recently, many autistic adults were a part of the community. The children knew about Collin, who was in his early teens, and about autism, but they were as yet unaccustomed to adult autism.

"I think I know who that man is!" exclaimed the eldest child, who suddenly appeared sandblasted at his parents' side with a sibling tagging close behind. "It was Santa Claus in the summer-time, because he had a beard, and he was fat and jolly, and he sure knows about slides! It works! It's really, really fast! "

"Hey mom!" interjected the other child, whose face was so full of sand that two eyes peered from behind a mask. "Can you tell it's me? I tried to cover my whole face!"

The children raced into the cool blue water and then back toward their slide.

The rest of the morning was uneventful. Later on, as the beach filled with tourists and local families, the children played with friends and the young man and the young woman chatted with neighbors and acquaintances. By mid-afternoon, the family stopped for ices at the pavilion and headed back to their Westhampton home.

Two weeks had passed and the young woman was at home reading the local Southampton Press. In it, an article appeared about a dramatic rescue at the beach; a seven year old girl was fishing with her uncle when she slipped from the rocks at the jetty and she fell headlong into the dangerous currents of the Cupsogue Inlet. The waters carried the struggling girl quickly away from her uncle, but incredibly, a young man further along the jetty dove fearlessly into the inlet after her. Deftly he turned her head and shoulders toward the sky and side-stroked away from the crags and rocks of the jetty to the safety of the sand in Moriches Bay. A fisherman in a small boat witnessed the whole ordeal, and he reported that he could not have imagined a more heroic rescue. The brave rescuer, who wished to remain anonymous, was quoted as saying: "I like to walk all the way to the jetty and back...I was walking and swimming...I love to swim...and I am a very good swimmer." The grateful uncle expressed the whole incident as a miracle: "Thank God the man was there to save her. I would not have been able to reach her in time."

Lost in Astoria - A Thanksgiving Story

"Thanksgiving is not all about food," lectured Sister Benedicta, pointing her authoritative index finger at me and at the rest of her first grade class. "Remember the poor, and give generously to our food drive," she commanded. "I want that crate stocked full of canned goods in two days. Do we understand each other?"

Sister Benedicta didn't mean to be mean, and she wasn't mean, but she was a tall woman, and when she stood in full habit in front of her six year old children (she never referred to us as students) with her finger wagging, General Patton could not have been a more imposing classroom presence. All of us, shivering from her decree, introspectively swore on our defenseless lives that we would empty our cupboards of every tin cylinder we could sneak out of our house. If anything in heaven and on earth was certain, it was that we were we going to fill that crate with peas, soups, beans, gravy, creamed corn, potatoes, pumpkin, cranberry sauce, and all things canned. I remember the next day Dennis Keeler whispering to me on the bus, "I am in *big* trouble when I get home," because he had loaded his back pack with so much iron that he dragged with both hands the dead weight across the hallway, finally hoisting it like a gunny sack into the classroom.

Dennis was the student who cried hysterically and with complete abandonment the first day of school; he scuttled from his desk all morning and howled so vociferously, that the rest of us could not get our complaints heard even if we did cry. We were grateful to him that day because his demonstrative outburst at this predicament called "school" was so excessive that the rest of us were simply astonished that so much noisy lamentation could be emitted by such a small frame. Dennis was crawling up the walls

15

in absolute terror, and compared to what *he* was experiencing, the rest of our class felt a soothing calmness descend upon us. By the next day, he was fine. It turns out that Dennis did everything in the extreme, and when he decided to help with the food drive, he donated everything he could get his hands on.

The whole school couldn't wait another minute for the Thanksgiving holiday break, and when the final bell rang at Stella Maris Regional School in Sag Harbor, uniformed children attacked the school bus like our soldiers at Normandy. We were free at last, and tomorrow, Thanksgiving Day, would mean turkey and pastry desserts for everyone. For my family, it meant a long car ride to Astoria, Queens to visit Grandma Honey and Aunt Marie and Uncle Joe and to run around all day unsupervised with my numerous cousins. My family was quite an addition to the bedlam at my grandma's house; eight of us tumbling out of a yellow Rambler, and including my other relatives on my mother's side, there were no less than twenty three cousins under the age of sixteen arriving Thanksgiving Day to run around unbridled at the large but unassuming house on Fourteenth Street near the Triborough Bridge. What a day to be a kid!

As one member of a very large family, pandemonium and chaos was fairly normal for me. It bothered my Uncle Joe after a while though; he didn't like the noise during the football game, so he gave each of us a quarter to disappear from the parlor for an hour. He did this every year, and I can't be certain, but it was possible some of my older cousins may have instigated some distractions during the game, inciting him to fork over the coin so they could go to the candy shack before dinner. "Come over here, you beasts!" was Uncle Joe's booming directive, and we lined up like dominoes. "Here's a quarter…Get lost!" It was all very amicable, and lots of fun. Uncle Joe always had enough quarters for everyone, and on occasion, to the older ones, he passed along a dollar bill, and so my elder cousins took care to remind us all to stay away for *an entire hour*, and that if we messed up this arrangement, they would have to kill us dead. I stuffed my quarter right away into my pocket, passed by the kitchen, and looked in to see my mom and all my aunts busily shuffling steaming pots and huge platters, so I headed outside to see what was cooking in the backyard.

Oddly, it was quiet back there. I looked around and decided that many of my cousins took to the street toward the candy shack, and I put it into my head that if I hurried, it was likely I would catch up to them. The problem was that I didn't really know where the candy shack was located, as I was far too young to have ventured there before, but I thought it was nearby, just around the corner.

They say that when one entered the labyrinth of Daedalus, upon taking just a few steps from the portal, one might wander aimlessly for a lifetime before discovering a suitable egress. When I trotted around the corner that morning, I lost my bearings in an instant. My mouth went dry and a sallow feeling descended upon me. I became anxious. It began as a pang of worry, but soon it was as though I fell into a fever; the landscape began to swirl as in a whirlpool, and from within the spinning currents, there appeared the bricks of unfamiliar row houses; the parked cars were lifted from the concrete and they whirled madly; strange chain-link fences that held nameless dogs barking from the recesses spun wildly before me and added to my growing confusion. "I must not panic!" I thought to myself, but I started to run frantically through the maze of jumbled sidewalks, and my fears broke through in one solid voice: "It is hopeless! You cannot find your way! You are lost! It is hopeless!" and I knew that my continued flight would end badly. I slackened my pace and my tears surged so suddenly I stopped moving completely.

As a six year old child thoroughly lost in a strange city, what else could I do? I sat at the curb's edge in the middle of a random street and I cried. With my elbows on my knees and my head in my hands, I wept. I can't be sure how long I sat crying, but before too long, emerging from the sobbing haze as it were, a thin voice prevailed:

"Little one! Hey there! Little boy! Are you lost?"

I turned, and from between the peaks of a shingled roof, leaning forward from a small, third-story window, a young man was calling to me. I brushed myself together, and I and shook my head, "*Yes!*" and in the briefest of moments, he was at my side speaking to me. I recall he was well-dressed, wearing a suit befitting the holiday, and he was perhaps thirty years old. His voice was kind and his countenance cheerful.

He may have asked all of the usual questions one would expect under the circumstances, and I am sure I obliged his every enquiry; my name, the description of my grandmother's house, and all things else. It was fairly remarkable what this stranger did next. Without fuss, he said something like, "Well then, young man. Let's find that house, shall we?" and he extended his well-groomed hand toward mine, and reaching up toward his hand, I saw that he offered to me two fingers to hold as we walked. In this manner we set out upon our search, talking all the while, and his voice was benevolent, and his gait was obliging to my tiny steps. I recall my fears had subsided, and when we arrived at the façade of each house on the street, with his free hand outstretched and finger pointing, the man asked as in a game, "Is this the one?" and when we approached another house, and yet another, he asked each time, "Is this the one?" and in this way, we searched. I can't say how far we walked or how many houses we surveyed, but before too long, there before me was a familiar house, and in the driveway was our yellow Rambler, and I was no longer lost.

In my excitement, I ran away from the well-dressed stranger toward the house and I did not have the wherewithal to be less than completely selfish and self-absorbed. I never looked back; not even to say thank you. I ran mightily through the gate and into the foyer. I burst into the kitchen, proclaiming: "I am safe! I made it back! I am safe!" and to my astonishment, my mother with my aunts, all bustling with platters now full to the brim with victuals ready to be served, repeated, as if spoken a hundred times: "No children in the kitchen!" My mother, grinning freely, addressed me directly:

"What on earth are you blabbering?" she asked, raising her forefinger and pointing toward the parlor. "Go to your cousins and tell everyone we will be eating in ten minutes…spread the word." And with that reasonable request from my mom, I left the crowded kitchen.

It took me a minute to realize that absolutely no one knew that I was missing. I tried to tell the story to anyone who might listen, but it was dismissed in a flurry, as my siblings with my cousins were still racing around enjoying all kinds of mischief. We still couldn't bother Uncle Joe, so the whole ordeal took less than an hour. My cousins did, in fact, go the candy shack, and they were keen to show me their sweet treasures. I was envious, I admit, but suddenly remembering, I checked my trousers and within my pocket, I still had my quarter. I was feeling pretty hungry by then, and I couldn't wait for the turkey and the pastry desserts!

Years have passed and I think about that man on every Thanksgiving Day. It bothers me a bit that I can't remember a single feature of the stranger's face; perhaps one cannot retain that kind of detail on a guardian angel.

The Acorns

When you are ten years old, you have several best friends all at the same time. For about two weeks, Glenn Larsen was definitely my best friend. It wasn't simply because he had the only in-ground pool in the neighborhood, either, though it was a pretty hot summer and the whole gang was determined to be Glenn's best buddy. It didn't matter much, though. Glenn and his sister Anita along with their parents were very generous by nature, and so, during the scorching afternoons, just about every kid on the block who could swim was diving into the clear blue water of their backyard pool. We were in heaven.

Of course, you couldn't just run over to their house uninvited and dive right in. There were rules; nobody could call for Glen or Anita to swim before nine o'clock in the morning, for example, and if there were chores to be done, then his mom or dad would scatter any visiting kid with a brusque wave, saying, "Come back in two hours!" and that was that. Also, as a matter of general knowledge, it was considered bad form to knock on their door with a pool towel in your hand.

One morning, just around nine o'clock, I stashed my pool towel in the bushes of Glenn's front yard as usual and knocked low on his aluminum screen door. My best friend burst through the entranceway with the energy of a tornado. In his right hand, held stationary in front of my incredulous eyes, he presented to me the most professionally-carved, exquisitely-laminated sling-shot on the entire planet. The handle was made of sturdy oak, and the band was a single stretch of rubber an inch thick; it was far superior to the clumsy ones we constructed with flimsy rubber bands and imperfect twigs found in the woods. It was a marvel to behold! Glenn let me grip it for a moment, and I was jealous. And then, my magnanimous friend did something momentous; with his left hand hidden behind his back, he revealed another sling-shot identical to his own.

"My dad made them on his saw last night!" Glenn said jubilantly. "He made this one for you!"

Glenn placed the magnificent piece into my hand and I accepted it as if it were the most precious gem in the world. I wrapped my fingers about the stem and I stopped breathing; it was the most generous gift of my young life. I looked into Glenn's face, and his grinning mouth was opened-wide with excitement and anticipation.

"Let's go!" he exclaimed, and the two of us set about racing towards the woods down the block.

"Hold on!" came a booming voice from the area of the garage.

It was Glenn's father motioning for us to hustle over to him immediately. We did so without delay, for to ignore a directive from someone's father was suicide. Glenn's father was a strong, muscular man with full hair and a tanned complexion. When he spoke, he said things only once, for such was the power of his presence. God help anyone who ignored his commands, and this was true for all of the fathers in the neighborhood. He addressed us directly, and it was clear he had something to say that was important:

"Now listen to me!" he warned, with his index finger pointing. "You are *not* to use rocks in the sling-shot."

I looked at my wooden armament again, and then looked to him to express my thanks without words; I think he could tell from my expression how grateful I was for the thoughtful gift.

"I cut up some balsam dowels into soft pellets," he continued, producing two pouches and handing one to each of us. "These alone will be used by you! If I find out you shot stones, I will take the sling shots away for good... and you will have to ...*deal...with...me!* Now be careful...and have fun!"

Inside the pouches were a gross or more of the light-weight projectiles. I recall placing the first one inside the leathery sleeve in the center of the thick band and stretching it back to my chin; the soft pellet flew between the forks with amazing precision. Glenn did the same...and we were in heaven. We scoured the woods for hours in pursuit of lively targets, and the whole morning was glorious. After lunch, we were careful to put our prized "toys" away until later to avoid confiscation by older bullies. For a few hours, anyway, the beautiful sling-shots were not to be shared with anyone, and together, we swore to keep their hiding spot an exclusive secret.

It wasn't long before we were out of pellets. Glenn's father was at work all day and fabricating more of them on our own was impossible. We knew we could not shoot rocks, and neither Glenn nor I wished to disobey his father; even the crushed bluestone pebbles from the driveway were out of the question. We decided to try to locate some of the spent pellets that lay scattered in the woods, and upon our initial search, we discovered very few of them. We both agreed that locating enough of them to go on a hunt was futile. Discouraged, the two of us made our way back to the shady part of Glenn's yard to wait for his father's return.

We decided to put aside our sling shots for a while so we could play with our black and silver pocket knives. Every kid had one. We challenged each other to a few rounds of *Dare*; a game that obliged each of us in turn to thrust the steely blade into the ground in the proximity of our opponent's foot. The idea was to get closer and closer to our adversary's toes until one of us declared cowardice.

After that, we moved to the soft grass of the lawn and started to wrestle. Sometimes I would pin Glenn's shoulders to the ground with my knees, freeing my hands to playfully smack his face around in victory. Other times he would do the same to me. We were getting bored quickly, so we rolled over on our backs and stared up at the clouds in the sky. "I see a fish!" Glenn announced, and then together, we identified the billowy shape to confirm the image.

Glenn took out his magnifying glass next, and we searched about the concrete walkway looking for an unlucky ant. We found a few, but the sun wasn't strong enough to bother them, so we gave that up in a hurry. Before long, we found ourselves back at the shade tree, and so we retrieved our prized sling-shots, examined them from every angle, and resigned ourselves to simple daydreaming about fresh pellets until Glenn's father came home after work.

As we sat on the ground brooding, something miraculous happened. It was difficult getting comfortable under the oak tree because of the round, pellet-like nuts that lay all about the shade in plain view. We swept an area free of the annoying wooden orbs so we could stretch out, and that's when it finally occurred to us. Acorns! Millions of them! All over! Everywhere! Glenn picked one up and looked at it the way a caveman might study a shard of granite when inventing a stone tool. I tried one out first to see if the acorn-pellet shot true. I dead-eyed the bird bath across the yard and let it fly; "Ping!" was all we heard. We looked at each other with expressions as dumb as oxen.

"They're not rocks, these acorns," Glenn uttered, dispelling any worries about compromising his father's plain words.

"Definitely not rocks!" I concurred, with enthusiasm.

We over-filled our pouches, and once again, we were in heaven. With endless ammo at hand, Glenn and I took to climbing the oak tree in his yard when hanging around doing nothing. We could search for rodents from up there, but we never did hit anything alive "*dead-on*" with the acorns. Later on, we practiced our aim by placing a tin soda can on the fencepost, shooting and keeping score as in a marksman's contest. That was fun for a while, but soon enough, we lost interest in the activity. Time passed slowly, and we were sitting up there in the tree with our sling-shots like a couple of hunters, when a huge UPS truck appeared up the road. It was dark brown and as large as an elephant, and we knew it was destined to pass beneath us within range.

Imagining we were primitive warrior-scouts securing food for our prehistoric village, we held still in the tree until the unsuspecting behemoth passed slowly below us. Anxiously we loaded our weapons, and when the instant arrived, and with singular purpose and steadfast resolve, we aimed and fired! The acorns struck the elephant-beast soundly, and immediately we reloaded and unleashed a second bombardment. "Ping! Ping!" clanged our attack! We had stunned the mighty mammoth!

Then something unexpected occurred. The wooly mammoth once again became a plain brown delivery truck. The driver halted with an abrupt screech and he dashed out of the cab. He spotted us in our perch straight away, and with fists upraised, he took chase. He was livid. We knew, then, we were in trouble. We fell from the tree limbs like dead crows and we scrambled across the manicured lawn like ambushed gazelles. The furious driver was cursing us both with unspeakable expletives when I saw him cut away from the oak tree in my direction. He was hot on my tail.

As every boy knows, when being chased by an enraged adult, or by a junk-yard dog for that matter, it is "every man for himself!" God knows where Glenn ran, but I bolted around the pool area toward the corner of the house leading to the bushes in the front yard. I dove as would Superman taking-flight, headlong into the shrubbery, and I rolled like a combat marine into the darkness beneath Glenn's front porch. With my chest to the ground, I maneuvered through sticky spider webs deep into the dank enclave and waited. My eyes peered out from the sanctuary as would a frightened opossum. The curse words were getting nearer:

"I will kill you when I catch you!" the driver shouted maliciously. "You better run!" he frothed, suddenly very near to the bushes.

I held my breath, when, in disbelief, I saw my pool towel dangling on an azalea plant in plain view. The driver approached it and he picked it up and looked farther into the landscaped bed where I was hiding. I could see his uniformed pant cuffs and black boots pass in front of the porch opening. I inched further back into the filthy recesses. He must have known I was nearby.

"You better run!" he shouted again, tossing my towel aside. He ambled slowly about in silence, listening.

I didn't expect what he did next. The angry man went to the front door and banged with heavy fists upon the aluminum screen door and waited... fuming. A second time he banged, and perhaps because Glenn's mother was in the basement doing laundry, or perhaps because she was busy on the telephone, she was slow attending to the clamorous entreaty at her door. The currier, continuing to speak with mumbled obscenities, finally stepped off of the decked entryway and headed back to his truck.

Minutes felt like hours, when, at last, I heard the engine start and the wheels of the elephant truck begin to roll. I waited. As one might expect, the outraged man circled the area. All was quiet. I exhaled. It was a close call. I knew I was safe, but what about Glenn?

I crawled out of the hole to survey the neighborhood. The angry driver was gone. Nonetheless, I stepped stealthily, like an escaped convict, back toward the pool. Glen emerged cautiously from behind the pool filter where he had found refuge. We were both shaken. I was filthy with soot, but unharmed. Glenn smelled of chlorine and he was sweating, but safe. In our shaky hands, neither of us had forsaken our sling-shots. We decided on the spot to put them away in our secret place. Suddenly, a voice was calling from the kitchen window. It was Glenn's mother:

"Were you banging on the front door?" she wanted to know.

Glenn was pretty quick-witted when he needed to be, so he dodged the question altogether.

"Can we go in the pool now, mom?" he asked innocently. "It has been more than an hour since lunch."

"Okay," responded his benevolent mother, "...but no diving until your father gets home...and go get the pool towel from the driveway...somebody left one out there...pick it up before your father runs it over with the car!"

With that simple request satisfied, and without a worry in the world, Glenn and I were swimming in the clear blue water of his backyard pool... and once again...we were in heaven.

Mademoiselle and Her Three Lovers

"Why must I choose among my lovers?" queried lovely Mademoiselle. "I love them equally in turn, and when I am alone with one, my passion becomes resolve to dedicate my love to him. But alas! When I am in the presence of the other, and yet again with my third lover, it is he that I must adore for a lifetime!"

Mademoiselle was not disheartened. Indeed, she should not have been surprised that her lovers would attend to her every desire, as she was an exquisite beauty whose grace emanated from her very soul. Her countenance was angelic and her spirit immaculate. Other women of lesser beauty might parade their attributes to ensnare such lovers as might provide for them a leisurely life; but Mademoiselle, she took measures to conceal her charms, as modesty and innocence flourished within her. She was lovely. Should occasion place her amidst the most attractive men and women of the world, all of them would be transfixed by her beauty.

There were three who brought to her a sincere love and a worthy entreaty for her devotion. Each was magnificent in his own fashion; each adored her and offered to her all of his wealth in a genuine appeal for her everlasting love. They knew that Mademoiselle was pure of heart. They knew that deception and deceit withered and died in her company and that it would be impossible to win her love by trickery. They loved her well and each one offered to her the very truth and substance of their being.

The first lover was a wealthy man. His empire contained all things upon the earth and he promised Mademoiselle the stars and the sun should she so desire them. All manner of treasure he could afford; all possessions of the world were within his reach, and he desired from her only her love and devotion. He was benevolent, but as befitting a king, he could be strict in the defense of his domain. Mademoiselle was in awe of his power. In all matters of humanity he was conversant, and his genius and his extraordinary wealth were appealing to her. He loved the world because Mademoiselle was alive in it, and it was his desire to provide for her an affluent life and a prosperous future. Her first lover would bestow upon her all things forever.

The second lover was a man of unrivaled beauty. His countenance could enchant any lover across eternity. His very presence was a wonder; his eyes were as portals to an enormous sea of love within his bosom. Women fell to his feet and adored him. He was all things sensual. His physique was sublime. Together, he and Mademoiselle were the most sensational lovers on earth! His manner of living was exemplary. He was honest and caring and his kindness was as a balm against cruelty. He could forgive Mademoiselle for any trespass. His appeal to her was as an ascetic without worldly riches or possessions; he did not treasure wealth unless one spoke of love, integrity, truth and fidelity. To be near him was to fall in love with him.

The third lover was an artist mad for all of existence; he was inspiration personified. His masterpiece was everywhere; his passion was without limits. All at once he presented to Mademoiselle the verses of the poet, the melody of the composer, the vision of the sculptor. He heard a symphony in the gentle winds and he celebrated the epic fury of the tempest. He was a compassionate lover who triumphed in his nakedness; his desires were the sustenance of life. He spoke only the truth, and his manner of living was impulsive, and his reply to heroic ventures was always an emphatic "Yes!" To be his lover was to exult in each moment forever. His appeal to Mademoiselle was not one of material wealth or an extraordinary physical body; he could offer to Mademoiselle his boundless spirit! Her third lover was the breath of life itself, and he promised her in each moment an eternity of divine ecstasy.

"Why must I choose among my lovers?" asked lovely Mademoiselle once again. "If only I could embrace all three together as one great lover!" she pined. "If they will not visit me as one, I will be content to receive them nonetheless!"

Faintly from within her chamber there was a sound as soft as falling snow, and Mademoiselle knew she was no longer alone. Mademoiselle closed her eyes in silent prayer. Presently, she felt the gentle hand of Mother Superior on her left shoulder.

"My dearest Mademoiselle," began Reverend Mother, with tender piety. "At the close of your postulancy, you were filled with perfect love. Joyously we celebrated your vocation to the life, and when I placed the white veil upon your temple, it was with perfect love that you accepted the habit of our order. I have observed your great devotion, and for two years you undertook the novitiate. Together we have prayed our three-fold vows of poverty, chastity and devotion. I have received from you the perpetual petition. It is time to join the others and declare your solemn vows."

Mademoiselle, who loved Mother Superior second only to her Lord God, turned to her and she spoke with her heart unveiled. "Reverend Mother," she began breathlessly, with eyes blurred with tears. "I have prayed and I have been visited by God our Father. When I am with Him my heart and my soul shall burst with love, and in His palm I am lifted to sacred heights of perfect security. His love for me is assurance and safety and I am awed by his power. He is omnipotent. He is my perfect Father. When I am with Him, I must love him truly."

Mother Superior bowed her head when she heard God the Almighty Father referenced thus, and strong emotions stirred within her. She loved her own moments spent in His presence. She remained silent.

"I have prayed and I have been visited by Blessed Jesus, Reverend Mother," continued the lovely disciple. "His beauty fills my essence with sensation. In His embrace I am awash in a sea of love. When I am with him, His voice enters my soul and He guides my life. He is my light; through Him I feel all things and with His love I seek to serve the sick, the poor, and the uneducated. His love is the love for all mankind. When I am with Him, I must love Him forever."

Mademoiselle let her tears flow and Mother Superior allowed her own emotions to swell with love for Jesus. So often had she asked Jesus for guidance, and when He visited her, she, too, trembled in His sublime love.

"I have prayed and I have been visited by the Holy Spirit, Reverend Mother," said Mademoiselle, with uplifted countenance. "His love and inspiration for us all is unremitting ecstasy. When near Him I am fulfilled. All living things are breathing His divine energy. I feel His ethereal spirit as divine purpose. He is passionate love eternal. Without Him, all of the artists in the universe would perish. Mankind would perish. When he comes to me at last, I am already in love with Him."

The Reverend Mother and the lovely Mademoiselle embraced then, and together, they gave themselves over to their lovers. They held dearly to each other and they began to sway with emotion. A rush of love took from them their breath and their thoughts; it took from them their earthly existence. Suspended in the glory of divine love from the Father in heaven and from his Son Jesus, and all at once from the Holy Spirit, they became angels on earth.

"I have prayed to Our Lady of Perpetual Help, Reverend Mother..." declared Mademoiselle at last, beaming with joy, "...and to St. Gregory, the patron of my calling. It is clear to me now Reverend Mother! I will impart to our children the secure love of our heavenly Father, and the beautiful presence of our Savior Jesus, and the sacred holiness of the Holy Spirit within our souls."

"Very well, Mademoiselle," said Mother Superior. "Let us join the others on this day of declaration, with your passion and your perfect love, and proclaim your sacred vows. Henceforth, let the world proclaim Sister Mary Gregory in His name...In the name of the Father, and of the Son, and of the Holy Spirit."

Three Rioters

It was a time of dread and disease and adversity. Death prevailed and his ugly head was reared with impunity. His gruesome presence was everywhere widespread, and a day would not pass that his ghastly parade did not carry the corpse of an innocent man whose family languished and grieved at his side. He was a ruthless and cunning schemer, this scourge named Death, and his delight was agony and affliction, and his favorite song was the wailing of forsaken children.

In the town of Huntington, inside of a rustic pub called *The Canterbury Ales*, three tormented men sat drinking beer to alleviate their misery; they could no longer bear the death-suffering inflicted upon the people of their countryside. Once again that day at noontime, the funereal carriage could be heard cricking along the main street carrying the dead body of a poor soul that was a victim of the wicked reaper. It was too much to bear! The three rioters, with unsteady wit and reckless bravado, raised their goblets together and they swore to the heavens that it was enough!

"Brothers!" bellowed each in turn. "Let us put an end to this hideous plague! Let us seek out our enemy Death and secure his fate! By Jove! Let us not be content until contemptible Death lay cold in the ground! Cruel enemy of the living! Brothers! Let him be outdone! Let us kill Death!"

The three men thus resolved raced out of the pub to the passing funeral procession and violently they accosted the driver. With angry fists and menacing taunts, the men bullied the innocent man: "You! Death's driver and deliverer! Show us your employer! Where is Death? We are determined this day to rid his wickedness from our lands! Tell us! Or fear for your own life!"

The driver was terrified by their aggressive threats. "Kind sirs!" he stuttered, seeking to thwart their terrible blows. "As you can see, Death has visited this pitiable man within my wagon, but now he is gone! Witness! Death has completed his work. I am but the courier who chaperones the lifeless to the yard. Death has gone! I know not where! Show mercy!"

"You shall tell us more, or we shall bring Death here upon you!" demanded one of the three rebels, slowly releasing his sharp weapon from its sheath. "Tell us! Where is Death?"

At that fearful moment, the defenseless driver saw an old man walking with a staff at some distance ahead of him in the meadow. With hand outstretched and with finger pointing, the driver pleaded again with panicked voice: "Show mercy! There is an old man in the distance. Look to him! Soon he will be visited by Death. Speak with the old man, for surely he will know more than I. Please! I beseech you!"

The rioters were satisfied. With renewed purpose, the determined trio covered the distance to the aged man and they were ruthless in their approach. As would murderous ruffians, the men trounced upon the grey-haired vagabond and demanded to know the whereabouts of deceitful Death. Throttled at the neck and jostled, the crooked old man nearly collapsed.

"Grey-beard! Take heed!" the rioters thundered. "It is our undertaking to find and to rid Death from our lands. You stand at his threshold. Tell us if he is at home or we shall knock soundly upon the door and bring Death upon you!"

"I am very old," replied the wrinkled traveler. "My bones are brittle; my countenance ashen and grotesque as a corpse. Each day with my staff, I knock upon the crusted earth, for I am weary with suffering. I knock soundly upon the earth and I plead, 'Take me! I am ready to rest eternal!' but each day passes into night and each morning I arise and await my fate once again. " The weary old man lifted his staff in the direction of a solitary maple tree as old as a century. "Behind that tree," he said with his ligneous staff pointing, "slumbering upon the knobbed roots…there you will find Death."

The three men were not convinced. With finger squarely forced upon the old man's chest, and with all the fury of declarations resolute, the rioters professed a warning: "Let those words be true or they will be your last! Death shall be resting there behind the appointed tree or we shall silence you forever!"

The ancient man weakly embraced each of them, and he swore to the veracity of his spoken words. "Be wary," he warned, "for behind that tree you shall surely find Death."

At breakneck pace the rioters approached the base of the lone maple, and with momentary trepidation, they removed their knives and prepared to slaughter that which lay reposed behind the massive tree trunk. Swiftly and upon a single command, the attackers leapt with vicious intent and they swung their sharp weapons freely.

Astonished, there in plain view, reposed upon the knobbed roots, a huge wooden treasure chest lay opened, and brimming within its sturdy frame, glistening in the sunlight, there appeared an incalculable cache of golden coins. They could not believe their good fortune! The three rioters were rich beyond all measure! They rubbed their eyes as to vanquish the dream, but upon opening them, there again lay the countless stash of golden florins! In a triple embrace, they danced and spun and twirled with unbridled joy! They were rich!

When with their sleeves they wiped the joyous tears from their faces, and when their raucous laughter subsided, the three men decided to divide the great fortune evenly. It occurred to them, however, that such sudden wealth would appear suspicious; the townsfolk would be jealous of their treasure and accuse each of theft, or worse, claim the coins as their own. A plan must be divined, they knew, to displace such mistrust with a solution less dubious than the one claiming they had found the coins behind a tree! They must take precautions and figure a way to safely transport the heavy chest. Such a plan would require time and much consideration.

The rioters had grown hungry and it was decided at last to draw straws to determine which of the three would take with him a coin into the marketplace to purchase nourishing provisions while the other two remained behind to guard the gold. The youngest drew the shortest reed, and it was just as well as he was the fittest runner, and so with lively tread and coin in hand, the youth sped toward the village. While on his lengthy trip, the two rioters that remained as guards kept vigilant and spoke again of their great fortune. Soon, however, with voices subdued, a pestilence invaded their thoughts, and after a prolonged silence, the elder spoke as one does when ruminating:

"My dearest friend," he began innocently. "How would it be if I should devise a plan such that we would divide the great store of golden florins *two ways*, instead of three?"

"You have my devoted attention, my dear brother," replied the other. "What are your thoughts?"

"Let us imagine together, shall we, that when our youthful companion returns with nutritious supplies, you approach him with jovial temper, glad for his safe return, and you reach out to him in the spirit of sport. Upon his arrival then, with merriment and playful jeers, you pretend to romp with him as frolic, and I, with casual demeanor, shall advance undetected. As you and he wrestle in jest upon each other, from beneath your arm, I shall raise my shiv and with deadly aim, I will strike him deep upon the vulnerable spot...and then, my good cousin, we shall pack our purses full with increased pleasures."

"It is a strategy that pleases me well," responded the listener. "Let us shake upon it and anticipate his ill-fated return."

Meanwhile, it took but one hour for the youth to enter the limits of the village, and as he trotted, he dreamed of the glittering gold and of his own great fortune. Soon, however, a venomous contagion infected his thoughts, and so enraptured by his meditations was he, that his lips moved in a murmur as he was deliberating: "What if I should have that great chest of golden coins to myself?" he whispered openly. "Indeed, let me not stop with considerations alone!"

Having cast all vacillation aside, the young rioter raced directly to the apothecary, and with convincing entreaty, he described to the pharmacist his pressing circumstance: "I have rats, sir, the size of house cats that plague my home both night and day! Can you help me rid the vermin, my good man, so my wife may rest with undisturbed thoughts?"

"I have just what you need, my friend," replied the goodly chemist, retrieving with his key a container secured within a locked cabinet. "Take caution! The poison within this vessel is so strong that a single drop would lay down for eternity the strongest man among warriors. Be wary and be assured. Mixed with a bit of cheese or mutton, the wretched pests you describe as rats will bother you know more!"

Having secured the other requisite supplies, the young renegade made certain to purchase among them an exquisite wine. Midway along the route, he carefully undid the cork and he poured the poisonous liquid into the bottle and shook it. "I have procured this potent fluid to extinguish rats...and so it shall!" he declared to himself as in a sudden madness. "Upon my return, in mock celebration, I shall but *pretend* to drink! Ha! Ha! Alas! I shall have the treasure all to myself!" The young scoundrel was beside himself with rapture; but nonetheless, he was meticulous to disguise any sign of tampering upon the cap of the lethal container.

Before long, the rioters spotted the young one in the distance approaching steadily across the very meadow where the old man with the staff had pointed to the lone maple tree. As planned, the guardian of the treasure came forward to greet the returning rogue, and as in good-natured play, he tussled and wrestled harmlessly with the youth. Indeed, the ruse was well-enacted and very convincing, displaying therewithal much laughter and childish mirth. Meanwhile, the elder rioter, with deadly seriousness and sweat upon his brow, prepared his steely blade. Moving as does a shadow to avoid detection, he quietly approached the tumbling pair. With a single swift stab into the chest, he did send the blade home! The unsuspecting youth writhed with pain for just a moment; the blade had struck true to the heart, and presently, the young man lay dead before them. The co-conspirators smiled then, for their murderous scheme had worked! Without remorse, they dragged the lifeless body behind the maple tree and turned their efforts to the nutritious provisions.

The two murderers were satisfied, and with their mood festive and triumphant, they proposed a toast to themselves and to their prosperity. Seizing the wine, the two remaining rioters opened it, poured an abundant quantity and raised their goblets high: "To sumptuous life! Forever may we evade Death's embrace! Let us drink!"

The rioters guzzled the toxic brew, and before they could wipe their mouths with the sleeves of their garment, the deadly beverage did its work. Falling one upon the other, the two poisoned scoundrels did fall directly upon the corpse of their recent victim. The three rioters lay lifeless upon the knobbed roots of the ancient tree.

In the distant meadow, ceasing for a moment his eternal journey, a crooked figure slowly turned a grotesque countenance toward the slain rioters. With his staff uplifted, the grey-haired old man, bearing a wry smile and then a ghoulish grimace, appeared disappointed with the fate of the three foolish rioters. He knocked upon the hard earth with his staff, and without recourse, he turned away and wearily he resumed his lonely trek across the countryside.

I Want To Hold Your Hand

It wasn't that often that Jeff held his little sister's hand, but if they were in a crowded mall or crossing a busy thoroughfare, he didn't mind doing it. When you are eleven years old, you can handle that kind of responsibility. Barbara, his kid sister, was only eight years old, and Jeff knew that soon enough, holding hands would be awkward because siblings stop doing that sort of thing as they get older.

Jeff remembered one time in particular though, when he and his little sister Barbara held hands. It was on February 9th, 1964, and he didn't feel awkward about it. After all, just after eight o'clock that evening, the *Beatles* would appear on the Ed Sullivan Show, and he and his sister, along with seventy-three million other Americans, could not wait to see the musical performance by the four talented young men from Liverpool. For Jeff and Barbara, it was a very big deal, and the two kids talked about it all week long. When Sunday night finally arrived, they sat down together with their noses a few inches away from the television screen. Jeff adjusted the volume on the old black and white TV to its highest decibels before the sound would cackle with distortion. Barbara arranged a few pillows from the couch on the floor. There were potato chips but no one dared munch them; the crunch would be too distracting. In fact, all disruptions of any kind were peremptorily disallowed; if the dog got loose, he was on his own until after the show.

Everyone knows that a tennis racquet is a sorry substitute for a guitar, but during that time, the neighborhood kids were swept away by *Beatlemania*. Jeff and Barbara, and many other kids on Long Island, sometimes used tennis racquets as guitars when pretending they were the *Beatles*. Other times, they might put a black sock over a lamp stem and pretend it was a microphone stand. No one thought it strange. Barbara insisted she was Paul McCartney and Jeff sang along as John Lennon or George Harrison. The two knew every song by heart. When even the least bit bored in the car, or on the school bus, or at home waiting for dinner, the siblings kept busy singing *Beatle* songs together, making sure of the lyrics. Jeff knew all the mannerisms and Barbara knew all the harmonies. Even at eight years old, Barbara was already more advanced musically than her older brother. She had talent. Soon she would learn to play guitar; she wouldn't need a tennis racquet anymore.

On that unforgettable Sunday evening, Jeff and his little sister were sitting cross-legged directly in front of the television when Ed Sullivan introduced the band: "Now tonight, you're gonna twice be entertained by them. Right now, and again in the second half of our show. Ladies and Gentleman, the Beatles! Let's bring them on."

It was then that little sister Barbara slipped her hand into her older brother's palm, and together they held on tight as the first song... *All my Loving...* flowed from the speakers. The two were swaying with emotion when listening to the second song, a ballad *Till There Was You*. When the Beatles rocked out with *She Loves You*, both kids were bouncing along slapping their thighs and shaking their shoulders. Their parents, who were watching the show from a respectable distance behind their children, also recognized the event. It was true; the *Beatles* were a remarkable act, and indeed; they were charming. Their performance caused everyone to smile. As a matter of fact, the whole country was smiling.

Timed passed and Jeff and Barbara matured and both had plenty of ideas they wanted to pursue. Jeff played sports with a passion, and in high school he earned a varsity letter for baseball. Barbara continued to perform in earnest, and her beautiful voice was locally acclaimed due to her outstanding stage performances in the musical-theater productions at school. As brother and sister, their behavior was exemplary. Jeff was grateful he had a young companion who would help him out and listen to his sports stories when no one else was around. He might prattle on about Mets' players and their promising batting averages, or complain about the Knicks who were underperforming during the previous few games. Barbara was grateful, too, for when she needed to rehearse for a play, Jeff was there, willing to play the foil if need be. Her greatest performance and most difficult one was when she played the role of the blind housewife Suzie Hendrix in the suspenseful thriller *Wait Until Dark*. Jeff rehearsed for many hours with Barbara, who mauled him during the violent physical confrontation in the dark kitchen, until together they perfected the unforgettable scene. Years later, Jeff openly maintained that Barbara's portrayal of the terrorized blind woman was as convincing as Audrey Hepburn's performance. He was not alone in his opinion. Barbara had talent.

During high school and for the years thereafter, the siblings naturally grew apart and they led separate lives. However, whenever they were together, they continued to share a *Beatles* thing. At any moment, one of them might launch into a *Beatle* song, and because they remained devoted fans, together they would sing. Barbara knew the harmonies. Jeff knew the mannerisms. They both knew the lyrics. It was their unique way of connecting with each other. And wouldn't you know? They were very entertaining and they were very good singers.

*****

Many years passed by and not much was going on. After college, Jeff worked near the Great South Bay as a physical education teacher and baseball coach for the Bay Shore School District, and he raised two children without incident. When he had some free time, he was occupied in particular with assisting autistic children, and it was usual for him to help fundraise on their behalf. Barbara also raised two children, and she was pleased to be the Sachem Public Librarian. Whenever possible, she was engaged with causes related to underprivileged children, and she donated her time and sometimes resources to eradicate illiteracy. The two kept in touch during holidays, and occasionally, the families vacationed together in Montauk. Always they sang *Beatle* songs when they were together.

That's when it happened. Barbara was speaking at Lynwood Elementary School when Principal Anderson realized he and his wife would be unable to attend an upcoming Paul McCartney concert at the Meadowlands Arena. Appreciative of Barbara's efforts as a guest speaker, and having overheard many *Beatle* tunes softly hummed and whistled by her over the years, Principal Anderson shrewdly delivered the two tickets to her. With casual banter and in an offhand manner, the administrator ascertained that Barbara had no specific plans for the upcoming weekend, and so he slipped the tickets into a thank-you note. "Enjoy the Show!" was scribbled inside, and it was signed by twenty-four second-grade students from Lynwood Elementary.

Barbara called Jeff right away. They would be going to a live performance at last! John Lennon and George Harrison had passed some time ago, and so a true *Beatles'* reunion was impossible. But it was rumored that Ringo was in town. Jeff was ecstatic! Of course he would go to the concert. Barbara's husband was not surprised or offended that his wife offered the seat to her brother. Jeff's wife was not surprised or offended because her husband would be attending the concert with his sister. After all, for as long as anyone could remember, the two sang *Beatle* songs together at every occasion. Also, unbeknownst to each other, both Jeff and Barbara had shared with their spouse the fond memory of watching the Ed Sullivan show. Of course they would go together.

A *Beatle* hadn't performed in the tri-state area for years and so it was a huge event. It was a Saturday night concert and the siblings crossed the George Washington Bridge with time to spare. The parking lot was jam-packed, as was the walking path leading to the crowded venue, and so Barbara casually slipped her hand into Jeff's palm, for they could easily have become separated and lost amidst the swift-moving throng. "Tee Shirts...Sir Paul Tee Shirts!" rang out wildly as they advanced toward the gate. Others approached covertly, "Tickets! Anyone need tickets? Tickets!" they hawked on the sly. It was very exciting. The stadium turnstiles were pulsating with energy.

Inside, the two were filled with anticipation until their tickets led them circling forever upward. The seats were among the furthest from the stage, and as they climbed to the outer ring, their enthusiasm languished. They were in the "nose-bleed" section. Both had brought binoculars, but as the opening act came on, it became clear how distanced they were from the stage. Jeff and Barbara were plainly disappointed.

"What do you think?" asked Jeff.

"This will not do," they both agreed.

Barbara knew exactly what her brother meant. "Let's go!" she declared, already on the move.

They weren't leaving the stadium; instead, they were determined to get better seats if at all possible. They headed straight for the mezzanine section. With a story about losing his seat stub and with some cash, Jeff was able to persuade an opportunistic usher that two seats were available after all. Bustling alongside the dodgy employee, it was unfortunate that the proffered seats were way off to one side of the arena. The new arrangement was much improved from the previous one, and Jeff and Barbara endured for a few more songs, but they were not content. However, because they were inside the mezzanine already, they realized it was conceivable they could access the lower floor level. Barbara took the initiative: "Follow me!" she said, and once again, the two were on the move.

When they loomed near the narrow tunnel leading to the valuable floor seats, Barbara approached the usher with her sweet voice singing. She placed her own breath inches from the attendant's face, and with gentle mien and affectionate embrace, she sang *Let it Be,* like an angel. The enamored employee was delighted. Meanwhile, Jeff had slipped past him like a shadow. Once inside, he turned back and he beckoned to his counterpart:

"Martha, my dear!" he called, and then he held two tickets fleetingly in the air toward the attendant before disappearing into the mob. Because it was evident to everyone they were together as a couple, and because Jeff seemed to have her ticket, the unsuspecting usher allowed her passage.

Things were going splendidly. These floor seats were prime and likely very expensive as well, so it was difficult to find two that were unoccupied together. The brother and sister ambled calmly along the stadium rows without a visible worry in the world as they searched frantically for two vacant seats. Fortunately, they were able to slip undetected into empty ones near enough to each other to make sense to the proximate audience. These were truly wonderful seats, but the likelihood they would remain unclaimed was remote. Taking stock of the situation, Jeff could see that below them, closer to the stage, a single aisle led to general floor-level seating at stage-front. If they could get there, they would be able to enjoy the show without concern. Addressing his sister from a few seats away, Jeff pointed to the astute usher and shrugged hopelessly. Barbara considered the dilemma quickly, for she knew the rightful purchaser of her seat would soon lay claim. They both understood they would be caught without proper tickets and be escorted promptly back to the rooftop, or possibly to their parked car in the lot!

The lights dimmed further and the crowd roared. The opening act was offstage. Colorful fluorescent beams of rotating strobe lights burst forth suddenly from every direction. The show was about to begin. Barbara was accosted by the rightful seat owner and she had to relinquish her seat immediately. She signaled to Jeff to follow her, and instead of retreating, it was evident she was heading straight toward the guarded aisle that led to the seats on the floor that afforded direct access to the stage. Jeff brushed against the rightful owner of his own seat as he exited the row to follow helplessly behind his sister. The bedazzling lights were ricocheting from the ceiling and the floor, and presently the arena erupted with applause upon hearing the deep rumble from a thunderous keyboard. Distracted momentarily, the attendant did not see Barbara until she was very nearly upon him.

All at once, Jeff was astounded and mortified. Barbara, in a panic and with arms outstretched, groped as does a blind woman in desperation. The confused usher rushed to her aid, and with entirely convincing execution, Barbara once again became the blind housewife Suzie Hendrix in the play *Wait Until Dark*. Others nearby came to help her, and Jeff seized upon the moment and came forth to her rescue:

"Lovely Rita!" he cried, with a good bit of acting on his own.

The startled attendant believed the blind woman had become disoriented by the blast of sound, and in the commotion, Jeff swiftly embraced her, and with obvious relief, he whisked her into the bedlam of the screaming fans. They disappeared into the standing ovation, for at that precise moment, with lights blazing and in dramatic fashion, Sir Paul McCartney had burst upon the stage. The adoring fans of the Meadowlands Arena erupted as does a mighty tempest, and Sir Paul, with perfect voice, sang out the very same song he performed first on the Ed Sullivan show.

Jeff and Barbara were center stage now, as near to the rock star as they once were near to their black and white television. Together they held on tight as the first song... *All my Loving...* flowed from the speakers. The two were swaying with emotion when listening to the second song, a ballad *Till There Was* You. When the *Beatle* rocked out with *She Loves You*, both Jeff and Barbara became as kids again, bouncing along slapping their thighs and shaking their shoulders. They sang along with all of the songs...Jeff knew the mannerisms...Barbara knew the harmonies...they both knew the lyrics...and they didn't feel the least bit awkward holding each other's hand.

Bully for You

Bobby Freeza's father was a broad-shouldered ex-boxer who made his living with his muscles unloading cargo. When he was a younger man, he had a dream; he named himself "Fists of Fury" and he set out to make himself famous on the Golden Gloves circuit. When he was inside the ring, he was known as a dirty fighter; outside the ring, in the neighborhood and at home, he was aggressive, mean-spirited and physically threatening. As a young man, many considered him a punk who drank too much and swore too often, and it was not uncommon at the local brew houses to hear that he had beaten some innocent patron with his fists. After he married, and his only child was born, he was elated; he named his son Bobby and he began immediately to teach him to be fearless and revered for his strength. At every turn, he encouraged Bobby to push back violently whenever anyone leaned on him. "*Stand up!*" he would demand with a shove. "*Don't let anyone push you around!*" he would command with an enraged look that landed like a sucker punch into his son's young soul. Bobby's father wanted his "little man" to become a tough guy; he taught his boy not to cry...ever... and he taught his son that with his fists, he would gain respect.

That's probably why, at eight years old, Bobby Freeza really couldn't help himself. He was confused; he couldn't disseminate a friendly gesture from a provocation. At school, Bobby challenged authority at every turn because he didn't quite understand the rules, and there were so many of them. Every day, with everyone, he was quarrelsome; wherever he went, there were altercations. As far as anyone remembers, he was the only boy who was kicked out of our parochial school.

I first met Bobby in the second grade before they showed him the door. He sat right next to me in class, and I talked to him once in a while, enough to know he was unhappy most of the time. He had a certain cold look that he borrowed from his father; it was a sneer and a glare that was confrontational. Sister Sophia, our second grade teacher, marked Bobby straight away as a bully, and as the school year progressed, she spent most days disciplining him because he just wouldn't sit still for long, and he was always grabbing more than his fill of snacks, and he wouldn't keep his head down on his desk during rest period. I'm sure the straw was finally broken when Bobby let loose a string of obscenities during a math lesson. The good sister yanked him out of his chair and she dragged him across the classroom by his ear lobe. Bobby broke free and leered at her and he smirked; it was the cold look that he learned at home, and if he had thought of it, I'm sure he would have spit on the ground right there in front of Sister Sophia, just like he said his father did when picking a fight. He glared at our teacher with insolence and fury in his eyes; the rest of us would have sobbed and whimpered in pain and humiliation, but not Bobby Freeza ...Bobby Freeza would never cry...ever!

Not long after, Bobby's desk was empty and everyone knew he was not coming back. He was transferred over to the public school, and no one heard another thing about him. No one cared, really, as Bobby Freeza was better off somewhere else, and we had our own lives ahead of us.

The years passed and I spent most of my time with my best friend Billy Crushack, a stringy kid who was good-natured and a little bit mischievous like me. We spent all of our free time together. Billy was naturally quiet and shy if he didn't know you very well. I was definitely more talkative than he, and physically stronger, until about the sixth grade. I remember wrestling on Billy's front lawn one summer afternoon, expecting to pin Billy to the ground as usual, when he let loose a surge of strength contrary to my objectives. Billy had definitely gotten stronger, a lot stronger, and he flipped me aside like a wet towel tossed to the sidelines.

"Hold on, Billy!" I exclaimed in awe. "Whoa! Don't hurt me now!" I pleaded jokingly. Remember...we're best friends!"

Billy smiled, and I got the feeling he had been letting me pin him down when wrestling for quite some time. I think he was very happy I called him my best friend. As for me, I know I was grateful he didn't have a grudge to settle with me...and that he wasn't a bully. We didn't wrestle that much after that day because I really couldn't challenge him anymore; he was too strong.

A year later, I guess I caught up with Billy *strength-wise*, because my shoulders filled out and my arms and frame acquired muscular definition.

I was brawny overall; beefy in the chest with thick, solid thighs, and my father told me I resembled his kid-brother Johnny when he was a teenager. By that he meant I had the frame of a boxer; my Uncle Johnny had won a few prize fights on the Golden Gloves circuit. Everyone in my family was proud of Uncle Johnny because years ago he had earned some modest celebrity in newspapers and on radio for his talent in the ring, and to be compared to him physically was a significant compliment.

My best friend Billy, on the other hand, still looked skinny as a string without much muscle mass; but he was strong to the bone, and his bones were made out of steel. I remember thinking that if I pounded him with my fist, I would likely break my hand. To look at the two of us side by side, a bully would have picked on Billy as the weaker one, but it would have been a mistake. My best friend may have appeared wispy and thin and gangly, but God help the unlucky fool who backed him into a corner and instigated a fist fight. Billy's bony limbs were made out of steel.

It was a year later that Billy and I graduated from parochial school and we transferred into the public high school. That's where I ran into Bobby Freeza. I took my seat in math class, and because we were seated alphabetically, I looked to my left, and there sat Bobby. He looked at me curiously, and I looked back at him in the same way. I nodded, and he nodded, and nothing was said. Class began as usual, and I couldn't tell if he remembered me. He was older by then, of course, and he was built strong and low to the ground. He looked tough. I kept well within my space, and occasionally, I tried to look tough too, but that was ridiculous, as I still had too many freckles while he was already mature with many features of a grown man.

Before long, I got the word that Bobby Freeza was the most feared kid in the school; a mean-spirited brawler to be regarded warily. Nonetheless, as the days passed, we became comfortable with each other. Occasionally, we would talk in class or work together as partners on an algebra problem. Sometimes we would move our desks together, and at close range, I noticed that he had marks on his body, either a bruise on his arm, or a cut on his eyebrow, but I never mentioned it. As math partners, we would lose ourselves in the task at hand, and I explained to him how to solve for x, or showed him why we needed to work out the equation in the parenthesis before we multiplied and so on. That's when he opened up a bit and told me about his life and how he wanted to be a boxer. I told him my Uncle Johnny was a boxer, and that he had won a few noteworthy bouts on the Golden Gloves circuit. I remember he smiled at me then, and this was not typical because Bobby never smiled unless he had just beaten someone down. But he smiled that day, and he told me all about "Fists of Fury" and all the rest. I guess we sort of became friends. He seemed tolerant of me anyway; but not with everyone. If someone bothered him in the least, he would flash that cold look he learned from his father, and the mettlesome intruder would fly out of his way like a flustered duck. He was okay with me, though, maybe because my uncle was a boxer.

As the school year rolled on, I heard all about the fights he won. "Bobby Freeza beat the daylights outta Timmy Marshall," I heard, or, "No contest! Bobby cold-cocked Matt Corrigan in the locker room...it was over in three seconds." Crowds would gather after school when rumor had it there would be another fight, and Bobby Freeza was in most of them, and he won them all. The sad part of it was that Bobby picked all of the fights, because if someone tough and strong was measured against his prowess, Bobby hunted him down in the hallway and started in with him. Bobby was convinced that with his fists, he would gain respect.

One time Bobby came to class with a butterfly stitch on his right eyebrow, and the wound was fresh. I leaned over to him and I whispered softly some unsolicited advice. It was a mindless gamble, but I did it anyway, in a gesture of friendship.

"Bobby...you have to stop getting in so many fights..." I said, pointing with my finger at his stitches. "You're always coming in to class all banged up!"

I saw immediately that I had upset him. His face flushed in anger and frustration, and he gave me the cold look that he had learned from his father. I pulled back instantly. I had provoked him. Why did I open my mouth? It was none of my business! Who was I to advise him how to live his life?

And then Bobby did something highly unexpected. He exhaled and relaxed his shoulders; he took a few deep breaths to allow the anger to dissipate from his body. With his eyes diverted, he leaned back over to me, and in a whisper, he said the most incredible words I had ever heard:

"You see this cut on my eye...and this bruise on my shoulder..." he said softly, "...they're not from a fist fight...they're from my father...."

He turned away and slumped back into his desk, exhausted. I kept my head down for the entire class. We never spoke about it again.

During the next few days, I pretended to forget about the whole thing. We talked every once in a while and we continued to work together as partners on the math. Bobby kept on fighting after school...he kept on fighting…and I knew that he probably would keep on fighting for the rest of his life.

I remember Bobby laughed only twice in all the time I knew him. The first time was when he came to class excited one day and he told me he had turned sixteen, and he was eligible to join a prestigious gym in the neighborhood; he was accepted into a competitive program, and soon he would be training to be a boxer. He chuckled when he told me the details. I was happy for him. I thought it was the best thing that could happen to him. His spirit was uplifted, and wouldn't you know? Once he started training, there weren't that many fights after school anymore.

The second time he laughed was when Mr. Benson, our math teacher, returned our algebra exams. I leaned over to Bobby's desk and I saw that he got an eighty-three on the test. It was by far the highest grade he had achieved all year, and with a nod in my direction, he laughed with satisfaction. His gratification was short-lived. Wouldn't you know? Mr. Benson crumbled his paper, and then he crumbled mine as well, and he accused both of us of conspiring to cheat. I looked at Bobby and I saw the enraged look in his face, the one he borrowed from his father, but before he could stand up and let loose a string of obscenities, I spoke up first:

"Wait a minute!" I stated, bewildered. "We've been working on these problems together all week…I didn't cheat…and Bobby didn't cheat either!"

Mr. Benson thought my reaction was insubordinate, and he was upset with Bobby because he had scowled at him, so he gave both of us detention on the spot. However, we were given the opportunity to prove our innocence.

"You will take the test again after school…both of you…right in front of me…and then we'll know the truth!" said Mr. Benson weightily, and then he walked away.

It was fortunate that the bell rang, because Bobby stormed out of the room, plowing through several desks on his way out. I returned after school to retake the test. Bobby never showed up. He took a zero for his grade, and he lost all interest in algebra after that day. His attendance fell off, too, and he was frequently cited for cutting class.

It was a few months later, on a Monday, that I was on the crowded lunch line in the cafeteria with Billy Crushack when Bobby Freeza nudged his way between us; he had muscled his way into the line. I nodded a greeting to him, but Billy thought differently. Bobby was caught off-guard when Billy shoved him with his shoulder, and with his thumb, he gestured for Bobby to "*get lost*" at the back of the line. Bobby slammed his lunch tray against the counter and flipped Billy's tray headlong onto the floor at our feet. The two of them squared off. Bobby spit on the ground and he glared at Billy with the look he had learned at home. Billy was indifferent to it; in his quiet world, he didn't know anything about Bobby Freeza or his reputation, and he didn't care.

Bobby struck first with a solid punch to Billy's chest; he wasn't about to let anyone push him around. Billy hardly budged. I could tell that my quiet friend with the limbs of steel had been backed into a corner. Billy responded with a powerful blow to Bobby's neck, and then all hell broke loose. Students on the lunch line scattered like frightened chickens. Fists were flailing from both fighters, but it was over quickly. Teachers and aides rushed to the brawl and they quelled the squall. The two were ushered away to the office, and each received a three-day suspension for fighting in school. Both would return on Friday.

News of the cafeteria clash spread down the halls and into the classrooms like a conflagration. Friday afternoon was the anticipated rematch. Very few students knew Billy Crushack before the incident, but now, everyone lay claim to some association with him. His tall, lanky frame had held its own against the bulky muscles of Bobby Freeza. Friday afternoon behind the bleachers after school; the bully Bobby with the fists of fury and the bashful Billy with the bones of steel would settle things. Attendance at the event promised to surpass the senior prom.

It didn't happen that way. Details of the "Big Fight" had drifted into the ears of the administration; announcements on the school PA system expressed that the cops would be at the bleachers on Friday afternoon, and three-day suspensions from school were guaranteed to anyone who was foolish enough to be there.

The fight took place without anyone in attendance except for me. I was talking with Billy on the front steps of his house during his suspension, telling him about the hullabaloo at school, when Bobby stomped down the street alone. When he got to Billy's house, he let loose a string of obscenities, and he raced up the concrete walkway straight at Billy. Bobby Freeza ambushed Billy Crushack on Billy's own front lawn.

I backed away and watched the battle unfold. The onslaught was immediate. Bobby slammed Billy hard to the chest and he let go a sucker punch that missed. Billy regained his composure and advanced upon Bobby, driving his punches forward like a machine. Billy's determination was resolute; he would not be intimidated by this bully, and he appeared undaunted by the blows that he absorbed or deflected with his iron limbs. Billy advanced and Bobby retreated. It was Bobby who had misjudged his adversary; with one powerful right hand to the jaw, Bobby was down, and Billy flew at him and pounced upon him. Bobby took a pounding to the body, but he would not yield. He was one tough fighter. The two of them thrashed on the ground for control, and Bobby reversed the momentum and he pinned Billy with his body weight, and then it was his turn; he blitzed Billy's body with a furious flurry of punches. Billy lay still, shielding his face and neck, and he withstood the barrage.

And then it was over. Billy let loose a surge of strength, and he flipped Bobby aside like a wet towel tossed to the sidelines. He overturned his attacker and he pressed Bobby's face into the grass as he unleashed his prowess. Billy pummeled him, and when he ceased punching, all became quiet. Bobby was defeated. He had fought with all his might, but now, his opponent towered over him. When Billy released him at last, Bobby lay sprawled on the ground. For a long time, he did not budge. The fight was over. Billy was the clear victor; the bully would fight him no more.

Bobby did not stand up. Instead, he simply lay there slumped and exhausted on his stomach with his face shrouded beneath his outstretched arms. He took a few deep breaths to allow the anger to dissipate from his body. Suddenly he appeared as someone who might fall asleep right there on the lawn. And that's when I realized that something remarkable had happened to Bobby Freeza.

In a moment of extraordinary effort, Bobby had pushed with all of his strength against his opponent, and when he could not gain freedom from the bonds that held him, there emerged from deep within him...from the very center of his being... a rush of emotion that found expression in an explosion. Incredibly, Bobby had burst out...crying...and he had hidden his face in the blades of grass to conceal his shame and humiliation. That's when I figured it out. Bobby hadn't stopped fighting because he was losing the fight. He quit because an eruption of outrage had risen up within him involuntarily, and because he was restrained physically, it found release in a sudden torrent. And here's the thing. Bobby's volcanic outburst came most unexpectedly...to him! The cry gushed forth, and no one was more shocked than Bobby! He had not cried due to pain; he was not hurt. He did not cry due to fear; he was unafraid. The cry was due to the sudden discharge of something profoundly disturbing deep within him. I walked near enough to his body to see if he was alright.

"Get away!" he shouted from beneath his arms. "Get away from me!" he demanded, burying his face further into the grass.

Billy and I melted away. We walked back toward the steps to allow sufficient time for Bobby to put himself back together. Even though it was only the two of us, we left Bobby alone so he would not have to endure humiliation upon his departure. In truth, a wave of shame overshadowed the whole episode. When finally we looked back, Bobby Freeza was gone.

School resumed for both of my friends on Friday, and the word spread quickly that there would be no fight after all. The matter had been settled, and no one knew any of the details. I saw Bobby a few times in class afterwards and I pretended to forget about the whole thing.

In a couple of weeks, Bobby's desk was empty and everyone knew he was not coming back. Bobby Freeza had quit school, and no one heard a thing about him. No one cared, really, as Bobby was better off somewhere else, and we had our own lives ahead of us. As for me, I hoped Bobby had found some success in the gym as a boxer because I knew that he probably would keep on fighting for the rest of his life.

As for Billy, he returned to anonymity, as he didn't have a grudge to settle with anyone ...he wasn't a bully. We keep in touch. I see him every once in a while, and he is still very quiet and shy if he didn't know you very well. When together, I do most of the talking...I am definitely more talkative than he...and he is still skinny as a string...and to look at the two of us side by side, a bully would pick on Billy as the weaker one...but that would be a mistake.

Jazzy

The old box truck was no longer white; rust had discolored the dented fenders and blotches of pale-grey coated the rest of the faded metal panels like dirty snow. The tires were too dirty to determine if they once bore white-walls, and the rims were filthy black and only three held hub-caps. The muffler beneath the box was secured with make-shift coat hangers and a metal strap, and the rolling steel door in the rear was in need of grease and it lifted with grinding tones that were shrill and painful to the ear. There was a deep ping in the windshield that webbed its way into a lengthy crack that stretched like a lightning bolt across the glass on the passenger side. The heavy passenger doors sagged from their own weight, and they groaned when opened, and they never closed properly unless slammed shut.

Inside the cab, the ratty seat covers were torn and rubber insulation peeked through the canvas, no longer able to conceal the iron springs. The windows rattled and they needed coaxing with a swift punch to open at all during the winter months. Knobs for the radio and the door locks went astray. Cigarette stubs clogged the sooty ash tray. Dried mud, paper rubbish and discarded coffee cups littered the floor. Once a week, the debris in the cockpit was swept away carelessly as a matter of convenience to make space for another weeks-worth of fresh garbage. It was too many years ago to recall when the old box truck had been properly cleansed.

Despite appearances, it was a bull of a truck, eighteen feet in the rear, and his owner, a bearded teamster named Steve, provided the essentials to keep it safe and operating reliably. Steve made his living upon the wheels of the truck's old frame, and he was careful to maintain the engine's health and to feed it diesel-fuel always quarter-full so the fuel pump would not suck grime into the fuel injectors from the bottom of the mucky gas tank. When in motion, Steve was attentive to the drive shaft as it spun, and he kept one ear upon the rhythm of the cylinders. He was vigilant to rotate the filthy tires and he changed the oil regularly. When his foot squeezed the brakes, he was mindful of their integrity.

This shabby workhorse of a wagon Steve gave a name; he called him "Jazzy" because the truck reminded him of a worn-out saxophone player he once saw in a subway station; the musician was tired but he could still play, and every day, he blew his horn for coins tossed to him by passengers on their way to work.

Steve could be affectionate toward his bedraggled vehicle, speaking to it on occasion as to a friendly partner in labor: "How 'bout it, Jazzy?" he would say in the morning. "Ready to go to work?" he would ask, with a tap on the hood before climbing inside.

Most days, Jazzy was ready, for like his owner, he was a dependable blue-collar worker who ceased resisting his fate. Jazzy was a jalopy alright, and sometimes he needed coaxing to start-up on cold mornings, but once revved against the elements, he did not deliberate when attending to his daily labor. In fact, he seemed eager to push on through the traffic that was his life on the roadway. If the square tin machine could think, he would have recognized that he was a box truck after all, and that it was best for him and for everyone involved to simply find purpose in the tumble of the work-week that rumbled one day after another as seamlessly as day fades into dusk and then into darkness.

Steve didn't want a new truck anyway. The neighborhoods where he delivered furniture were among the most dangerous in the city; an expensive vehicle would only alert the punks who sidled in the shadows of the slums. If the gangs spotted a truck with an unlocked entry door, for example, particularly a late-model one, they would ambush the box, even when in motion, and scatter its cargo upon the roadway. Thus pillaged, the contents would then be whisked away down dangerous alleys. It was modern-day pirating. Steve knew from experience it was a risk to chase after the rogues in their own waters, so to speak. Consequently, he was always diligent throughout the day about security, asking repeatedly, "Did you lock the truck?"

I first met Jazzy when Steve dated my sister. The first time I actually got inside the truck was after he married her. Steve was my brother-in law who offered me a job. I would be his helper. We would deliver wall units and dining room tables with chairs throughout the city. There was some assembly required. Upon delivery of a dinette, for example, it was necessary to screw the legs to the table top. Upon delivery of chairs, the cushions needed to be fastened to the frame. This we did with electric drills that we carried with us in a leather tool belt in the fashion of a six shooter thrust inside of the holster of a cowboy.

I was not a trucker like Steve. I was in my second year of college studying philosophy, much to the dismay of my parents. My mother thought it might lead somewhere, perhaps to a law degree or a teaching position, so she was tolerant of my studies. My father was a bit more skeptical. He was a contractor who supervised the installation of concrete foundations for skyscrapers. His firm, Tully and DiNapoli, had worked on the footings of the Florida Building at the '64 World's Fair in New York City. When addressing my choice of majors in college, my father could become sarcastic, saying things like, "Son...I suppose one day you will join the Local Philosopher's Union 10211?" I knew what he meant. Usually, he would follow with a bit of practical wisdom; "You better get a job in the meantime... just in case things don't work out."

So between college semesters and during the summer break, there I was with Steve and Jazzy delivering heavy furniture to apartments throughout the five boroughs of New York City. Typically, we would get on the road at seven o'clock in the morning, and I would check the manifest to help organize the day's deliveries. What frightened me most were the apartments that were located on the sixth floor, because in the boroughs, a building with six stories or less did not have elevators. These we called six-story walk-ups, and when hauling weighty boxes, it was with sweat and grimaces that we would negotiate the narrow stairwells.

Early in the day, we delivered the furniture to the poor sections of the Bronx or Harlem or Brooklyn because we had little cash with us in the morning, and because our arms and legs were not exhausted from heavy lifting and from climbing stairs all day. In the afternoons, we delivered expensive wall units to fabulous apartments whose doorman would escort us in air-conditioned elevators to wealthy patrons who served us iced-tea and gave us hefty tips. It was a pleasant way to end the work day. I understood that wealthy people could afford new furniture, but I was puzzled by the impoverished recipients. I asked Steve about it.

"How is it possible that people who live in poverty can afford to buy a new dining room table and chairs?" I asked.

Steve looked at me with interest. "I thought you knew," he said. "In a welfare situation, a kitchen table and some chairs are considered a necessity...everyone needs a place to sit and to eat for heaven's sake...and so the state will provide for them."

That made sense, but it didn't seem right that people had to rely on the state to provide furniture. It made more sense to provide work and education so people could get out of the ghetto for good. Some of the residences on the manifest were flat-out unsafe, and living there was worse than jail.

One morning, on our way to the day's first delivery, Steve warned me about our immediate destination. He was anything but casual about the delivery. "Be careful with this one," he cautioned. "We are going into hell itself, so do as I say, and keep a close watch on Jazzy."

We pulled into a spot in front of an abandoned brick tenement that appeared to me as a building shelled by firebombs; broken glass and litter was everywhere evident. "You're kidding?" I asked incredulously. "Nobody lives here!"

Steve knew he had parked Jazzy in one of the most dangerous neighborhoods in the city, and I could see he was nervous; all manner of his speech and demeanor was sober and humorless. He told me we needed to get in and out of the building, and the vicinity, as quickly as possible.

"I'm going up to see that the owner has the paperwork in order. Stay near the truck until I return ...don't lift the tailgate...and try to look tough... you are the only one around here without a weapon. I'll be right back."

Steve was gone in an instant. I got out of the truck and looked around. A starved dog and a derelict lay sprawled together near a wall; a woman wearing a ragged wool coat pushed a shopping cart across the courtyard; a few dirty-brown sparrows searched for tidbits on the crumbled concrete pavement. It was quiet. I scanned the recesses for hoodlums.

Steve re-emerged from the entranceway, and with purposeful strides, he hustled to the truck. "Let's do it!" he declared, and straight away the tailgate was up and the cardboard cartons containing a table and four chairs were placed on two hand trucks heading inside the perilous apartment building.

Once inside the foyer, the smell was nauseating. Down the hallway, I witnessed a drug addict urinating on an interior wall. The building had an elevator, and Steve had wedged a screwdriver between the doors to keep them open to save time. Our destination was on the third floor, and as we turned toward the apartment, the whole of the building smelled of feces. We passed several occupied residences, and one dwelling was without a front door. From inside, two children peered at us through the opening as we passed. At last, we knocked upon the bolted entry of the household where the dweller was waiting to receive a new kitchen table and chairs.

A portly woman, well-dressed for business, was waiting for us. She appeared eager to return to work. It was dark inside the apartment. I set up quickly and began assembling the chairs. A bead of sweat appeared upon my brow; I never worked more intently.

"Steve!" I called out, as I set the padded cushion upon the aluminum frame. "I need light! Turn on the lights so I can see what I'm doing!"

The woman who resided in this space moved slowly toward the switch on the wall; she was reluctant to comply with my request. I looked to her and she appeared despondent. After deliberating for several seconds more, she flicked the switch. All at once light flooded the room, and I was stunned! In all directions on the floor, cockroaches scattered for the cover of darkness. I looked to the kitchen sink, and clogged as it was with dishes, countless roaches leapt and scurried in panicky flight all about the counter. I very nearly staggered, and Steve looked at me sternly.

"Get a move on!" he demanded, and I resumed my work with fervor.

We completed the assembly and we rushed back to Jazzy. Fortunately, the old box truck was unscathed by vandals. I reached for the door handle to jump into the cab when Steve collared me, slapping my arm away from the lever. He was breathing heavy and his voice was hoarse:

"Shake out your cuffs!" he shouted.

"What do you mean?" I asked.

"Your clothes...dust away any cockroaches... shake them out!"

Steve was disgusted. I followed his lead and I shook out my clothes as requested. Satisfied we were roach free, we jumped into the cab together and sped away.

It was quiet inside the cab. Steve was upset and he banged once with his fist upon the steering wheel. He rolled the window down and he spit on the roadway. When we were some distance away from the filthy location, driving on a familiar thoroughfare, I broke the silence:

"How can she live like that?" I asked. "That place is disgusting! Why doesn't she spray pesticides to get rid of the cockroaches for God's sake?"

Once again, Steve looked at me with interest. "Get rid of the cockroaches?" he snorted, his face contorted. "The whole building is infested with them! She can't get rid of the cockroaches!"

I let his comment sink in. He was right. The residence was verminous, and likely rat-infested. I wasn't going to ask another question, so I stared blankly out the window. Eventually, Steve asked me a question. There was sadness in his voice.

"Did you notice how she manages the cockroaches?" he asked.

I admitted I did not know what he meant.

"The cockroaches...she kept them hidden by keeping the lights off in the apartment...that's why it was so dark in there...that way she could ignore them...keep them out of sight."

Quiet returned to the truck. I remembered the woman's behavior when I asked for light in the room. She appeared despondent. I thought long about the appalling conditions of the building. It hit me hard, because until I saw it for myself, I could not have imagined that people lived that way. I was thinking it was shameful and humiliating for anyone to smell the urine and the feces and to live with the drug addicts and the cockroaches.

And then I remembered the two helpless children who stared at us in the hallway as we passed them. I felt sadness, too. I wondered if anyone would provide for them the essentials to keep them safe and functioning well. Who would maintain their health and feed them always quarter-full so they would not suck grime from the mucky bottom of the filthy ghetto? Would anyone speak affectionately to them or coax them to start up on cold mornings?

I wondered if the children huddled in the dwelling would turn out to be punks in a gang of pirates who sidled in the shadows of the slums waiting to ambush late-model box trucks. And then I wished that Steve and I could have scooped the children up right there in the hallway and given them a ride on our hand trucks to some place far-away from the drug addicts and the cockroaches.

Jazzy picked up speed as we entered the Cross Bronx Expressway. Steve crushed his empty paper coffee cup, tossed it carelessly upon the floor, brushed his pants' cuff again, and let out a sigh. It was quiet in the truck for quite a few miles.

The Bedroom Window

One thing you want to have in a Linden Cape on a freezing January evening is plenty of insulation between the rafters. You might also want to consider caulking the windows, checking for leaks around the exterior doors, and making sure that the oil burner is working at peak efficiency. Ken Wilson didn't think his house on 28th Street had received any of these considerations against the cold. In fact, when the winter winds assaulted the modest frame house and gusts blasted against the cracked seals of the old window frames, a rustle of the curtains within the cozy residence revealed the inefficacy of the caked casings to combat the frigid air. As for the front door, when snowstorms pounded upon it, the blustery flakes like tiny spirit-soldiers would advance stealthily under the doorsill, leaving their downy presence melting on the living room carpet. One might suppose correctly that the interior of the Wilson house was sometimes chilly during the winter months, but no one in the family complained, as this seasonal inconvenience was expected and accepted by everyone.

Of course, there were plenty of ways to keep warm inside the home, and Ken took advantage of the most obvious one when he wrapped himself warm with a brightly-colored knit blanket his grandmother had crocheted during the summer months. In fact, there were no less than eight such blankets available, not including those that were ready in storage as gifts for Christmas and birthdays, as Ken's grandmother, when she wasn't reading, could be found in her comfort chair with a pair of long wooden knitting needles and a bundle of colorful yarn on her lap. And on this particularly cold winter evening, he was grateful of her efforts.

At about 7:00 pm, Ken plopped his weary fifteen year old body onto the sagging couch in front of the television and he flitted through the channels before the hockey game came on an hour later. His mother was in the kitchen cleaning up dinner plates and his brother and sister were nowhere near the TV. With his blanket wrapped cozily about him and with the couch all to himself, Ken let a sweet grogginess take hold of him; the full comfort of his dinner eased him into a sleepy stupor, and soon the glare of the lights in the living room dimmed gently into a haze and the drone of the television voices sank softly into a whisper. Before long, he was sound asleep.

Ken was sleeping for only a few moments when he was awakened without warning by an uproar; an ear-splitting, blood-curdling scream the likes of which he had never heard before came blaring from the staircase. Ken reacted to the shocking outburst by springing from the sofa in disheveled confusion to witness his sister Nancy rushing down the steps with tears flooding her cheeks. She was panic-stricken. Nancy was a petite fourteen year old girl, and with her eyes wild and her voice terrified, she was shrieking frantically for her mother.

"Mom! Someone is at the window! I saw someone at my window!" she cried, and through her hysteria, it became evident that a stranger's face had peered at her from an upstairs bedroom window; a terrible face staring at her through the glass.

With his sister sobbing uncontrollably in her mother's arms at the bottom of the stairs, Ken abruptly bolted. Taking two steps at a time, he sprinted up the stairwell into his sister's bedroom. The window was without curtains and he could see a hint of his reflection in the window pane. He rushed to the window's edge and tried to open it. Quickly he abandoned the effort, and at close range, he cupped his hands about his temples and pressed his face against the glass. Into the darkness he searched, but as expected, he saw only his neighbor's house illuminated by residual light from the streetlamps.

Satisfied that the danger had passed, Ken stepped back from the window and stood in the center of the bedroom, and with the light emanating from the ceiling lamp, he saw that from within the windowpane, his own reflection was gazing back at him. Bobbing his head back and forth like a pigeon, he could see his own bobbing image replicated as in a dark mirror; he could see also how someone might be startled, mistakenly imagining that an intruder was staring inside the room when all the while it was one's own reflection in the glass. Further, the window belonged to a second story room without a balcony, and it was not possible for anyone to reach that height. Ken realized that his younger sister may have grown nervous momentarily and her own reflection frightened her, appearing in the window as the face of someone else.

Ken relaxed his shoulders and he adopted the persona of a clever sleuth who had solved an important mystery. He descended the stairs nonchalantly and explained the whole circumstance to his mother, careful to relate all of the details that caused his sister's erroneous conclusion that someone was there in the first place.

"There wasn't anyone at the window," Ken said, by way of explanation. "It was a reflection from the lamp. You saw your own image in the glass, you silly fool. You frightened yourself! Ha! Ha!"

Ken's comments were received awkwardly as there was nothing to laugh about, and Nancy remained inconsolable in her mother's arms. Ken decided to put the whole thing behind him and he made his way back to the couch and to the start of the anticipated hockey game.

A few minutes passed and his sister's anxiety was unrelenting. Ken's mother appeared dissatisfied with the explanation and she ordered Ken off the couch to scout around the house perimeter to "take a look around." Ken thought differently about the request and he foolishly informed his mother that it was very cold outside, and because the hockey game would start any minute, he preferred to stay near the television. His mother turned her head in disbelief; she was a strong woman, and as a parent, her authority was not to be challenged. In fact, she could hardly believe her own ears, and with one look at her son, Ken vaulted from the couch.

"Okay! Okay! I thought you were *asking* me! I'm sorry. I'll check it out," he said.

Ken couldn't get his shoes on fast enough, and he was relieved when his mother spoke to him softly.

"I just want to be sure," she said, and it was clear to Ken that his mother and his young sister were still very upset by the ordeal.

His jacket was inadequate to the twenty degree temperatures when Ken looked about the front yard, but he was only going to be scouting for a minute. He went to his left beyond the garage and he turned the corner of the house to survey the area where the threatened bedroom window split the peaks of the roof. When he could ascertain a clear view of the section of the yard where the intrigue allegedly transpired, Ken was shocked and his knees buckled; he could not trust what he was seeing. "Oh My God!" he whispered in disgust as he backed away, observing incredulously. He could no longer feel the cold; his breath ceased and his feet moved mechanically as his brain processed what lay stark and undeniable in front of his disbelieving eyes. Propped tall against the house and angled directly to access his sister's second story window, an aluminum extension ladder appeared abandoned, and it leaned there as undeniable evidence of Nancy's horror. Here was the proof that a criminal did indeed glare at her through the glass, and what's more, Ken understood that the immoral interloper could not be too far from the ladder.

"Mom!" Ken exclaimed. "Stay calm! There is a ladder leaning against our house...there is a ladder there...and someone was at the window...I didn't see anyone because..."

"Get your brother up here right now!" interrupted his mother, and she was all action; she was fearless and she was immediately on the telephone.

Ken's older brother Jack was in the basement all the while, and having sensed some commotion, he was already up the stairs and standing with Ken outdoors, staring at the dreadful ladder. Jack was a powerfully-built athlete and a star wrestler on the varsity wrestling team, and he was on his cell phone without delay. The police were notified, and the immediate danger probably had passed, but there in the darkness, Ken could see that his older brother was beginning to boil over. Jack was nineteen years old and already a man and he did not take the assault of an intruder calmly; one part of him recognized the trespass as a personal insult. Suddenly, his friend Jason appeared from out of the shadows of the yard.

"What's going on?" Jason asked, and then he saw the ladder.

Jason was a neighbor whose property was adjacent to the Wilson's backyard; he was also a talented wrestler, and having received Jack's distress call, he flew to the scene to offer his assistance. In the meantime, no one expected his shocking declaration:

"That's our ladder!" he shrieked, pointing. "My dad keeps it lying outdoors along the foundation of the house. It's aluminum and will not rust. That's our ladder!"

This news confounded everyone until it was decided that the creepy prowler had lifted the ladder from Jason's concrete foundation and transported it through the yards for access to the window.

"*Let's get him!*" was declared by all, and in the company of these two strong young men, Ken felt suddenly emboldened. The three of them began searching the neighborhood in the manner of a military operation. They circled nearby properties. They were going to get this guy, and if they did find him, it would end badly.

Unbeknownst to Ken, his brother Jack with his neighbor Jason were texting other wrestlers all the while, who notified other wrestlers, and still others, and it would be accurate to imagine careening cars belonging to high school seniors racing towards 28th Street that cold winter evening, for quickly the word had spread and Ken realized he would soon be a part of a small army. Cars began pulling up to the house; unfamiliar athletes joined in the search. "Over here!" came one of the masculine voices.

Oddly, an old worthless mattress was discovered hidden in a corner of the yard, and with it were stained and filthy clothes as befitting a homeless person. The police arrived, and Ken and the wrestlers circled back to the house. Unfortunately, it was evident to everyone -- including the police -- the lawbreaker had escaped.

Nothing happened for several weeks, and with time, some confidence and optimism returned to Nancy. Her brothers remained vigilant though; each evening they were sure to safeguard the premises before retiring. The family pretended the ordeal was over, but still, with the darkness of night, an icy draft wafted into in the Wilson's home, and there wouldn't be relaxed warmth within it until the police rang the doorbell with some news.

Finally, the doorbell rang. The Corona family lived one block away, and Lori Corona was a fourteen year old girl who ran terrorized from her bedroom window. She had seen a stranger's face looking in at her, and this time her brothers tackled the scoundrel in their yard. The bruised intruder was arrested, and his identity established.

The criminal was a quiet teenager who had recently moved to the neighborhood. He seemed to be a loner. He made some money as a paperboy, and no one suspected that upon his daily deliveries, he had identified the homes of his female victims. Ken and Jack were outraged; their intentions of physical retaliation upon the trespasser had been voiced from the beginning; each had openly sworn revenge upon the culprit for what he had done to their sister. They remained furious, but emotions changed when the police presented a very somber version of the ruined future that lay ahead for the disturbed boy. Ken and Jack listened attentively to the police officer at their door.

"It's very sad," the officer began. "He's a troubled fourteen years old kid who only sometimes attends the ninth grade. He has a history of bizarre activities and his family circumstances are unspeakable. His childhood has been tragic and cruel, including physical and mental abuse by his parents. Recently, he ran away from his violent home, and he has been living in filth, sleeping on a dirty mattress he drags to various places in the neighborhood."

The policeman presented an official document to Ken's mother verifying the criminal episode at the Wilson residence. "You must file charges; it is for his own safety," insisted the official plaintively. "He needs help. By signing this document, the authorities can provide assistance."

The officer's words had a calming effect upon the family. He turned to reassure Nancy directly: "Rest easy, young lady, we caught him. Eventually, he will be relocated to a facility for rehabilitation; he will not be on these streets again for a very long time."

Eight Ball

It was a steady unrelenting rain. In Suffolk County, homeowners took note of their vulnerable outdoor umbrellas and they worried about flooding in their basements. Commuters checked the news concerning road hazards to avoid timely delays. Slickers and boots were worn by everyone. A thick grey fog coated the community. On such a day as this one, parks were deserted; birds were silent; pets were sheltered; children were ushered along sidewalks without mirth. It was a day to remain indoors.

Mr. Carlos Rodriguez and his eleven year old son Emilio decided to make the best of things. After securing candles for Mrs. Rodriguez in the event of a power outage, Carlos good-naturedly challenged his son to a contest.

"How about it, then?" he asked Emilio. "Perhaps the thunderstorm will put some fury into your game."

With a smile on his young face, Emilio descended the stairway with his father to the finished room below the den. A regulation-sized pool table purchased second-hand from a billiard gallery in town lay majestic beneath a stained-glass ceiling lamp. With his father's old cue in his hand, the young boy asked:

"What shall it be then, father? A few games of Eight Ball?"

Without waiting for a reply, Emilio twirled his fingers deftly inside the leathery pockets and promptly he filled the wooden triangle rack with ivory billiard balls. He banked the lively white cue ball off the cushion near the side pocket to his patient father waiting at the other end of the table.

Carlos chalked his cue and took note of the exquisite pearl inlay on the birch shaft. He placed the expensive pool cue horizontally upon the expansive cloth and rolled it like a cigar to reaffirm its integrity.

Meanwhile, Emilio removed any dead space within the rack, and with solids and stripes as neighbors, he liberated the colorful spheres upon the designated spot. This was a pleasant ceremony enjoyed by father and son, and as much as the pool game itself was always enjoyable, the activity overall provided time for both of them to talk 'man-to-man' so to speak, and to share informally all things, no matter how frivolous, that might be on their minds. Young Emilio was usually quite competitive by nature when engaged in sport with his peers, but he cherished this time with his father, and both of them understood the value of this time spent together; it barely mattered to either of them who won the contest.

Emilio had something on his mind. In two short weeks he would be going to a prestigious summer camp for boys in New Hampshire. He would spend three weeks, and he was feeling insecure overall; he had little preparation for the kinds of competitive activities that took place there. He read the brochures and spent hours checking over the webpage, and in his opinion, things looked pretty bleak. He didn't mind that eight boys shared a cabin, or that a single bath was provided for them, or that meals were served from a buffet line. What concerned Emilio in particular was the strange nature of sport that was commonplace at such a camp.

"*Crack!*" sounded the break as Carlos Rodriguez sent the balls scattering across the table. The three ball scurried toward the corner pocket and it found refuge inside.

"Solids!" declared the indomitable patriarch, strutting about the table surveying his options. Emilio leaned back and attentively considered the table as well, and he developed a preliminary strategy as if it were his privilege to score next.

"Father?" asked Emilio, waiting patiently for his turn after the break. "I am afraid to be embarrassed when I am at camp. What good am I at such things as archery? How can I compete at horse-shoes? At kayaking?"

Carlos was a man who had not attended a summer camp as a boy and he had not ever visited one. He could not speak from experience. His family lived in the suburban town of Brentwood on Long Island, and his youthful environment was vastly dissimilar to the pastoral farmlands and the primitive woodlands of a remote sanctuary in rural New Hampshire. He considered his son's concerns as reasonable and authentic and he was not about to dismiss them perfunctorily. He listened carefully, as his son voiced his worries:

"I am afraid because I am not a great swimmer, and I don't know about snorkeling," Emilio continued without emotion. "Dad... what is tetherball?"

Carlos did not know anything about tetherball. What he did know was that camp offered other familiar and enjoyable activities for his son. Carlos was thoughtful when he finally responded. "There are many other things there, Emilio. You can play baseball and soccer there, as well as volleyball and lacrosse. Why are you worried about these things?" he asked with genuine empathy.

Carlos took the long shot at the five ball, and it hung wedged at the pocket's edge without falling. Emilio's turn was at hand. The young boy already held the cue as would a skilled adult, having spent hours perfecting a professional stance and approach to the table. His aim was flawless as the cue ball kissed the striped nine ball and it plopped obligingly into the side pocket. For a few seconds he stood alert to the play-options open to him on the table.

"I think that I will be good with the team sports alright," Emilio replied. "I am worried when I am alone and I cannot perform well in front of everyone. I don't know how to water ski or to wakeboard. I don't know about rifles or dramatics."

Emilio solidly bit into the glossy white cue ball with a dashed stroke, hurtling it into the eleven ball, and the intended English reversed the pearly cue ball back toward the rail. The fourteen ball was a ringer hanging precipitously close to the edge in the far corner.

"Lots of green!" said Carlos, attempting playfully to rattle his son's confidence by pointing out the extensive distance between the cue ball and the target ball. Emilio bent low and gently he nudged the white cue ball toward the far end; lazily it rolled across the emerald expanse and softly it kissed. The striped ball fell at last into the leathery nest.

"Good shot!" affirmed his father. "As for the individual sports and events, I think, Emilio, you will have a choice. You may avoid unpleasant ones and remember...there will be other campers who will not know these things either."

Emilio was disappointed when he missed a bank shot into the side pocket. He stood back with his cue held upright like a soldier's musket held at his side.

"I was thinking I might win a trophy at something," Emilio remarked. "I want to win *at something*. I will try not to be embarrassed, but, do you think maybe we could learn how to play croquet and shuffleboard before I go there?" Emilio hesitated before he went on. He thought his father should choose the one-ball combination off the four ball instead of the banked four ball in the side pocket. "And dad," he said, "they do an awful lot of things with horses."

The two players completed six matches before they returned to the kitchen. The fierce rain had not diminished and it would continue to rain steadily for the rest of the evening. Emilio and his father had struck a bargain. There were still two weeks remaining before the start of camp, and Carlos promised his son he would find time away from work in order to alleviate some of his concerns. They would make an effort.

Over the next two weeks, Carlos and Emilio could be found together all over Long Island. They journeyed first out to Montauk to the *Deep Hollow Ranch* where scenic horse-back riding was available; they spent an afternoon in the stables at the *Thomas School* in Woodbury. At *Bethpage Golf Course*, they practiced at the driving range. Kayaks were rented in Riverhead and they went fishing at *Connetquot State Park* in Oakdale. At dusk one evening, Emilio practiced casting lures from his lawn to his driveway. Mrs. Rodriguez found an old croquet set and a ruffled badminton net at a flea market and everyone played a few games in the yard. The family roller-skated and played tennis and they tore up the turf playing horse shoes. They visited the shore at *Robert Moses State Park*, and with bruised knees, they wobbled on bogey boards until the sun set. They wore goggles when they swam in the pool. They hiked the *Sunken Forest*, and they studied the geology and the flora of the woods at *Cedar Point*. The family lit a campfire at night in their backyard. They ate smores. Carlos even tried to tell a frightening story, but gave it up for a joke instead. The family laughed. By the time camp registration arrived two weeks later, the family had experienced more fun-filled activities than they had in the previous three summers combined. Emilio still had his doubts about camp activities, but he was having so much fun, he forgot about negative things altogether. When the time finally came to leave home, the sun was shining. Father and son loaded the Chevy Tahoe and headed north toward New Hampshire. Six hours later, they arrived at camp.

A long row of century old maples lined the drive to the camp headquarters. In the distance, the cool blue waters of the lake glistened. Cabins stood like boxes under the pines and there in plain view could be seen all things rustic. Campers circled cautiously with their parents, and each of them wondered which young person might become a significant friend. Emilio was grateful to his parents for the efforts they had made on his behalf. At last, Carlos said goodbye to his son. Emilio waved to the retreating Tahoe before he disappeared inside his cabin.

It did not take long for Emilio to become comfortable with his surroundings. He had met two friends who were more reserved and shy than he, and together, they had climbed Peacock Hill. He soon discovered that many of the sports at the camp were not very competitive after all, although there were a few events that were spirited and even cut-throat, and so quite naturally, at some events he thrived, and at others he barely survived. Emilio was determined, nonetheless, to make a mark for himself; it was his intention to win a trophy if at all possible. Try as he might, however, the young competitor fell short of the prize in each contest.

At home, Carlos knew from the old-fashioned, hand-written letters he received from Emilio (computers were off limits at the camp; it was part of the appeal) that his boy was pleased with the camp. Emilio wrote enthusiastically in much detail and he had conveyed in each correspondence a healthy enthusiasm overall, and his reassuring words were sufficient to dispel any angst related to his camp experience. Carlos had every reason to think positively. Things were going very well.

During the final four days at camp, it rained. It was a steady unrelenting rain. The campers were soaked to the bone and activities shifted indoors. Carlos and his wife wondered if Emilio was able to keep dry, and suddenly they were unsure if their young son had brought sufficient rain gear. Camp was ending in a couple of days, so the notion of bringing Emilio clothing immediately was not sensible. The boy would simply have to make the best of things.

It was still raining when Carlos reentered the promenade of maples to pick up Emilio on the final day. Campers shuffled about the grounds with sagging heads and with drenched backpacks searching for their families. When reunited, Emilio lunged at his father and Carlos lifted him high into the air. Quickly they dispatched the wet gear to the rear of the SUV, and together they rushed across the soggy field to a short farewell presentation already underway in a tarp-covered outdoor amphitheater. Huddled close under the make-shift canopy, the parents and the campers listened as best they could to the closing ceremony. The water droplets fell noisily upon the canvas and the rain trickled like a curtain about the perimeter of the improvised structure.

On a small stage, the camp director was intent upon thanking everyone. It had been another successful summer session. Eventually, he announced that he wished to recognize with trophies and plaques a few lucky campers who had been noteworthy for various accomplishments. Michael Calloway was far and away the best swimmer at camp, and he received thunderous applause from his family and friends when his name was called to pick up his prize. Kevin Sheehan was a born camper, and by all accounts, he was the reincarnation of Daniel Boone. He received a prize. Mark Hanson ran faster than anyone had a right to, and he could catch, punt, throw and wrestle better than anyone in the country, or so it seemed. He sprinted like an Olympian to the stage, and he waved his trophy for all to envy. At all of the contests, Emilio knew he had done his best, so he didn't really feel very disappointed after all. Carlos wasn't disappointed either. He was proud of his son's attitude, and he didn't need a plaque to hang on the wall anyway. Father and son turned to one another, and without words, they read each other's satisfaction. They were ready to go home.

"As you know," boomed the voice of the camp director. "It has been raining steadily for the last four days. Each rainy day we did our best to keep busy inside the main lodge, but our indoor activities were stretched to the limit. Campers were teetering upon inconsolable boredom until one young man's extraordinary skill created quite a stir here at the camp."

Carlos and Emilio stood together, listening attentively.

"As everyone knows," he continued, "we don't access the internet here at camp, and there are no video games and such, so during each waterlogged afternoon, many campers tried their skill at checkers or at chess, at ping pong or at board games. It was getting a bit dreary; let me tell you, until one young man with his astonishing accuracy captivated the attention of everyone during the stormy days."

Carlos' knees buckled with pride when he heard the next pronouncement.

"Emilio is the best darned pool player this camp has ever seen! After thirty-seven matches, he remains undefeated at the game of Eight Ball! Emilio Rodriguez! Come on up and take your trophy! Congratulations Emilio!"

The Girl with the Scars

Young John Dennison was feeling pretty accomplished for a fourth year teacher, as well he might, for he had worked diligently and his proficiency in the business was being acknowledged by nearly everyone. It was not easy though. He remembered his first year as especially difficult; he taught English literature to five classes with roughly 27 students per class, and he had little time for himself. He spent many hours preparing exhaustive lesson plans that were only sometimes effective, and most of the remaining time he spent correcting papers, as it was his practice to return to students each writing essay *with detailed corrections* without delay. As for classroom management, he studied how to be consistent and fair under adverse circumstances. When addressing disruptive student behavior, for example, he learned not to be accusatory without offering to the student a way to amend the situation. Concerning curriculum matters, there were times he led his students astray; sometimes he made sudden turns without looking and he headed the wrong way down one way streets that were dead-ends anyway. There were other times he escorted students to places unforgettable and exhilarating; the literature he presented danced and sang and spun within the impressionable minds of everyone inside his classroom. He didn't know it then, but administrators had recognized a natural talent in the young man, and he received favorable evaluations and well-deserved encouragement from experienced staff. His students knew he was sincere, and he was popular; he was all-business when necessary and he never made the rookie mistake of trying to be his students' friend. He understood his purpose was to model successful behavior and he knew that students had plenty of friends already. Nonetheless, he stumbled often and he felt his heart ache with self-doubt.

His second year was much improved; he corrected curriculum misjudgments so that students better grasped the strategies needed to perform well on state exams, and he was feeling comfortable enough to gradually release aspects of his personality into a few lessons. He still had problems, of course, but he understood systemic procedures better and he grasped the wisdom of many of them. He called a student's home for both positive and negative behaviors; he was on time for meetings and he listened attentively; he was careful to avoid office gossip and he rarely spoke negatively about anyone, especially his students. It helped that he loved the literature he taught, and without knowing how exactly, his enthusiasm for *Macbeth* and for *The Grapes of Wrath* was so naturally evident in his lessons that students rarely interrupted him without genuine questions entirely on task. He found the classics so entertaining that given the opportunity, (which was his job) he was able to animate the text with great voice and vibrant demeanor. The year went well overall, and as he improved his craft, student performance improved as well.

In his third year, Mr. John Dennison could address his students as an educator with some confidence and skill. His determination to succeed never wavered. Having shaken procedural inhibitions and generally mastered time-management issues, he was determined to pull together all of his resources. He was great with technology; his readings of the literature were engaging yet he knew very well the value of variety, and many times he presented a professional's voice and interpretation of the literary work via the smart-board. His graphics were current and awash with dynamic visuals always relevant and delivered with rapid-fire precision; his lessons were sometimes turned over to students in groups to evaluate controversial themes enabling all to comment and to discuss personal connections to the literature. On most days, before a class lesson became in the least stagnant, the forty-two minutes were over and students were dismissed. He also displayed a clever and charming sense of humor.

By the end of his third year of teaching, Mr. Dennison appeared suddenly to everyone as a consummate professional, and when he walked the hallways before and after lessons, his demeanor was that of millionaires, though money was unrelated to his accomplishments. No amount of money can purchase charisma, and this young man had plenty of it, and many parents in the district were spreading the word that he was gifted.

In September of his fourth year and during the first days of classes, something very disturbing jolted Mr. Dennison out of the academic ivory tower he had constructed. Without realizing it, the developing teacher had focused primarily on the success of each of his lessons; he was not adequately-attuned to the recipients of them. No doubt his tutorials were impressive, and most students accepted them gratefully. But when Mr. John Dennison exited his classroom that first day of his fourth year, something had changed.

The semester for students began mid-week on a Thursday as usual, and Mr. Dennison was early to his classroom preparing for a class of tenth-graders with varying language arts capabilities. Across the hallway, the talented Ms. Angela Flinta could be heard introducing Standard Algebra to freshmen; she spoke with formality and acuity and her confident voice was appealing to her students that first day of classes. She was beckoning each to remain attentive during her lessons. Her alluring voice drifted across the hall to Mr. Dennison as would a pleasing melody.

"The basis of algebra is found in arithmetic," she explained sweetly, "and the student will find in algebra many things familiar to him in arithmetic. In fact, there is no clear line of demarcation between algebra and arithmetic. The fundamental principles of each are identical, but in algebra, their application is broader than it is in arithmetic."

Her euphonious words bolstered John's enthusiasm for his own lesson, and so he put aside his lesson preparations to listen further.

"To illustrate, arithmetic teaches the meaning of 5 minus 3 and so does algebra, but it will be seen that algebra is more general than arithmetic in that it gives a meaning also to 3 minus 5, which in arithmetic is meaningless." Ms. Flinta lingered for a moment for a heightened effect. "In algebra, my young scholars, addition does not always mean an increase or subtraction a decrease."

"Bravo!" thought Mr. Dennison, and he was glad to be working near Ms. Angela Flinta again this year. She was a supportive friend and a marvelous teacher.

When Mr. Dennison's own students filed past him into his classroom that first day of his fourth year, he instructed each of them to check their schedule for accuracy and he announced that the seating would be arranged alphabetically until further notice. Students were accustomed to this assembly but they grunted anyway because it sabotaged all hopes of sitting with a distracting friend. Once settled, My Dennison addressed his students by reviewing briefly the literature from the previous semester. He reviewed because he knew it was comforting for nervous students to hear familiar themes and characters, as familiarity always reduces stress, and right at the beginning, he wanted to establish a comfortable setting overall. One strategy he employed, for example, was when he pretended a hazy remembrance of a specific character or event in a novel they had read the previous semester, thereby inviting a confident student to volunteer a suitable response, and in this manner, he could open things up a bit. Outspoken students offered the appropriate specifics for everyone in the class, and the shy ones were grateful to be left alone. The skilled instructor then worked the lesson forward by outlining with enthusiasm the major works of literature the class would be enjoying during the upcoming semester.

Mr. Dennison next addressed his expectations for writing assignments, and perhaps inspired by the punctilious Ms. Flinta, he was relatively thorough from the outset when he spoke of them.

"Writing assignments will fall under four categories," he began. "The narrative and the descriptive essays will demonstrate specific literary devices when completed; dialogue will delight us and add variety to our composition; meaningful details will enhance our comprehension; rhetorical questions will invite us to participate in the effort; metaphor and simile, personification and sentence variety will reveal something about the author and his or her skills."

He paused, then, to allow students a moment to process his academic barrage.

"The expository writing and the persuasive writing will be supported by relevant facts and current statistics; the student will proffer believable exemplars and be prepared to argue capably both sides of a worthy thesis; the authority one cites within the text must be a creditable scholar or established expert, or indeed, a reliable witness or unfortunate victim… and then there is the research paper, a world unto itself!"

Having dispensed with content matters, Mr. Dennison rested another moment, for he understood that in the performing arts, including his own, stillness and silence are as important as movement and sound, particularly during a monologue. He picked up a piece of white chalk from the sill.

"Oh yes," he continued, feigning his next point as an afterthought. "Spelling errors by tenth graders will not be tolerated. The idea that one is a life-long spelling dyslexic will not cut it on the English regents, or on the SAT examinations; both assessments will be hand written by you without the spelling, grammar check or thesaurus you rely upon when communicating your thoughts with words on the computer. Unfortunately, one's poor handwriting can negatively affect overall scores as well."

Students believed correctly that these archaic hand-written exam practices should end immediately, and Mr. Dennison sided with the use of technology; he believed, as did his students, that no one on earth communicated with pen and pencil anymore, except to express an appropriate sentiment on a postcard.

"Let me illustrate," Mr. Dennison said as he slowly wrote large letters on the blackboard appropriately choreographed to his anecdote. "A previous student of mine wished to describe a furry rodent that thrived in the suburbs. It was a small animal with large gnawing incisor teeth, an expert climber and gatherer of the hard edible fruit from a plant or tree, and this athletic inhabitant of the canopy he named ...SKWIRL..."

The enigmatic instructor stepped away from the nonsense spelling example on the board for all to witness. The class chuckled as they understood the calamity of his former student's spelling error. Beneath that word, Mr. Dennison then wrote the following error: ...PEPUL...and students were astonished.

"Can anyone tell me what these misspelled words are supposed to represent?" he asked with affected incredulity. The class responded appropriately appreciative of the humor of the misspellings, but Mr. Dennison resumed quickly and he did not acknowledge a student response.

"What is this?" he queried, and he saw that his students were curious and smiling when he wrote... "JEET YET? NO, JU?"... on the blackboard. When no one had it figured correctly, he explained that the garbled interrogative statement intended to ask, "Did you eat yet?" and the response was "No. Did You?"

He spoke further about words often misspelled in general, and he invited students to add to the list. "Everyone has a license," he offered for consideration, "but I assure you, the word *license* is frequently misspelled, as is the word *misspelled* itself. Can anyone spell the word *cemetery*? How about the words *calendar... amateur... sincerely... pastime ... receipt... leisure ... jewelry...sergeant*? Want to try?" Mr. Dennison, in the manner of a game-show host, allowed a few eager students to air out their skill. It was fun.

"Let me offer something else for consideration," the teacher stated, rapidly changing the focus to analogies. "How would you respond if I asked you to identify the object that does not belong in the following collection of objects? Tell me, won't you, which one does not belong? Ready? Choose the one that is dissimilar to the others; ... banana... orange...grapefruit...baseball..."

Hands shot into the air willingly now, as most students recognized the witty ruse as superficial and easily solved; the baseball was not a fruit and the banana was not round. Unfair question! There are two answers!" shouted one student in protest, and another added that "orange" was also a color, establishing yet another disassociation altogether.

There was but a minute remaining in class when Mr. Dennison instructed students to copy the supply list he had written on the board. Students complied hurriedly as the bell would ring momentarily. It was then that the skilled teacher felt weak and his knees buckled; the air grew thin and the shuffling ruckus within the room vanished.

In the closing moments of the first day of class, Mr. Dennison spotted among the busy scribblers, a female student three seats from the front and two rows left of center of the room. She was blonde and otherwise plainly dressed with uneventful make-up and with a few blemishes on her skin. She was tall, and she wore a blue silken blouse with wide lapels. The young lady was not copying from the blackboard; instead, she was clearly distracted and her fingers were unhinging the top button of her shirt. Her breastplate was revealed, and she lifted her lapels away from her skin, and her neck and upper chest exposed a nightmarish horror. In the briefest of moments, Mr. Dennison witnessed upon her bosom an extensive blotched redness of sores and raw, mutilated skin; he saw multiple wounds and they were not bleeding, though they certainly bled when inflicted. It appeared they were caused by the repeated slashing of a sharp knife, though there was no visible crusting. It took another moment, but then the shocking lacerations and terrible slashes appeared to him suddenly to be the result of the sharp edges of a razor blade. So disfigured was her chest, that Mr. Dennison stopped breathing, and when he looked away from the abrasions to her face, he realized she had unwittingly disclosed the abusive scars.

The bell rang and the unknown student covered up quickly as she sprinted up the aisle toward the doorway. "Miss! I wish to speak to you!" called Mr. Dennison, but his entreaty was blocked by another student who approached him and physically stood in his way. He hurried to the door, but she had dashed away and he lost her in the crowded hallway. Students in his next class were already filing past him, and the corridor was clearing as classes would begin momentarily. She was gone for now, and he knew he would find her upon his first opportunity. He glanced finally at the innocent boy who had approached him and he accepted the note that was handed to him. He turned his attention to the note and he read it silently:

Dear Teachers,

I am sorry to inconvenience you concerning the notebooks and supplies Justin Crane needs for his classes. Unfortunately, I do not get paid until Friday and Justin will have a notebook on Monday. Justin is a good student. Thank you.

Sincerly, Mr. Crane

"I need the note for my other classes," the young student named Justin explained sheepishly. "I have to go. Thanks."

Mr. Dennison assured Justin that Monday would be fine for his supplies, and with the note back in his hand, the young boy hustled away. It took a minute for Mr. Dennison to shake free the paralysis caused by the dreadful scars of his unnamed student. He brought his mind back to the more immediate tasks. The Crane family, he realized, didn't have the money for a notebook.

The bell rang and his class sat respectfully next to friends and each pretended they were ready to go. Mr. Dennison explained that the seating arrangement would be alphabetical, and when the groan subsided, he began his lesson. Undetected by his students, Mr. Dennison was rattled to the core. He was perplexed and troubled; but nonetheless, in the delivery of his lesson, he was as expert as a marksman. He had the experience and the maturity he needed. He would find the girl with the scars upon his first opportunity.

When his lunch break arrived, Mr. Dennison headed straight to the guidance office to ascertain the location of several female students in his class. He guessed her name was either Valerie Connors or Kristina Calabrese, as the alphabetical seating arrangement had helped to narrow things considerably. He needed to speak to her before reporting the incident, for in the interim, his own distrust hampered his recollection of the upsetting ordeal. Did he really see what he thought? Did she have a rare skin condition? It was important not to overreact and to embarrass a student unnecessarily. He only saw the injuries for a fleeting moment. He might have it all wrong.

Mr. Dennison found her sitting attentively in room 216, a science classroom. He knocked politely on the door and opened it, interrupting the lesson. He excused himself and surveyed the students inside the room; there sat Valerie Connors, the girl with the scars. Deftly, Mr. Dennison pardoned his presence, explained he had mistakenly entered the wrong room, begged forgiveness of the rude interruption, and he closed the door.

He would not embarrass her by calling attention to her. He would return when class dismissed and he would speak privately with her then. He did exactly that. He returned and he was waiting for her when her science class dismissed.

"Miss Connors," he stated with authority. "You are to come with me. I need to speak with you." It was not a request but a statement of fact from an experienced teacher, and the obedient student complied. The teacher and the student walked in silence to a quiet alcove where they could speak without interruption. Valerie Connors was nearly as tall as he, But Mr. Dennison's authority towered over her, and she listened and accepted the inquiries and concerns for her well-being.

"I am alarmed by the scars I had seen in class this morning, Valerie," Mr. Dennison said, and he was empathetic in his expression. "You must tell me...who did this to you? What is going on? Are you alright?"

Valerie Conners looked past him dazed, and the hard shell she had worn all morning suddenly fell apart, and the tears and sorrow emerged because she was vulnerable, and her face immediately reddened and her countenance appeared flushed. She secured her blouse tight against the reality of her wounds and she began to whimper. She slowly stuttered her words..."It...it is...my....my...It is..." she stammered, turning her face away from her teacher with eyes filled with crying. "I must go to class, Mr. Dennison, please...please..." she said, and it was clear that she wished to be somewhere else.

Mr. Dennison reassured her with comforting words but Valerie was inconsolable. There was nothing else to do or say. Together they walked to the office of the nurse and there the teacher spoke to an assistant without revealing the specific nature of the circumstance. Valerie was better composed there and she settled herself in the office. The assistant whispered to Mr. Dennison that Ms. Garrison, the school's nurse, would be returning to her office before long.

He felt better, for he knew Valerie was in the appropriate place, and he understood that the many legal and practical procedures for caring and protecting potential victims of abuse were available to her here, and he knew it was correct for him to have set them in motion. She would receive attention. Valerie would no longer suffer and her abuser would be identified and arrested. All would go well.

Instead of returning to his classroom, Mr. Dennison went directly to the Main Office to formally report the ordeal. Details were recorded.

Guidance was notified. The administration had experience in these things. Mr. Dennison felt assured that all would go well with Valerie Connors.

All did not go well. The school day ended and the afternoon turned into evening and it was no longer the injuries that haunted Mr. Dennison; he was disturbed by the moment in the alcove when his student very nearly expressed to him the name of the abuser that inflicted the wounds. He sensed, or rather something in the formulation of her last sigh expressed to him, that it was her *father* that was criminally involved. He did not realize it until time had elapsed and he replayed the conversation repeatedly in his mind. He thought Valerie may have formed with her lips the first syllable of a word suggestive of "*fa*" when she broke into sobbing. He could not recall with certainty. Was Valerie beginning to say *fa...ther*?"

The next morning brought renewed vigor to the young teacher. On his way to the building, he stopped at a local outlet and picked up a few supplies, and he entered his classroom prepared to discuss literary terms with his students; they would record definitions made succinct by him into their notebooks while he discussed their applications. His students entered, paused momentarily, and then settled alphabetically into their assigned seats. Mr. Dennison immediately composed a seating chart and he called each student's name to verify pronunciation; in this manner he could also elicit preferred nicknames and begin to visually associate a student's facial characteristics. He knew Justin Crane, of course, and with the dexterity of a sleuth, he slipped imperceptibly to the boy at his desk and slid to him a fresh notebook. Justin accepted it. He also knew Valerie Connors, and he recognized instantly that her seat was empty. She was absent from his class.

At his first opportunity, Mr. Dennison ascertained that she was legally absent from school. Later in the day, he approached Nurse Garrison for information and she informed him that she was aware of the student, and that Valerie's parents were contacted yesterday in the afternoon.

"She is absent from my class today," John Dennison stated. "Do you happen to know why?"

Nurse Garrison was clearly busy with students who did not have proper vaccination documents, and her office teemed with students withheld from scheduled classes. It was evident she was unaware that Valerie Connors was not in school.

The concerned teacher made his way next to the guidance office. Valerie Connor's guidance counselor, Ms. Garvey, and the school's social worker, Ms. Reardon, were responsive to the situation, and he felt better for it. They were aware that Valerie had not attended classes that day.

The weekend was busy for Mr. Dennison and the uneasiness concerning his student abated considerably due to pressing personal matters. When class reconvened on Monday, however, the disquiet returned when Valerie Connors was again absent from his class. At his first opportunity, he was back inside the guidance office inquiring about his troubled student.

"Have a seat," offered Counselor Garvey, "I have something to tell you."

Mr. Dennison sat and listened attentively. Ms. Garvey was an experienced professional with twenty years of experience. She spoke directly:

"Valerie Connors has withdrawn from the school district...we have tried unsuccessfully to contact her parents again this morning. It will be difficult to locate her as she is no longer in our jurisdiction. Valerie is no longer a student in your class."

Mr. Dennison attempted to process this unexpected news. He was clearly confused. "We spoke about my concerns, did we not?" he asked in response, and his dread took expression suddenly. "She may be in trouble, or worse, she may be in danger," he said, and his words did not reveal his suspicions concerning her abusive father. "Is there anything we can do?"

"I understand," replied Ms. Garvey, barely above a whisper. "Be assured that we are obliged legally to follow up on her welfare. We will do everything we can...you see...we know very little about her, as she was a new transfer to our school."

Mr. Dennison's uneasiness was palpable, and with frustration mixed with indignation, he decided to come forward with a specific point: "I have suspicions that her father may have something to do with the abuse. I can't be certain. Surely, someone will find her?"

Ms. Garvey decided then to tell him more about the circumstances surrounding Valerie Connors as she knew them. Ms. Garvey had been anything but casual about the reported abuse, and she had spoken at length with administrators and the nurse, with the social worker, and the school's psychologist on the previous Friday, and she, too, was upset and determined to do her job. "You should know," she said gently. "We suspect the scars on her chest were self-inflicted. Did she tell you otherwise?"

Mr. Dennison admitted that Valerie had not confided any details of the abuse to him at all. He was stunned to think she had done the offensive deed to herself. He stood back confounded by the complexity of the possibilities. It took a few moments; he realized then he could do nothing for her if she had inflicted the scars upon herself. Perhaps Valerie had not intended to implicate her father; she may have been saying, "It was my *fa*...It was my *fault*!" He looked directly at Ms. Garvey, and he nodded. An awkward moment elapsed. He would leave, he knew, the welfare of the student named Valerie Connors in the experienced hands of Ms. Garvey.

"Self-inflicted?" he whispered in disbelief.

"We will locate her, Mr. Dennison. Be assured," replied Ms. Garvey. "But you should know there are legal matters of confidentiality in place here to protect her. She is a minor; it's unlikely I will be sharing with you many specific details."

Mr. John Dennison collapsed back into his chair. He knew Ms. Garvey would handle things from this time forward. With a sigh, he let it all go. John left the office dispirited, and his mouth was dry. He sipped from the water fountain, and then he shuffled with downcast demeanor back to his classroom.

Something had changed within himself. As a teaching professional, young John Dennison matured. He would observe his students independent of his own commendable lessons and search vigilantly for the troubled ones among the recipients. He had previously thought of teaching as a performing art; one staged and play-acted according to witty lesson plans designed to improve test scores; he had desired the accolades of colleagues for exhibiting some dazzling wizardry with technology. Mr. Dennison knew what it was that had changed. He realized that the finest execution of a perfect lesson is worthless when the student is indifferent or distracted by crippling personal issues. He was moved to repeat these words in a whisper to himself:

"...the finest execution of a perfect lesson is worthless when the student is indifferent or distracted by crippling personal issues..."

Mr. Dennison better understood the purpose of the sports and the clubs, the theater, the arts and the music, the after-school competitions and the field trips. He acknowledged the benefits of spirit week and the senior prom, the homecoming parade and all of the other festivities. When the continuity of his own lessons were interrupted by assemblies, he was certain to remind himself, as with a mantra; ...it is not about me...it is not about the curriculum...it is not about the test scores. Mr. Dennison could properly identify the refrain of his professional life; ...it is about the student...the learner...the child.

In May of that same school year, Mr. John Dennison was called to the office for a brief meeting with his principal. Due to budget cuts on the state and local levels, his teaching position would be eliminated. Unfortunately, the Board of Education had no alternative but to increase class size and eliminate programs at the high school. Of course, recommendation letters would be provided.

The entire school district was in a depression due to budget-related layoffs. Ms. Flinta was similarly notified.

With Extraordinary Dexterity

Dr. Anthony Falco woke up early, and as usual, he acknowledged a small thin scar, barely perceptible, upon the palm of his left hand. Every morning he took note of the blemish, and occasionally again when he was scrubbing for surgery; otherwise, he ignored it completely. It never bothered him in the least. Instead, curiously, there was a pleasant remembrance associated with the mark. It was the vestige of an important event that happened to him many years ago.

Dr. Falco was a talented pediatric surgeon whose specialty was repairing damage to the human eye. Indeed, this very morning, he would be restoring vision to a beautiful eight year old girl named Mary Cavanaugh. On such a day as this one, he was grateful for his own professional capabilities.

By all accounts, the surgeon was a gifted ophthalmologist. During medical school, his colleagues were duly impressed with the steadiness of his hands and with the uncanny precision with which he performed his delicate operations. His hands exhibited extraordinary dexterity, and his instincts were nothing short of astonishing. Upon graduation, he was offered several opportunities immediately and he accepted one in Nassau County near his home in Baldwin. As his practice grew, his name and his reputation became fixed among the nation's leading practitioners. Esteemed colleagues did not overstate his skill when they would reference his techniques as genius.

Everyone assumed that Anthony Falco was among the lucky ones. Some may have believed that God had bestowed upon him a natural predisposition for the profession, and that he was *born* to work miracles with his fingers. And this may be so, but not without deference to the life-experience of the man.

At the age of seven, Anthony had been diagnosed with a rare bone-condition. He complained to his mother that he had "rocks in my knees" and it was determined that the boy's hip was deteriorating from lack of blood flowing to the femur. His hip was decaying as would the bone of a corpse. Dr. Riesman performed the surgery, and with prescribed physical therapy, Anthony made a full recovery. However, for eleven months, the seven year old spent all of his waking hours lying flat on a foldable army cot. His activities were extremely limited. There was no pain or discomfort; he simply was under strict orders to keep off that hip. Because he could not sit or stand or walk or run, his arms and his hands naturally assumed heightened importance; for months on end these appendages alone were able to dance, to play, and to discover. He spent hours manipulating objects of interest placed within his reach upon the floor. He worked tirelessly at puzzles and plastic models. He played video games; text-messaged with the nimbleness of a wizard; solved the Rubik's cube; he spun a basketball on his finger until it bled beneath the nail. The days crept slowly by. He read books. Carol Tully, his tutor, shared with him her capabilities as a calligrapher. Sometimes, when frustrated and bored, the boy turned to his journal for comfort. His mother recognized despondency then, and with resourcefulness, she brought things to inspire his imagination. The carpet beneath his cot became a backdrop upon which fancy items magically appeared; tricks and coins, jacks and all things tactile.

Something else was happening. "*Anthony!*" his mother would call to him. "*Anthony Falco!*" she would shout, even when standing a few inches from his cot. Her son did not answer her; he was far away in a fog, quite unaware of her close proximity. It was times like these, when in a deep concentration, that Anthony would block it all out. He was so focused upon the immediate task that he would completely disallow petty distractions. All extraneous sights were relegated to the distant grey shadows in his mind and all superfluous sounds were distanced into the faraway muffled background. "*Anthony Falco!*" his mother would beckon to him again, but her son would not respond. He had constructed about himself a bell jar within which he lived and breathed. What's more, his hands and his fingers began to appear strangely to him as impartial mechanical extremities that worked as would meticulous robotic limbs. He examined them with bemused detachment when they were sketching with crayons and pastels; he was entertained by them when they worked with clay. The weeks turned into months. All activities remained sedentary. He was alone much of the time. *"Anthony!"* his mother would call to him. *"Anthony Falco!"* she would shout.

There were other things going on as well. Anthony learned patience; the feverish longing for juvenile activities subsided; a soothing relaxation took its place. When it was snowing, he asked to be brought to the window. During a warm rain, he wished to be on the covered porch. When the trees were full with leaves, he was satisfied to be in the yard. There was no more ennui. He had accepted his handicapped condition. As the blind person listens attentively to the songs upon the wind, and the deaf child observes alertly the movement upon the landscape, so did young Anthony Falco develop an extraordinary dexterity with his hands. His handicap was temporary; he was grateful to know that one day soon he would once again be able to run and play without disadvantage.

It happened at Babylon's Cedar Beach when he was not yet a teenager. Anthony was with his Aunt Susan near the marina on the bay side of the park. Strolling barefoot on the old wooded boardwalk, Aunt Susan skimmed her right foot carelessly, and in a pain-filled moment, she was clutching her ankle, unexpectedly immobilized. With the shriek of the wounded, she hobbled to a nearby bench, lifted her foot and revealed a splinter deeply embedded. Without recourse, Anthony's aunt took from her purse an ordinary safety pin, handed it to her nephew, and she winced. It was Anthony's first surgery. With a shake of his shoulders, all nervousness left his body, and with steadfast purpose and with singular intent, the young man set upon the pressing business at hand. All extraneous sights were relegated to the distant grey shadows in his mind and all superfluous sounds were distanced into the faraway muffled background. With keen execution, he carefully unfolded each layer of skin. His voice was calm: "Tweezers," he requested, and from within her pocketbook, his aunt provided the crude cosmetic tool. Deftly, he isolated and removed the invasive sliver. "We have it!" he heard himself whisper. The wooden fragment was nearly two inches in length.

At the age of fourteen, a neighbor asked the young man if he would work with his crew as a landscape assistant. Anthony was too young to operate power tools and machinery; he would work instead with a claw cultivator and with the steel-shafted, half-moon lawn edger in the flower beds. It was a summer job and he was obliged for the opportunity.

His neighbor would not regret hiring him. Anthony worked the tools tirelessly, without fuss, and soon he was building strong shoulders and wrists. With remarkable accuracy he would dig with the half-moon edger at the perimeter of each flower bed. He walked miles on manicured lawns stabbing the sharp tool at precise outlines in the soil and he commanded his arms, his hands, his wrists to consistently hit the mark. He took extraordinary pride in his ability to clear the tumbled soil from the edges of each flower bed. He allowed a single bead of sweat to linger on his brow. He lost himself inside the simple task: "*Faster!*" he thought to himself giddily. "*Strike as would the archer!*" he pretended imaginatively. "*Be the warrior upon the battlefield!*" he commanded arrogantly, as in a video game. In reality, at the end of one month's time, Anthony Falco was the most efficient landscape assistant with a hand cultivator and steel edger anyone had ever seen.

That's when it happened. A clumsy co-worker who knew nothing of restraint was carelessly cutting corners with his mower. Always impatient and agitated, the co-worker would scuttle pig-headed about the landscaped yards blaming others for his own shabby work. "Pick up the pace...slackers!" he would shout in an attempt to bolster his self-worth.

There was a small round shard from a discarded metal soda can lying on the lawn in plain view near the curb. Rather than pick it up, the obstinate fool ran it over with his lawn mower, and the rusted lid was lifted into the blade housing; it whirled as would deadly shrapnel. Violently, the tin projectile was hurled outward and it bit into his co-worker's naked interior thigh; it had penetrated deep into the flesh as would a bullet. Anthony Falco was nearby. Rhythmic spurts of blood spurted from the laceration, and with his tee shirt and a sweat cloth, Anthony tightly affixed a make-shift tourniquet. He settled the victim on his back and lifted the leg above the heart. All extraneous sights were relegated to the distant grey shadows in his mind and all superfluous sounds were distanced into the faraway muffled background. He applied pressure to the wound and patiently waited. The EMT's arrived. Anthony rode inside the ambulance. He was extremely curious about all things medical inside the speeding vehicle. Thereafter, he spent hours investigating medical topics on the internet.

That winter, Anthony's received a call from his uncle who knew someone who was hiring a part-time worker at a busy restaurant on Hempstead Turnpike near Hofstra University. He was grateful for the opportunity. Every Thursday and Friday afternoon, Anthony worked at Triple-Crown Pizza; it was one of the busiest pizzeria restaurants on Long Island. Anthony did not make pizza; instead, he folded the squares in each corner of the flat cardboard pizza boxes for hours on end in preparation for the enormous weekend demand. On Friday and Saturday evenings, hundreds of them were needed to be stacked like skyscrapers along the back walls of the establishment. At first, bending and creasing the flat cardboard boxes was tricky. Anthony found it awkward but not in the least tedious. He studied the mechanics and practiced at it the way a determined card handler might work his trade when dealing poker at a casino. Anthony accepted the challenge. He lost himself in the rote activity. Without realizing it, within a few months, eyebrows were being lifted on the faces of customers in the restaurant. People picking up their pizza order would silently signal to each other to check out the kid working the pizza boxes. Across the counter, toward the rear corridor, Anthony Falco could be seen assembling cardboard boxes with such extraordinary speed and dexterity that it was evident to everyone that his performance at the simple task was possibly the most efficient in the entire world. He was popping them out with such masterful assemblage that Henry Ford himself would have observed with admiration.

And then one night, regrettably, it simply happened. A friendly co-worker who was easily distracted was openly flirting with an attractive patron when he lost his footing near the stove where boiling water was set waiting for fresh pasta. The inattentive co-worker's torso twisted into the heavy pot, and with his left hand, he grasped the red-hot container, overturning the boiling water. The injury was catastrophic. His skin peeled and melted from his fingers as would thin plastic wrap under fire. His countenance became pale and his breathing weakened. Anthony moved quickly. "Call 911!" he shouted, and he lifted his injured friend restfully inside an unoccupied booth. He placed a towel beneath his head for comfort for he knew that swelling and shock would ensue. He removed the victim's watch and he isolated the oozing wound. Patrons in the restaurant stepped forward. Anthony's voice was mixed with shouts for specific action: "I need clean towels...moist...with cold water!" Two waitresses were at his command. He elevated the afflicted appendage above the heart. "First aid kit!" he bellowed, and it was bought to him instantly; from within it he removed the cool moist sterile bandage.

He examined the third degree burns. All extraneous sights were relegated to the distant grey shadows in his mind and all superfluous sounds were distanced into the faraway muffled background. With a wet towel, he prepared a suitable dressing until the EMT's arrived. This time, Anthony did not ride in the ambulance.

In high school, Anthony witnessed a sad event indeed. A close friend named William played varsity basketball and he had ignored a small blister on his right foot. It became infected. William failed to bring the matter to the attention of his coach. The talented athlete played for a few games more. He began to limp noticeably on the court. Before long, the ankle had swollen badly and the poison in the wound was travelling up his leg. William was hospitalized, and Anthony visited him often. It was decided that his friend's foot would be lanced and drained. The procedure did not go well. Things became seriously grave. In the hospital, William caught pneumonia and his lungs collapsed. His body was weakening and a fluid was leaking from a mysterious source into his abdomen. Things became critical. William might die. Anthony was visiting him when a priest arrived. The entire tragic collapse occurred in only three weeks' time. Treatment was speculative among the doctors until one brilliant physician, Dr. Samik, correctly diagnosed the cause of the toxic fluid as spinal discharge originating from William's lower vertebrae. Surgery revealed the truth and drain tubes were positioned. Recovery was prolonged but successful and Anthony spent many hours at the hospital with his recovering friend. While visiting, Anthony witnessed the routine of the staff. He was attentive to the medical procedures in the adjacent rooms. He imagined he was a physician. His friend William recovered but he would not play competitive basketball again. For the first time, Anthony Falco seriously considered the medical field as a profession.

It happened that same year on one lazy Saturday afternoon that Anthony Falco lost his balance when cycling near the harbor. He mindlessly pedaled into a pile of sand at the curb's edge and he fell headlong into a hedgerow of briars. He was alone. A rusty barbed fence was hidden within the leaves and Anthony cut the palm of his left hand. He was bleeding. As did his friend William, Anthony foolishly ignored the wound until it swelled and his hand appeared webbed between his distorted fingers. He finally showed a physician who commented that the inflammation was severe; it reminded him of wounds common upon battlefields where treatment was scarce or non-existent. "How could you let this go!" scolded the attending doctor in the emergency room. Anthony looked at his swollen hand with the same bemused detachment as when he lay prone on the foldable army cot. He saw it as a foreign limb and he wondered when the inflamed and disfigured joints would return to normal size. It would not be until his hand was lanced and a draining tube inserted. It took several months to recover completely. A small thin scar barely perceptible had remained there. Never again would he delay treatment for himself or for another. Anthony Falco had decided. He would become a physician.

As an undergraduate at Stony Brook University, Anthony Falco earnestly pursued his ambition. To help offset expenses, he worked briefly in the school book store at the cash register. Brilliant in all matters of mathematics and sciences, Anthony was promoted to the Bursar's office for accounting purposes. One year later, a biology professor recommended a modest salary be provided to him as an assistantship during crowded lab sessions. It was granted. Subsequently, by recommendation, Anthony worked at the desk of the provost. His undergraduate requisites were completed with the nimbleness of a wizard. It would be a shock to everyone should he be denied admittance to several prestigious medical schools.

Anthony Falco graduated Fordham University Medical School with honors and he established a successful practice. Years passed.

Dr. Falco was comforting a patient at Long Island Jewish Hospital when he was called upon to perform an emergency surgery. An accident had occurred to an innocent young girl in her home. A large glass container smashed upon the granite countertop and it shattered explosively. Countless sharp fragments were propelled like shrapnel about the room. It was catastrophic. A lengthy splinter of glass became lodged in the child's left eye. Dr. Falco responded quickly and when hastily scrubbing for surgery, he took note of the small thin scar on the palm of his left hand. In minutes he found himself comforting his young patient with a calm and soothing voice.

"What is your name?" he asked her, smiling with reassurance.

"Mary Cavanaugh," replied the shaken little angel.

"I am Dr. Falco...and you are going to go to sleep now...and when you wake up...you will be well."

The surgeon had spoken these words with complete confidence. He nodded to the anesthesiologist, and to both of his nurse assistants. Mary Cavanaugh could be heard counting backwards:

"Ten...nine...eight..." and there was silence.

Dr. Anthony Falco lost himself in the immediate task. All extraneous sights were relegated to the distant grey shadows in his mind and all superfluous sounds were distanced into the faraway muffled background. Hours passed and he allowed a bead of sweat to linger upon his brow. His strong shoulders and wrists did not tremble from fatigue. He observed his hands with bemused detachment and his fingers appeared to him as impartial mechanical extremities that worked as would meticulous robotic limbs.

"We have it!" he heard himself whisper. The glass fragment was nearly two inches in length.

When the procedure was completed, the talented surgeon emerged as from a thick fog. The nurse assistants and the anesthesiologist welcomed him back. They had witnessed the successful procedure and they were impressed with steadiness of his hands and the uncanny precision with which he performed the delicate operation. His hands exhibited extraordinary dexterity and his instincts were nothing short of astonishing. On such a day as this one, Dr. Anthony Falco was grateful for his professional capabilities.

Kelly and the Birds

The first time Kelly took an interest in birds was during one ordinary summer afternoon when her eighth birthday was exactly twenty-two days away. She and her best friend Francine were nearly the same age, except Francine's birthday would be in twenty eight days. The two girls were discussing the matter while they walked leisurely toward the ping pong table that was set up inside the elementary school gymnasium, where every afternoon a young school counselor opened the doors to local kids who could not afford to attend an expensive sleep-away or day camp. Kelly looked up for a moment, and that's when she spotted *Inky the Crow* perched on a telephone wire about seventy feet above them.

"Isn't that *Inky the Crow*" asked Kelly, squinting through the sunlight and pointing. "He's been following us. I see him nearly every day now."

Francine agreed it was Inky the Crow, and she didn't seem too surprised, as it had become predictable for the neighborhood kids to notice the curious bird somewhere, and the older kids claimed that *Inky the Crow* had followed them past the pond all the way into town. Even some of the parents nodded with surprise, allowing that this intelligent fowl certainly did seem to be keeping a vigil on their progenies.

"Has anyone seen *Inky the Crow?*" Kelly might ask if she hadn't seen him for a day or two, and before the day was through, someone could attest to his most recent whereabouts. This attentiveness to the neighborhood pet went on for all of July and August, but waned in September when the cooler autumn winds arrived and the rumble of school buses could be heard, and he was seen less frequently and by fewer children.

Kelly had taken a keen interest in the crow that summer, for she recognized it as a very intelligent and alert bird, and through the winter months into the following spring, she paused at times and she searched the lonely horizon, envisioning his potential whereabouts, but to no avail. *Inky the Crow*, her free-range companion, was seemingly gone for good, and by the following summer, Kelly began to accept that it was unlikely he was ever coming back.

Kelly forgot about birds altogether until a year later when she entered the third grade; that was the year Dr. Peterson left the high school and joined the ranks of the elementary teachers at Cayuga Academy. Dr. Peterson was an expert at test preparation, and in order to ensure strong results on the state exams, she was brought in to consult with educators and to model best practices for the entire teaching staff. In August, Kelly's mother expressed modest apprehension to her husband during dinner one evening that Dr. Peterson may be unaccustomed to the nuances of third grade instruction, but that concern was short lived. Dr. Peterson was a twenty-year veteran teacher and she quickly established her expertise at all levels of instruction. In fact, it was Kelly's good fortune to have been placed in her class, as it became evident to everyone that Dr. Peterson was talented and very personable, and soon she became one of Kelly's favorite teachers. It was no coincidence either that the school's state exam results improved dramatically that year, or that Kelly's test scores reached into the top two percent in the nation.

Fortunately, Dr. Peterson was not all about test preparation; she had a terrific sense of humor and she was quick to laugh. She told the most engaging stories with great enthusiasm, and in the sciences, she could invent jingles for memorizing facts. She often employed visuals in her lessons and she encouraged group activities. Not incidentally, she was expert with technology.

"Tomorrow," Dr. Peterson promised, "I have a surprise for you. I have invited two special guests to our classroom, and they are especially dear to me, so when we arrive to class in the morning, we must behave in a particularly respectful and courteous manner." Dr. Peterson smiled reassuringly. "They are going to entertain you with their singing; and their songs will be delightful."

It should be noted that at Cayuga Academy, it was generally true that hamsters, fish, gerbils and guinea pigs were the preferred classroom pets. Dr. Peterson was different. The next morning, as usual, Kelly and her classmates bustled clumsily into the classroom, but alas, something had changed. In the rear corner of the room near the water fountain, an extraordinary multi-tiered brass cage sat impressively on a plain but sturdy wooden table. Inside the cage, a glimpse of crimson and emerald, light blue, soft tan, and breathtaking yellow could be divined; no one dared to get close to the exotic structure. Instead, the children clustered in small groups at a safe distance and whispered to one another pointing. Presently, the colors took form, and the furtive movements settled both within the cage and within the classroom, and a hush remained therewithal. Any students entering the room late slowed their pace and also whispered, as no one wished to disturb their guests; within the enclosure, settled peacefully upon a long balsam dowel, two brilliantly-colored songbirds perched side by side.

Dr. Peterson introduced them as Passerine finches, and our response to their arrival could not have been more heartfelt and genuine. A contest was held to ascertain appropriate names for each lovely finch, and at the behest of our esteemed teacher, we named one "*Jem*" and the other one "*Scout*" after characters in a famous novel called *To Kill a Mockingbird* that Dr. Peterson promised would be our favorite book when we reached the tenth grade. Before long, the amusing finches with the colorful plumage were ours to enjoy, and as expected, our teacher established a schedule for students to partake in the necessary responsibilities related to the care of these sometimes messy, seed-eating birds.

Specifically, each morning, a student was selected to assist Dr. Peterson with the replenishing of the seed bin and water basin, and with the cleaning of the paper-lined bottom of the cage. It was important, also, to faithfully examine the interior for anything unusual. This inspection was done because, on occasion, though rare, someone lucky might discover miniature finch eggs concealed inside the brittle grasses, straw and hay that draped inside. So each morning, with gentle fingers, the student of the day searched the disheveled nest. On most occasions, the disappointed pupil had to return quietly to his or her desk. When Kelly's designated hour had arrived, her circumstance was the exception; she discovered within the tangled straw the precious eggs, and with a shriek, she proclaimed the news to the delight of everyone. Her classmates hustled to her side to marvel at the fragile pearls, and to congratulate her on her good fortune. Kelly was thrilled and she never forgot the experience.

After that privileged episode, Kelly thought about the finches often, and she knew that Jem and Scout could not be left forsaken in the classroom during the Christmas holiday. Kelly hoped she could bring them to her home, so she asked Dr. Peterson weeks in advance if she could take on the responsibility during the recess. Kelly asked few favors of her parents, and she was seldom denied, but some caution was voiced by them because within Kelly's home there resided a cat named *Frisky*, and that could be a problem. Kelly convinced her parents that it would be possible to avoid conflict by keeping the birds at a safe distance from the predatory *Frisky*, and so the birds, along with the elaborate brass cage, were brought to Kelly's home. *Frisky* seemed acutely interested at first, but perhaps persuaded by the invincibility of the protective brass, the feline mellowed considerably and took on all manner of disinterest about the feathery guests.

All was quiet and things went well for a week; the family enjoyed the pleasant songs from these lovely birds, and their faint presence blended seamlessly into the warm melody of the comfortable family routine. It wasn't until after the fireplace mantle was decorated with festive stockings and the Christmas tree glistened with sparkling ornaments and colorful lights, that the family, resting peacefully upon the sofa enjoying the music of the joyous season, first sensed that something might be askew. No one had seen *Frisky* for a while, until she trotted proudly through the den, prancing like a tabby on display. To everyone's horror, inside the cat's mouth, held by her razor-sharp incisors, there lay lifeless the body of one of the finches.

Kelly's father reacted quickly; he leapt from his armchair and caught *Frisky* by surprise, swatting the cat's hindquarters with a jolt. *Frisky* took off to find sanctuary, and in her haste, she let fall the dead finch. Kelly rushed to the carpet whereupon Scout lay motionless, and she cried plaintively "Oh No! Please No!" and her mother comforted her there. Meanwhile, Kelly's father raced to the battered cage and discovered the metal door hinge opened and the interior ravaged. Fortunately, however, cowering in the upper corner of the enclosure, a distraught finch fluttered in a panic. Immediately he reset the cage and fastened the hinge and lifted all to the center table. Satisfied that *Jem* was safe and unharmed, he hurried to the unhappy circumstance in the den, and he knew that Kelly would be inconsolable with grief at the loss of the bird's life.

Huddled low around the unresponsive finch, a most remarkable thing happened next. Kelly's mother had cupped her hands and slowly stretched her arms to gently lift *Scout* from the carpet when the finch suddenly righted itself. It stood upright as stolid as a wooden soldier. Startled, Kelly also reached out her cupped hands to collar the bird, when suddenly, shaking- free the shocking death-stupor, *Scout* took flight. At full speed, the frightened finch flew directly into the dazzling Christmas tree. Astounded, the family in full pursuit chased the revived bird to the tree and they searched frantically about the branches. Soon, the absurd prospect of locating the colorful finch within the flickering iridescent bulbs and glittering ornaments became apparent, even laughable; the garishly decorated Christmas tree provided flawless camouflage for *Scout* to remain undetected. Kelly's father reasoned correctly that the bird was likely stunned, so searching low on his knees near the tree stand, he found the finch trembling in the recesses. This time he carefully cradled the bird with both hands, and with renewed hope, the family glided as gently as possible to the table in the adjacent room where *Jem* fluttered nervously within the birdcage.

All manner of precautions were taken by Kelly's father, but before they reached the table, the resilient finch escaped his cautious grip and Scout once again took off in flight. The panicky bird again whizzed past them at top speed, but this time, it flew nonstop directly into the glass mirror that hung in the entrance foyer. Bang! Thud! In an instant, *Scout* lay stunned and unconscious on the hardwood floor beneath the impenetrable looking glass.

Speechless, the family huddled low once again, and *Scout* was clasped more securely this time, and his recovery was remarkable, for when he was returned to his cage and his general condition carefully inspected, it was evident that the finch would make a full recovery. In fact, not a feather was damaged! Kelly's father voiced wonder at the exactness of the cat's sharp teeth when clasping the delicate prey; perhaps *Frisky* intended to taunt *Scout* as a plaything in a deadly game. Needless to say, from that moment on, extraordinary care was taken to secure the whereabouts of both the cat and the occupied cage.

It took a few days to process the alarming events, but Kelly's composure soon returned, and with some relief, the finches were returned to her classroom the following week. Everything was fine. Kelly kept the events a secret, not even to be shared with her best friend Francine, until years later at a sleepover with girlfriends in the seventh grade. By then, it wasn't much of a story; it was just another funny anecdote shared among laughing teenage girls.

Kelly's mother, however, had a secret of her own and she didn't share it with Kelly. After a year had passed, she ran into Dr. Peterson at the market, and after some pleasant talk about things in general, she asked the educator about the birds. Dr. Peterson hesitated as she considered whether to speak of their demise.

"Oh my!" she began. "I suppose I shouldn't tell you, but the birds were tragically lost this past summer. I'm afraid it was my own negligence."

A moment elapsed and Kelly's mother waited courteously; she was unsure if Dr. Peterson would continue with the details. She was curious, and she was pleased when Dr. Peterson resumed speaking.

"I had rented a home in Westhampton Beach and foolishly I thought to bring the birds outdoors to the deck for a few hours. It was a warm summer day and the cage sufficiently secure, or so I thought. During the late afternoon, I dashed out for an hour nearby and I was unexpectedly delayed; dusk turned into darkness and soon thereafter I returned home to the backyard to bring the finches indoors to the safety of the kitchen. Unfortunately, I discovered an empty cage knocked on its side and damaged; the water bin and seed tray was gashed and destroyed, and bits of paper debris and straw lay shredded about the deck." Dr. Peterson paused a moment to express sympathy. "It was sad. I hope the birds were able to fly to safety because they were missing without a trace."

Kelly's mother was nonplussed at the remarkable irony of their fate. "Do you imagine that a neighbor's cat may have discovered the birds?" she asked innocently.

"It is possible…" replied Dr. Peterson, preparing to leave the market, "… but local residents and friends thought it was more likely raccoons that were the culprits, because the misfortune occurred at night and there was considerable damage to the brass cage."

Kelly's mother decided to share this dreadful update with her husband, and together they agreed to keep Kelly unaware of the fateful departure of the beloved finches named *Jem* and *Scout*.

******

Kelly's curiosity with birds continued through her formative years, and because she took an interest in literature, she was keen to notice them when studying the classics. Shakespeare was fond of birds, for example, and upon the death of King Duncan in *Macbeth*, Kelly noted that the owl did scream, and the obscure bird clamored the livelong night, and a falcon, towering in her pride of place, was killed. In *Animal Farm*, Moses the Crow was there to lead the animals to the promised land of Sugar Candy Mountain. Coleridge's poem featured the albatross, of course, and Poe's narrator despaired alone and grief-stricken in his haunted chamber when visited by a ghastly raven. An unusual film by Alfred Hitchcock portrayed birds as deranged assassins, and as Dr. Peterson had promised so many years ago, *To Kill a Mockingbird* was Kelly's favorite novel in the tenth grade, and it was then, too, that she realized that *Jem* and *Scout* had a fitting last name, indeed, as they were the children of one Atticus *Finch*. Kelly loved reading the novel, and discovered that the story wasn't about birds in the least, nor was another book she read in the eleventh grade, entitled, *I Know Why the Caged Bird Sings,* by Maya Angelou.

When not reading, Kelly kept with her the *Roger Tory Peterson Field Guide* as her reference when she searched for the native and accidental birds of her Long Island home. She received the influential book as a gift from her parents for her twelfth birthday, and she was fascinated by it and she soon became an avid birder. She could identify the swimmers and the long-legged waders, the aerialists and the birds of prey, the fowl-like birds and the passerine land birds. Before long, Kelly was spotting birds everywhere, and automatically she processed the tail formations, field marks, eye stripes and rings, wing patterns and the shapes of the bill. Kelly learned expeditiously and she also understood that successful birders needed to listen as well as observe; she was forever attentive to the owls and the woodpeckers, the jays, the mockingbirds and the doves.

During her third semester at Sachem East High School, Kelly accepted an unusual poetry assignment from Dr. Paley, her literature professor. The task for the poet was to personify something in nature and bring to it a voice and a personality. The trick, however, was to describe the chosen object in verse without directly identifying the entity, leaving the reader of the poem the delightful task of guessing the subject by examining clues and references within the poem. Kelly wrote the following verse:

Good morning, Early Riser! I wave to you and salute you!
I stretch and return to you my warmest greeting!
Each morning I am renewed by your presence, Oh God of the Innocents
Adored by all that run and climb and fly,
Adored also by all like me, who remain at one station
a lifetime as testament to your glory.
Sometimes I am jealous of those who freely roam,
And I dream that I can wander from my home
To explore, to learn, to experience
to run and to climb and to fly
But it not so, as I cannot wander free
There is no sadness!
For my soul is rooted to the truth that everything I desire will come to me
at last!

Everything I have and will ever have is already with me!
And so I wave to you and salute you Early Riser!
I stretch and return to you my warmest greeting!

Kelly thought about writing a poem about a bird, of course, but because she was studying the correlation between birds and their arboreal habitats at that time, she chose, instead, to assume the identity of a tree. She thought the word "rooted" was a dead giveaway, but she was surprised that some students in her class thought the speaker in the poem was the sun itself. She was joking when she read it to Francine, and asked, "Are you stumped?" Francine gave her the look that said, "I get it!" and she quickly changed the subject.

"Will you ride with me to my Aunt Laurie and Uncle Frank's house later today?" Francine asked that afternoon. "They keep as a pet the most beautiful blue and yellow macaw named *Ruffles* that sometimes talks. I get jumpy near her because she is a *huge* bird, and quite noisy too, but I think you would love her, the way you love birds and all."

Kelly agreed right away, and when classes were through, she and Francine headed to a small salt-water sanctuary named *Idle Hour* in the town of Oakdale. Here existed an expansive marsh preserve with wetlands and waterways fashioned years ago by immigrants brought in by Vanderbilt when constructing his south shore mansion. And it was evident to Kelly that here, too, did birds abound in great numbers and variety; within a very few moments inside the scenic enclave, she spotted several cranes, some red-winged blackbirds and the talented kingfisher. In the distance, she heard a common flicker still at work on an old rotted maple, and she listened to the thin shriek of the osprey flying overhead, but the hawk was not in distress and was gone in an instant.

Deep within the neighborhood, the roads narrowed and Francine's aunt was outdoors waiting. Something was wrong; her demeanor was panicky and she shuffled nervously and called the girls to her side. Aunt Laurie explained that the great macaw was out of its cage, and regrettably, the bird had flown through the open sliding door to the edge of the canal. With a nod she indicated the locale and we could see the brilliantly-colored yellow and blue bird easily, as its tropical hues clashed with the pallid bark of the pines and the tannish scrub brush of the salt water marsh. The accident of her freedom had occurred just moments before, and Francine's uncle was across the road cautiously approaching his domesticated pet; he spoke soothingly as he walked slowly toward the edge of the preserve, calmly enticing his bird to return to his own familiar outstretched arm. In his open palm, he held nuts, some seeds and bits of fruit.

The frightened macaw had perched itself perhaps fifteen feet above the earth upon a naked tree limb that lurched over the canal. A supportive neighbor joined in the suspenseful endeavor from a safe distance, and he spoke once to Francine's uncle to express his whereabouts and his encouragement: "Frank...let me know if you need a ladder...good luck." The neighbor stood quietly then and observed, and perhaps he was considering the value of the bird, both as a pet and as an investment, for these tropical parrots routinely cost thousands of dollars.

Kelly and Francine with her Aunt Laurie watched from the porch, and all motion appeared as in slow motion. "*Ruffles*...come on *Ruffles*..." was heard repeatedly from Uncle Frank as he inched his way forward across the lawn until he stood directly beneath the bird. He turned then, and he indicated in pantomime for his neighbor to get the extension ladder. Things were going well as Ruffles held steadfast to the tree limb.

The two men placed the ladder gently upon the outstretched branch and Uncle Frank began his ascent. Unfortunately then, displaying an enormous wingspan rivaled only by the great blue herons and egrets within the marsh ecosystem, the majestic macaw fell forward and descended, plummeting headlong first to capture the essential wind and air beneath her wings, and as suddenly as before, she lifted herself impressively above the pines, and the resplendent bird appeared to Kelly as both glorious and troubling, and curiously, as she witnessed this impressive bird's ascension, she thought for a moment of the fabled wings of Icarus, and the disastrous consequence of his inimitable flight. Suddenly, all was mayhem.

The adults sprinted to ascertain the bird's location. The macaw turned abruptly east, away from the residential streets, and she chose to fly instead directly into the heart of the natural preserve. It appeared certain that she had selected a tall roost in the interior of the wetlands, and getting to her would be problematic, but not impossible. Uncle Frank with his neighbor were already in pursuit, and together they speedily untied a neighbor's skiff, pushed their way across the canal, and struggled hurriedly through the prickly thickets and mucky soil of the sanctuary in the direction of the lost macaw.

It happened slowly then. Kelly noticed it before Francine or her worried Aunt Laurie. Minutes ticked and everyone searched the open sky for the disoriented parrot, fearful it might take flight again, but Kelly perceived something else; her years of birding were attuned to the sky of course, but also to the sounds from the environment. It was a single calling she heard from a distance that drew her attention, and then came the sequence, "caw…caw…caw…" and in a moment, the first ones appeared. Kelly tried to remain hopeful, but in vain. As feared, there came another, "caw…caw…caw…" and then several more, and the sky became a cacophony of sound and activity, and Aunt Laurie was nervous with doubt, seeking to know specifically what was emerging before her eyes. She sensed the danger now as well, but unacquainted with the territorial imperative of the species, she could not articulate her fears.

"What does it mean? All of these crows. What does it mean?" pleaded Aunt Laurie.

Kelly knew the answer, for she knew that these resident birds were intelligent executioners, scheming and strategizing creatures, and she knew they had identified a threatening interloper. "They are crows," she began. "There will be dozens of them, and they will shriek their warning, and other crows will heed the distress calls, and they will join together."

Kelly paused as she worked out the details in her mind. Already the sky revealed an overabundance of the ebony warriors, and the raucous calls from each foreshadowed a horror unfolding.

"The macaw is an exotic trespasser in these wetlands," Kelly continued, "and the crows will regard her as an enemy, and they will challenge her into desperate flight. If she cannot be rescued soon, she must find sanctuary from the crows…they will not yield…and they will not be intimidated."

Kelly stepped back to witness the intensity of purpose, the savage skill and merciless dexterity of the deadly crows in flight; some put down on limbs on the perimeter as sentinels; others honed in upon their target like fighter pilots, and Kelly knew it would end badly.

The three women moved away from the dreadful scene into the kitchen and waited anxiously for more than thirty minutes, trying their best to remain hopeful. Kelly wanted to go, and Francine felt awkward as well, and mindful of her aunt, she asked her if she wanted them to stay with her.

"No, you two should be going anyway," her aunt replied, trying her best to smile through her worry. "Thank you for visiting and I will let you know how all of this turns out in the end."

Francine and Kelly moved to say goodbye, and they expressed their empathy and best wishes that things would turn out well.

At that moment, however, from the kitchen bay window, Aunt Laurie spotted her husband with his neighbor emerging from the wetlands on the same path they had forged previously. With hunched shoulders and heads bowed, their manner of progress was altogether grave. In his left hand, held low, Uncle Frank carried a bundle that was a forgotten sack he found within the marsh. With crusted blood about the edges of the burlap, he stopped at the edge of the preserve, and he stowed the bundle behind a thick covert. He crossed the canal then, and his face and voice could not disguise the tragedy. Aunt Laurie met him near the bank of the wetland, and her sorrow became tears. Kelly and Francine watched all of this from the bay window. Uncle Frank and Aunt Laurie embraced, and his neighbor held his distance too; he had gone to his home and he emerged from his garage with a shovel, and he was also overwhelmed with grief.

The two men retraced their way through the estuary and they retrieved the dead bundle. Soon, they disappeared within the unspoiled acreage and they were set upon finding a suitable burial site.

Kelly and Francine were dumbstruck for most of the trip home. Francine was clearly upset and thoughts of the painful experience were tormenting her; she thought of her aunt and uncle and their heartache and her genuine sympathy went to them as it would to anyone who had unexpectedly lost their beloved pet. It was insufferable to see them so aggrieved. Kelly was similarly distressed, but her thoughts were splintered; she was attuned to the irony of the macaw's sudden freedom; how its demise occurred in a virtual bird sanctuary, and she wondered how in the world a healthy blue and yellow macaw named *Ruffles* got into this deadly predicament. She knew the answer, and the death and sadness of the afternoon seemed to her bizarre at its very core. She discovered herself thinking about all of the birds resigned to cages, and she thought about *Jem* and *Scout*, and oddly, her thoughts returned to a time long ago when she and Francine had walked together leisurely toward the ping pong table that was set up inside the elementary school gymnasium, where every afternoon a young school counselor opened the doors to local kids who could not afford to attend an expensive sleep-away or day camp. She heard herself speaking with the voice of a child in a soft whisper:

"Isn't that Inky the Crow? He's been following us. I see him nearly every day now."

Award's Night

Ms. Dayton, an esteemed English teacher at the middle school, poked her head into the office where the selection committee was in session. Everyone looked busy pouring over guidance records, report cards, extracurricular activities, teacher comments and so on. Ms. Dayton was hoping Janette Sheldrick would receive an academic award; stopping by the office and letting her presence be known was all the lobbying she could do.

In the morning during homeroom, Ms. Dayton received the committee results. She was disappointed. Her nominee would not be receiving an award this year. She wasn't the least bit angry because she understood that another worthy student had earned the recognition, but she felt a tender sadness when she saw Janette in her class later in the day. She walked over to her desk and gently rapped upon it in a gesture of greeting, and sighed, but she remained silent. She knew that Janette was overlooked for an award because the student was very quiet and reserved in demeanor. Janette returned her teacher's pattering with her usual delightful smile.

A few days later, Ms. Dayton could hold back no more. She ambled over to Janette's desk once again, but this time, with an extemporaneous comment:

"Excuse me, Janette?" she began, in a whisper. "I couldn't help but notice on the award's program that you were not among the winners at tonight's ceremony. What were the judges thinking? Anyone with any sense would have selected you for recognition."

The bashful student politely lowered her dispirited face. She accepted the compliment timidly. Ms. Dayton waited for Janette to look up at her before continuing with her opinion:

"If it were up to me... with your top English Language Arts score... and your ability to learn... and your enthusiasm to help others... well, you would be on that stage tonight, young lady."

The teacher sighed once again, and then concluded her heartfelt statements with reassuring words and with another soft tapping upon her student's desk. "Don't be discouraged...you will get your recognition in high school....everyone knows how talented you are... I'm sorry, but I guess sometimes gifted students don't always receive an award...even when they may deserve it."

Ms. Dayton felt better for having shared her assessment with her brilliant student. Janette felt better too, even though there lingered within her a pang of emptiness because many of her closest friends would be receiving awards; that's the tough part for exceptional students who do not receive recognition, learning to be happy for their peers when they had worked so hard to be in their place.

That evening, as was her custom, Ms. Dayton attended the annual Middle School Award's Ceremony. She had arrived early, and she took her usual seat in the rear of the auditorium, and she waited in near darkness for the proceedings to begin. It was a particularly important event for her this year because she had nominated another special student for the *Poetry Award*. The student's name was Amanda Colson, and she was the first winner of any award from a particularly challenging English class she taught, entitled, *"Eighth-Grade Revisited."*

The auditorium began to bustle with activity. Parents, siblings, relatives and friends of the award recipients ambled noisily inside and they jockeyed for seats. Ms. Dayton took little notice of their arrival. She remained seated, obscure in the darkness, and she let her thoughts drift unbridled to the circumstances pertaining to Amanda Colson's success.

The *Eighth-Grade Revisited Class*, as everyone knew, was a particularly difficult teaching assignment because the group consisted of a very rough mix of troubled kids with strong-willed personalities. In fact, all seventeen students enrolled in the class had failed the course the previous year. Ms. Dayton was chosen for the demanding assignment because administrators and colleagues believed she possessed a charismatic teaching personality that would be especially effective with these students. She was warned, nonetheless, not to let her guard down and to remain tough as nails: "Be wary...they are clever to challenge everything..." she was told by some. "Try to win them over," was suggested by others. "Good Luck!" was voiced by all.

Ms. Dayton took the advice very seriously. For days she poured over lesson plans, and she took note of her students' disciplinary documentation from the previous year, which were quite numerous, and their attendance record, which were quite poor. As she prepared, she thought that she would begin with a writing assignment, one that she had taught successfully before, so that she could get a feel for the students' interests and their capabilities.

On the very first day of class, Amanda Colson had distinguished herself from the rest of her students. Amanda was tall girl who sashayed into the classroom room after the bell wearing too much make-up, a blouse too skimpy to cover her breasts, and designer jeans worn snug to attract the attention of young men. What's more, she was a student with the unmistakable arrogance of a bully. She took one look at Ms. Dayton, chewed her gum condescendingly, flirted with Craig Robinson, and then walked arrogantly to her desk as if she was Madonna. Ms. Dayton knew straight away that Amanda Colson was going to be a rough one to win over.

Without a notebook, without concern for her lateness, and apparently without much regard for protocol, Amanda spoke suddenly:

"You must be our new English teacher," she said, stating the obvious.

Ms. Dayton stared at her, and Amanda stared back at her, and curiously, after some tense, uneasy moments, the two of them allowed a slight smile. For some reason, Ms. Dayton appeared to Amanda Colson as a person of interest, and surprisingly, Ms. Dayton felt the same way about her, as Amanda resembled a wild schoolmate she had befriended when attending Hofstra University many years before. And then Ms. Dayton spoke:

"Put your gum out and let's get started," she commanded with just the right authority.

The two glared at each other. Finally, Amanda did as directed and removed the gum with a tissue. The lesson went off without a hitch.

The assignment for students was to write a narrative about an unforgettable moment in their life. Ms. Dayton instructed her students to introduce themselves in some detail and to be absolutely certain that all events depicted in the story were tactful and appropriate for school papers. She explained she would be keeping a portfolio of their writings. After reviewing expectations of length and structure, she reviewed a few fundamental matters of writing mechanics before the class came to a close. Upon leaving, she encouraged all to submit a worthy example of their writing capabilities.

At week's end, Ms. Dayton surprised her students. With conspicuous fanfare, she took from her folder a student essay. She held it high as a flag for all to witness, and then she took a deep breath and waited for attentive silence. Ms. Dayton knew it was a gamble, particularly when she surveyed the terrified faces of her students who worried they would be embarrassed had their teacher selected their own writing sample to read to the class. Students held their breath because Ms. Dayton's intentions were clear to everyone; she was going to read a student's essay... aloud!

In lively fashion and with great enthusiasm, she read the title, "A Moment That Changed My Life," and her diction was formal and her voice was as perfect as any author might so desire. The narrative was exquisite; it began with rhetorical questions: "Should I tell you the whole story about my best friend and her untimely death? The true story when my life was shattered to pieces like the broken glass at her death scene?"

Students were spellbound. Ms. Dayton read to the class the sad story of how a teenaged girl named Pamela was running barefoot across Portion Road when in the darkness of night she was hit by a speeding motorist. How the author was there running barefoot beside her that night, and how, as in a recurring nightmare, the author could not forget the terrible sounds...and the horrible lights...and the dreadful moments she spent kneeling at her friend's side, calling to her, pleading with her...to live...to survive the terrifying ordeal. She read to the class how till this very day, the author could not cope with the tragic loss or the excruciating memory of the night her best friend lay lifeless on the roadway.

When the narrative closed, no one in the classroom dared to make a sound unless it was to sigh. Ms. Dayton let the silence linger. "Now students," she remarked with emphasis in a most complimentary fashion, "*that*...is great writing!"

After a moment more, she calmly returned the paper to the portfolio. Indeed, the storyline was superb. Students were dumbfounded to realize that one of their classmates, one of the *"Eighth- Grade-Revisited"* kids here in the room had penned such a capable and moving tale. Bedlam ensued:

"Who was it?" the students demanded to know at all once. "Who wrote that story? Wow! You must tell us...Please!" they clamored.

Some of the rogues in the room began to guess at those among them that might be capable of such a feat. All but one began to deny such an author existed within their ranks, and some suspected it was a ruse, and that the story was fraudulent because it was the work of a professional. Ms. Dayton intervened and she retrieved the paper, and once again she waved it high to halt further suspicion. All the while, with her legs outstretched and with her arms folded across her chest, the normally loquacious Amanda Colson reposed at her desk, silently observing. The attention of her classmates shifted in her direction. For the first time in anyone's recent memory, the usually brash leader appeared shy and reserved, perhaps even a bit embarrassed. Suddenly then, the truth was there to behold. Everyone knew it now. It was Amanda's paper that was read with such passion; it was her writing that had held them spellbound.

All of this Ms. Dayton replayed in her mind while sitting there in the darkness of the auditorium. It was among her most pleasant remembrances. She allowed herself a few moments more of pleasure, and so she recollected further how Amanda Colson had changed after that day; how she became a formidable ally in her class for the remainder of the semester. The gamble had worked.

Afterward and forevermore, Amanda was regarded differently by her peers. Amanda Colson was smart, very smart, and she was a wonderful writer, and now everyone knew it for certain. As the semester progressed, Amanda accepted many compliments from her friends and she fused them into a refashioned self-image. Her demeanor became more respectful, and even her manner of dress changed. Her academic rise was unmistakable; Amanda's grades took flight. Regarding her behavior specific to Ms. Dayton's class, she became proactive; should any miscreant presume to show disrespect during a lesson, Amanda collared the troublemaker without delay. What's more, Amanda Colson no longer chewed gum with disdain in front of her superiors, and the transformation in her attitude and academic performance was not restricted to English class alone. Other teachers took note of the extraordinary surge. By years end, she had regained the respect of all of her teachers.

Ms. Dayton, seated contentedly in the auditorium, reminisced further how during the poetry unit, Amanda had transformed her short story into an expressive poem. It was a wonderful effort. The elegy was submitted for consideration for the *Poetry Award*, and her poem had taken the honor.

Ms. Dayton let the memory fade when she and the other attendees were requested by Principal Thompson to rise from their seats to recite *The Pledge of Allegiance*. The proceedings advanced in splendid fashion, and once again this year, as in all previous years, it was evident to everyone that there are few events in a young person's life as emotionally heartfelt and as profoundly influential as when receiving an academic award.

When her name was called to accept the *Poetry Award*, Amanda Colson appeared on the stage as a lovely young woman, impeccably-dressed, demure, and grateful. She accepted the recognition gracefully, but suddenly and without forewarning, the brashness returned to her, but only for so long as it takes to seize the microphone for a few moments to thank a special teacher who had changed her life. Her short speech was carefully rehearsed and filled with accolades exalting Ms. Dayton and her positive influence upon her. When she had finished, thunderous applause and a standing ovation for exemplary achievement ensued, sanctioning the evening forever as an unforgettable moment in both of their lives.

The next morning, Ms. Dayton was taking attendance in homeroom when she was handed a note by one of her students. It was a plain envelope delivered to her by the talented but shy Janette Sheldrick, who spoke to her sheepishly, saying only the simple words: "It is from my parents." Ms. Dayton accepted the sealed message and she was curious to open it, as she could not imagine what communication lay inside. It read as follows:

Dear Ms. Dayton,

I just had to let you know that your acknowledgment to Janette about her accomplishments with reference to her English Language Arts score was very much appreciated. Janette was very disappointed that she wasn't receiving any awards this year. In fact, just the other day I was trying to convince her that many very intelligent students don't get any recognition for their hard work. Then the next day, you tell her that she should have received an award. You have no idea how that simple acknowledgement was appreciated. I just had to tell you because without you even realizing it, this is the second time you have done this for Jeanette. The first time was when she was accepted into the National Junior Honor Society and wanted to give a speech but wasn't asked to. Then one day you asked her if she was giving a speech and when she replied, "No" you simply said that you thought she should have been asked. So you see? You had unknowingly made a difference in a person's life and I just wanted to let you know that the Sheldrick Family thinks you're great too and hold a compliment from you higher than the award itself.

Sincerely,
John and Susan Sheldrick

Four years later, Principal Thompson entered the classroom where Ms. Dayton sat alone at her desk grading student essays. He was carrying with him an ordinary white envelope.

"Excuse me, Ms. Dayton?" he asked hesitantly, aware that his conscientious colleague was hard at work. "I have very good news. Your presence at Senior Awards at the high school has been requested by one of your former students."

The administrator waved the plain envelope high as a flag for her to witness. He was grinning playfully at Ms. Dayton as would someone who was about to share a bit of juicy gossip.

"Your former student has written to me about your positive influence upon her," he continued, "and she expressed that she would be honored if *you* would be the one to deliver her award to her during ceremonies. I dare say, in her letter, she was *very* complimentary of your positive influence upon her life and her academic success."

Ms. Dayton reached to accept the mysterious envelope that her principal fanned so manifestly, but Mr. Thompson withdrew.

"Can you guess the student's name?" he quizzed teasingly. "I will give you a clue...she has won the *English Language Arts Award*...and she said that it was something that happened during the eighth grade that made a real difference in her life."

Ms. Dayton remembered the letter from John and Susan Sheldrick, and she believed it was Janette who had won the prestigious honor. But before she could speak her name, she wondered...had Amanda Colson turned things around to such a degree?

The Persuasive Letter

There was a time when it was assumed by many that in all manner of communication, the human voice would triumph over the written word. It was thought that computers would become voice-sensitive machines such that the keyboard would go the way of the typewriter. Michael Olsen knew that if the people of the world wanted their voice to replace their fingers when writing, it would be so. It didn't happen. He was glad it didn't go that way.

Michael was infinitely more astute when writing at his desk than when publicly speaking. He dreaded having to speak in person during the occasional conference calls he made at the office. It was too spontaneous, he thought. He enjoyed e-mails and text messaging for business and personal communication. It enabled him and everyone else the needed time to thoughtfully assess the tone of the message, and to edit the length to avoid tedious repetitions of the same points over and over again, as is common when speaking. He liked to sketch out a message on his monitor for a while, and he was secretly envious of the authors he had studied in college who were forever composing masterpieces and sending them off by pony to some distant friend.

Michael's letters were often scripted for the benefit of disadvantaged children. As an attorney working the Suffolk County Courthouse in Riverhead, he managed successfully to raise funds on their behalf. Because he worked closely with wealthy Southampton developers, Michael often composed a letter suggesting a donation on the behalf of the handicapped kids at the Riverhead Youth Center. The letters he wrote were always a personal appeal for assistance. Wouldn't you know? His affluent clients frequently managed to find some money to help the disadvantaged kids. Michael could write a very persuasive letter.

Michael Olsen was born and reared in Riverhead. He knew Polish-Town, he shopped at the Tangier Outlet, and he attended the town's blues festival each summer. He was a community-oriented guy. He loved boating. He loved cycling. But more than anything else, he loved Scrabble. That's right, Scrabble! That's why he came up with the idea to create the Scrabble Club at the Youth Center. He could never have imagined it would be so popular. If he had thought about it, he shouldn't have been surprised that a board game consisting of simple words would be rewarding to children who could not otherwise afford to participate in expensive team sports.

Many of the kids who joined the club were handicapped in one way or another, either physically or by depredations caused by poverty. Some were emotionally distraught because of abandonment. The Scrabble Club provided a warm place to be during the winter months. Michael thought perhaps the youngsters were gambling, but he was wrong; it turns out they simply needed a place to hang out with words. They didn't gamble, but the kids weren't saints either; sometimes someone would be caught cheating when selecting Scrabble tiles by inspecting the letters in the cloth sack. Other times, friends would team-up by endorsing ridiculous nonsensical words like "trouse" or "obilgy" and so on, but that's the case wherever Scrabble may travel. Overall, everyone kept things more-or-less honest, and given time, just about everybody won at least once.

There was plenty of community support. Retired adults would stop by when they could to encourage everyone. Sometimes they brought pizza. Music blared from donated stereo speakers. In bad weather, kids got a ride home. Overall, the Scrabble Club was working out very well. Michael liked to say that the club was as well-received by the community as a red triple-word square! --as sought-after as a seven-letter word score! Ha! Ha! He thought he was being clever.

On every other Wednesday from November to April, Michael brought nine deluxe Scrabble games to the Youth Center's cafeteria. When it rained or snowed, the place was mobbed! Children played for two hours with their friends; the physically handicapped kids sometimes played with their aides; and once in a while, Michael Olsen sat in for a few rounds. He really didn't play that often; he was satisfied that the club was running smoothly and he liked drifting to the various boards to help those kids who were really stuck with difficult letters. One day, someone decided to distribute tee-shirts to everyone. The Scrabblers of Riverhead were born, and they were ready for a contest.

Michael Olsen was elected the official Scrabble Club President, and he considered it an honor. He contacted Newsday about the newspaper's annual Scrabble contest only to discover that they had discontinued the friendly competition. Everyone was disappointed. The club was planning a field trip to the contest in Melville. Michael wrote a very persuasive letter urging the paper to reconsider. He suggested he could get his clients to help subsidize the event. It was a very persuasive letter. Unfortunately, it didn't happen. The newspaper would not be able to sponsor the event. "Perhaps next year," was their official response.

The Scrabblers were disappointed. It remained in everyone's head, however, that they should go on a field trip anyway. But to where? It was decided that an old-fashioned baseball game at Citi Field Stadium would be just the thing. The Mets, considered by many to be the major-league team of Long Island after all, had struggled in recent weeks and seats were readily available the very next weekend, and so it was arranged. It would be a Sunday evening make-up game against the Atlanta Braves. If the Scrabblers delayed, the team would be out-of-town for the following two weeks on the West Coast. Michael Olsen convinced a few well-heeled clients they should bankroll the event. He wrote a few persuasive letters.

When field-trip day arrived, the weather forecast was for a miserable drizzle all evening long. Helpful parents had commissioned a luxury coach, and with the fund-raising money, fourteen scrabble players with entourage boarded the bus. The ride on the Long Island Expressway was pleasant except for the rain. It appeared certain the game would be cancelled.

All manner of wet-weather gear was worn by everyone. Bath towels were touted along to wipe dry the wet seats if needed. Clear elastic shower caps were placed over Met's caps and Hefty bags were fashioned into make-shift raincoats, and a plastic sheet draped Jeff Colson's wheel chair. It was a steady rain. At the turnstiles, the friendly attendants predicted the game would not be played due to the mushy field conditions; they allowed the Scrabblers passage anyway. Everyone entered the arena soaked but happy and all hoped for the best.

The stadium was practically empty. No one in New York expected the rain to stop anytime soon, and from the radio broadcast during the bus ride, even the sport reporters spoke about the game as if it had been cancelled. Because the field was nearly unplayable, most fans of the team stayed home. The Scrabblers held tickets on the Mezzanine level, but sympathetic ushers escorted the entourage to field level seating, inviting the group to "take your pick" of vacant seats as there were so few people attending the soggy game.

The Scrabblers found a dry spot beneath the Mezzanine overhang and everyone waited for the announcement that the game was a rain-out. It didn't happen. Surprisingly, the protective tarpaulins were removed from the infield. Field hands with metal rakes groomed the pitcher's mound. The few thousand people in the stadium stood and recited the National Anthem. The ballplayers took the field. All the while, an unrelenting rain persisted. It was not a downpour, but it was more than a drizzle. What was going on?

Michael Olsen was upset. "*Play Ball!*" was announced by the umpire, and sure enough, the first inning was underway. The second inning was uneventful except for the rain. The top of the third inning was lackluster except for the showers. The sky was dark grey. Droplets of water were plopping like custard from the empty balconies of the stadium. Finally, a chill arrived. Everyone was wet and cold and extremely uncomfortable. Michael Olsen had had enough. It became evident to him that the Mets' management was determined to play this game in spite of the discomfort to the fans. Why would they not reschedule the game? What about a rain delay? Retreating to the concession area, Michael asked an attendant about the situation.

"Everyone is miserable!" stated Michael. "It is wrong that the game is played in these conditions! What is going on?"

The Citi Field attendant knew that Michael did not fully understand the predicament. His response was empathetic to the patron's plight.

"Don't you know?" the usher asked. "In major league baseball, teams must play five innings for it to be considered a complete game. The Mets are heading to San Diego tomorrow. It may be inconsiderate, but management is determined to get five innings completed tonight. Don't you see? Right now, they are not concerned about the fans...they want to get this game completed before the team boards the plane."

Michael returned to his seat with the Scrabblers. He understood that the game would be cancelled only when five innings had been completed. It was the top of the fourth inning. Both teams were scoreless. The rain continued. "Why won't they at least delay the game?" was voiced by annoyed fans nearby.

It didn't happen. The baseball game was not relegated to rain-delay status because during the top of the fifth inning, as if on cue, the rain stopped. In fact, through the field lights, it could be seen that the storm was completely over. By the start of the fifth inning, all of the few remaining fans, including the Scrabblers, had descended to the rail seats on the baselines. The ushers encouraged everyone toward the best seats in the house! Further, the sky cleared and the moon peeked from behind hastening clouds. Even the ballplayers took note of the change in the weather, and they seemed to play with renewed zeal. During the seventh inning stretch, it was evident to everyone that it had become a wonderful evening for a baseball game! Who would have imagined? The Scrabblers, with a few thousand other devoted fans, practically had the whole stadium to themselves!

Even though things turned out splendidly, something was bothering Michael Olsen. The concession attendant had struck a nerve. It was an injustice to the fans, he thought. If not for the change in the weather, the outing would have been insufferable and regrettable. Michael decided to keep his thoughts to himself for the time being. Everyone had a good time, he reasoned. On the ride home on the bus, he tried not to let it bother him too much. The New York Mets had won the game, but for Michael, the Mets' organization had lost a fan.

The next couple of days brought little relief. Michael recognized an injustice and he was determined to make things right. He decided to write a letter. It may have been a masterpiece. In it, he introduced the Scrabblers by name, all fourteen of them. He outlined in detail the circumstances of the rainy conditions, and without naming the attendant, he described their conversation. The Mets were more interested in the business of flying to the West Coast than providing a suitable make-up game for their devoted fans. He wanted management to make things right for the Scrabblers. He wrote a very persuasive letter.

It took a few days. The phone rang in Michael's Riverhead law office. He was informed it was Customer Service from the Mets' organization. They had received a letter. Michael took the call. The voice was sincere and belonged to a woman.

"Mr. Olsen?" she asked. "This is Anita Ryerson of the New York Mets Customer Service Division. How are you today, sir?"

Michael answered courteously. Ms. Ryerson informed Michael that he was speaking to a senior officer of the aforementioned department.

"I am in receipt of your letter, sir," she continued, "and I wish to apologize on behalf of the Mets' organization. What's more, as you so aptly suggest in your letter, we wish to make things right for...is it...the Scrabblers?"

Michael authenticated the club's name.

"If you would be so kind as to accept complimentary tickets, sir, it is our hope that we can encourage each one of the children in your organization to remain a life-long Mets' fan!"

Michael Olsen was satisfied. The Scrabblers, with their entourage, would attend another home game at Citi Field, compliments of the Mets' management. When a day in August had been agreed upon, Ms. Ryerson asked only for receipts, as she had promised to cover all expenses related to the field trip.

What tickets they were! Upon their return to the stadium, the Scrabblers were escorted to VIP seats located directly behind a row of professional sport announcers from popular radio and television shows. Everyone could get the expert play-by play right there in person! All amounts of food and beverages were provided. Ms. Ryerson stopped by to greet Michael and to say hello to the children. Everyone was wearing their tee shirts! It was a great day to be a Scrabbler.

Michael Olsen could write a very persuasive letter. They were often scripted for the benefit of disadvantaged children. Many of the kids were handicapped in one way or another, either physically or by depredations caused by poverty. Some were emotionally distraught because of abandonment.

Interstate 95

It would be impossible for Brian's mother to be more firm when she declared to her son that he was absolutely forbidden to drive that car to Florida.

"You are sixteen years old! I am keeping your driver's license here on the kitchen shelf! I may have lost my mind when I agreed to let you go in the first place!" she stated emphatically. "You are *not* to drive that car!" she repeated, and it was evident to anyone listening that she meant it.

She was referring to the questionable arrangement engineered by her son and his best friend Marty. The teenaged boys had pleaded incessantly for six weeks for parental permission to travel south from their Long Island home during the week-long holiday break in December. Their specific destination was sunny Margate, Florida, birthplace of Alligator City, a senior citizen mobile-home community where Marty's grandparents drove their golf carts to an epicurean clubhouse surrounded by three luxurious pools. From the perspective of the adventurous boys, it was a mere one thousand four hundred miles away from Babylon, New York. "What *is* the problem?" each naïve teenager sincerely wanted to know.

Brian was a broad-shouldered, sluggish kid a few weeks shy of seventeen and Marty was a lean, bespectacled teenager turning eighteen in a few months, and their age was the problem. Neither of the boys had extensive driving experience, or any other kind of experience, but the validation for going on the trip was skillfully-orchestrated by both youths. It was true, for example, that the teens had earned adequate funds and that Marty's four-door Toyota wagon was in reasonable shape for a road trip. Further, as a decisive consideration, the boys would be lodging with Marty's benevolent grandparents who were genuinely elated to entertain their grandson and his best friend. It was pivotal, in fact, when Marty cleverly solicited his grandmother's influential input by tenderly repeating with heartfelt metaphors how much he missed her.

"We would love to have them stay with us!" affirmed Marty's grandparents from Florida.

"Don't worry!" pleaded the boys in New York. "We have cell phones! We have GPS navigation in the car!"

Surprisingly, like finding a note inside of a walnut, the boys were granted permission. A note inside of a walnut is what Brian remembered about Marty's grandfather, who was a well-known prankster. It was his practice to carefully open a walnut, remove the seed, stuff a small note within the carapace, and then glue the shell closed. Marty's grandfather was forever asking people if they wanted a walnut.

The teenagers would be going to Florida after all. The plan was to leave December 23rd to return December 31st in time for the New Year. The boys were excited and they spent hours in their room mapping out the trip. They discussed the food and beverages they would bring. Pillows, blankets, magazines and all such things were readied. The anxious adolescents began packing the car two days in advance. Their exodus was set for six o'clock sharp Friday morning, and they were thrilled to be leaving behind them the miserable drizzle of their beloved Long Island homestead for a week-long hiatus in the Sunshine State. "Let's go!" they exclaimed to everyone, and with broad smiles, they were on their way.

Inside the car, Brian and Marty were safe as in a cocoon; however, they were a bit fidgety at first and they did not play the radio. Navigating the Belt Parkway near the Verrazano Bridge is a challenge for experienced drivers, and maneuvering through this segment of the trip for the boys was intense. The two worked in tandem as co- pilots and they were careful to remain alert in the slow lane as many other confident motorists making the same trek sped recklessly on the congested highway. Once the boys crossed the narrow Goethals Bridge from Staten Island and finally reached the Jersey Turnpike, the white-knuckle driving was over and they could settle themselves and allow some excitement to return to them.

"Glad that's over," commented Brian.

He pulled a donut from the food stash.

"Hungry?"

The trek on I-95 from New York to Florida, as legions know firsthand, is a fabled excursion that has been celebrated and dreaded simultaneously by several generations since the 1950's. While many families, including their own, opted to fly into Florida on the affordable South-West Airlines, both boys as children had travelled to Disney World by car, and each had similarly visited Kennedy Space Center. Both remembered Carolina's 'South of the Border' for example, and because they had taken the road trips, they understood the mayhem of interstate rest areas and so on. Obviously, this solo trip was different. They were cruising without parents to make the easy decisions for them.

"How we doing on gas?" asked Brian frequently. "Sleepy?" he enquired repeatedly. "Car running well?" he wondered aloud more than once, and even though they had GPS, Brian held the road map open on his lap.

"Washington DC is always congested," remarked Marty. "Let's make sure we stop at Chesapeake Rest Area and gas-up before we cross the bridge."

The adolescent voyagers sailed smoothly south through Baltimore and Washington D.C. without issues, and together they enjoyed the scenic proximity of Richmond. Before long they noticed a culture shift when roadside advertisements for tobacco and fireworks began appearing regularly. After scurrying through Virginia's capital, interstate traffic thinned considerably. With the afternoon warmth rising, Marty began to feel a bit fatigued. They decided to take another short break.

"What do you think, Brian?" asked Marty during the hiatus at the rest area. "I'm getting pretty tired."

Both boys remembered the straight ribbon of roadway through southern Virginia and North Carolina as easily navigable, and that's when Brian exchanged roles with Marty and he took the wheel.

"It's not like I don't have a driver's license!" voiced Brian with shaky conviction, principally because the material document was at home on his mother's kitchen's shelf.

"Hey! It's just for a couple of hours," both declared confidently.

It wasn't a surprise. The two of them had always known they would share some of the driving despite their assertions to the contrary, and because outright deception made both of them uncomfortable, they avoided discussing the matter. Brian didn't want to worry his mother unnecessarily, and that was the end of it.

Marty slipped into the passenger seat and set it all the way back as far as it would go. He squeezed his head and bed pillow awkwardly into the corner of the passenger door jamb and he hoisted one skinny leg onto the dashboard. Brian took the wagon steadily southbound and he cracked the window summoning the cool refreshing air. He did not welcome too much heat within the cocoon as the warmth might bring to him a dreadful drowsiness. Marty, on the other hand, relished the lethargy, and he allowed a satisfied sigh to escape into his pillow. Soon, he was asleep.

Brian was careful to keep his speed steady and before long he approached the North Carolina border. As he passed yet another billboard for *South of the Border*, he took note of the clever advertisement; *"Pedro says, Chili Today - Hot Tamale! – 180 miles"* and he guessed it would be another three hours to the theme park hotel. The boys had made great time overall and they were in the ninth hour of the journey. After an hour or so, Marty awakened and adjusted the seat and took his position as co-pilot. All was well.

The first night the boys slept soundly in an inexpensive room at the Marriot Courtyard and the evening was uneventful with the exception of one harrowing experience at a flea-bag motel called *The Willow Motel*. The boys kept noticing signs offering overnight accommodations at twelve dollars a night; a forty dollar savings. By chance they were topping off fuel on a remote stretch of roadway a few miles from the interstate when there it was, behind the gas station, plain as day, the dilapidated *Willow Motel*.

Brian strolled inside the dumpy convenience store behind the fuel pumps and he wondered if they stocked a few of his favorite pastry snacks. A wrinkled woman with a nasty cough sat slouched and hidden on an old wooden chair behind the cluttered counter. Thick cigarette smoke masked any oxygen in the decaying market and residual tobacco resin had painted the walls and shelves the shade of sticky amber.

"Excuse me," Brian asked politely. "Do you sell Yankee Doodles?" The smoke-intoxicated woman looked at him as if she discovered the whereabouts of a cut-throat traitor.

"Yankay Doodles?" she replied in utter disbelief. "We don't carry no such things that say Yankay Doodle in heeya ...boy!" she hollered, and she stood up to have a look at him.

Like an idiot, Brian made another enquiry quite innocently: "Alright then. Do you have any Devil Dogs?" he asked.

The yellow-skinned cougher was perplexed by this weird reference to the devil and his dogs, and by his reference to Yankee products in general, so she scowled at him to see if he was intentionally harassing her. "We have no Yankay Doodles and we have no Devil's Dogs heeya... boy. What is it you want?"

Brian recognized that he had unwittingly insulted the woman. He had assumed all retailers nationwide carried the same products. He realized, finally, that he was in a different culture. The boy nodded, smiled sheepishly, and backed away toward the door. "Thank you, ma'am," he heard himself say to the cantankerous woman, and he quickly slipped outside.

At the gas pumps, a crusty red-beard gas attendant who owned the ramshackle establishment was filling up the Toyota's gas tank when he asked with a straight gaze at Marty: "You boys lookin to stay the night? Twenty bucks git ya a de-lux room overlikin the crick." The proprietor nudged his chin toward the decrepit fleapit motel behind the pumps.

"Yer sine says twelve bucks," answered Marty smartly in a dangerously sarcastic southern accent. "You tryin to cheet us?" he blurted out, like an idiot.

Fortunately, red-beard was not feeling particularly bad-tempered, so he looked at the New York plates and turned a cold shoulder to the boys. He spit once, replaced the nozzle and was silent. Marty paid the gas tab and the boys hustled out of there.

Back in the car, Brian chastised Marty for acting as someone who had completely lost his mind. "I can't help myself," Marty explained. "I don't know what is wrong with me. When I hear a foreign accent, I spontaneously take on that accent!"

By foreign accent, in this case, Marty meant southern accent. "Well, get a grip!" warned Brian preposterously. An absurd moment elapsed. "Listen to what I did inside the store..." Brian guffawed as he spilled the details about the snacks and the smoke woman. Euphoric, the two sped back toward the interstate and the safety of the Marriot Courtyard. Marty drove and they rolled down the windows, and with elbows dangling, the young men bathed in the flowing warmth of the southern evening air.

They awoke early and headed toward Savanna, Georgia. To their delight, a bright sun at daybreak promised a glorious day for travel, and they were refreshed and alert. Roughly seven more uneventful hours passed when they crossed the border into the Jacksonville, Florida area. Unfortunately, the roadway in the small city was impassable due to construction. The delay would be substantial so the two navigators changed their route to one that passed through the scenic back roads of central Florida.

On the quiet gravel streets that wound through the remote residential areas, Marty and Brian observed the southern lifestyle as one quite apart from the previous views from Interstate 95. Their progress was sometimes slow, as was the pace of the inhabitants, and they witnessed many modest dwellings as raggedy homes, dusty and empty of wealth. Everywhere, Spanish moss dangled helplessly from trees, and on one crooked porch, a solitary mutt lifted his muzzle and considered a bark, but gave it up.

"Pretty poor around here," commented Marty, breaking the silence.

Brian was pensive overall; he was preoccupied with the communities he saw along the route. The mood in the car was subdued, and for hours, the two boys passed by numberless houses and kept watchful.

It was Saturday, and by mid-afternoon, they reached the robust city of Gainesville, Florida, and the commercial main street was uproariously jubilant. A holiday parade was in progress, and the locals, especially children, were clanging and tooting everything noisy. The high school band in full regalia with tuba and all things festive were drum-beating alongside huge "floats" constructed by area students. Athletes and cheerleaders were dangling like Broadway stars from their rolling paper-machete flatbed; grade-school children were dancing pirouettes as ballerina's on their dolled –up trailer; swirling red and green elf-children were tossing tightly-wrapped, hard-candy from a snow-frosted village, and the police and fire trucks were blaring their sirens until Santa could be seen waving to everyone. It was Christmas Saturday, and as chance would have it, the two boys from Long Island had arrived precisely on time to partake in the merriments. The parade set them back a few hours but they didn't mind. It was a good parade.

Later that evening, things were much less entertaining when a homeless degenerate accosted Brian in a bizarre happening near the forsaken town of Calico. Marty was driving route 25S and he followed several highway signs to Budd's Convenience and Package Store. Because Marty had sat on his sunglasses and crushed them, and because Brian was hungry for another snack, they decided to stop there for a comfort break and to get some more fuel. Budd's enterprise was in desperate need of restoration, but it was too late to back away when they pulled in headlong into the parking lane directly in front of the front door of the grimy retail establishment.

At the store's entrance, two irritated young men were shouting at each other in apparent frustration; each was demonstrably upset with each other and it looked like trouble. With violent gesticulations, they were pointing and hollering obscenities and causing a commotion. They appeared angry and short-tempered and it seemed certain to Marty and Brian this dispute would end in a fist fight. Smartly, the boys remained seated in their air-conditioned vehicle and they dared not happen upon the unpredictable violence. Cautiously, Marty shut the radio and he let the driver's window slip down imperceptibly a few inches so he could hear the details of the volatile situation as it unfolded.

Astounded, Marty and Brian looked at each other speechless. The fiery men were screaming about "the Lord" and both were fanatically railing against "cursed sin" and "Satan." Curiously, these impassioned men soon thereafter rejoiced with frenzied gestures by swearing, "Praise the Lord!" and "Amen!" The anxious boys had completely mistaken their riotous exclamations! Once properly understood, they exited the car with renewed purpose.

Inside the seedy establishment, Marty picked out some sunglasses and Brian decided on a Snickers candy bar and they left the dirty market together. A young vagabond appeared suddenly in their stead, and with his braided, Rastafarian-styled brown hair and with his worn-out leather back-pack, he introduced himself on the spot, and he asked if he could travel a few exits south with them. He was not a physical threat to anyone, but he was pushy and he opened the rear door to sit inside the car without waiting for a reply.

"Just two exits on the expressway," he insisted, and just like that, the boys were riding with a pot smoker named Carson; a name one may correctly assume he invented for himself while on the road.

Carson didn't have any marijuana with him, thank goodness, as the last thing the boys needed was to spend some time in a southern jail, but he did display an awfully disturbing thing to Brian as the three youths headed steadily south. Carson was a drifter who travelled for months on the road, and he wanted ultimately to get back to Bahia Honda in the Florida Keys where he could find shelter and food. He was friendly enough and he spoke incessantly the whole way about grandiose adventures befitting a dharma bum, but most of it was obvious balderdash. While listening politely, Brian noticed the raconteur was scratching himself all the while he was inventing stories. Before exiting the car, the braided Carson picked from his lower waist area, below his belt, a tiny creature and he held it steadfast before Brian's widespread eyes. Suddenly, Brian's head and frame bolted back as if a firecracker had exploded in his teeth. On Carson's finger, Brian discerned a perfectly-shaped miniature crab.

"Damned crabs!" exclaimed Carson as he pinched it to death before Brian's sickened gaze.

Finally, hoisting his dirty back-pack out from the rear passenger seat onto the roadside, Carson grinned.

"Thanks for the lift. The name's Carson James, great grandson of Jesse James..."

Marty reacted badly, and he ransacked the car interior with intent to throw away all things that may have been in contact with the infested

Carson. He tossed a blanket, a small pillow and even a magazine before spending an hour with a rag and a hand-sized whisk broom thoroughly sanitizing all things in the rear compartment.

Dusk turned to darkness, and because of the parade delay, their progress was delayed as much as four hours. They were still quite a distance from Margate. Satisfied that the car was not contaminated, Marty drove until they reached a popular rest area jammed with eighteen-wheeled tractor trailers whose drivers had already bed-down for the evening. In a quiet covert near a swampy thicket at the perimeter of the truck stop, Marty and Brian prepared to sleep until early morning. It was Christmas Eve.

This tranquil evening would be a memorable one for both of them. Marty could not rest inside the despoiled Toyota wagon until it had been thoroughly detailed, so he considered setting up with blankets an open camp on the ground nearby. Brian was inventive when he suggested the roof of the car; it was high and flat and distanced from the native ground insects and other nocturnal pests in the unfamiliar ecosystem. It was a great idea. They spread layers of clean cushiony blankets between the roof racks, and with bed pillows and fresh coverlets, the two wanderers rested comfortably atop their vehicle beneath the illustrious starlight. In the heavens, the timeless display appeared spectacular. Their young minds were attentive to the dazzling stars set against the black vastness. Resting in perfect comfort, they allowed a transcendental curiosity overtake them. They spoke in whispers. Eventually, they slept.

Alligator City was everything the brochures and the internet had promised it would be, and the first thing Marty did when they arrived was to have the car thoroughly vacuumed and sanitized at a local car wash. The Margate weather forecast was for sunny days all week long, and soon Marty and Brian settled into the laid back warmth of the community. Most days they spent tanning at the pool or cycling around sidewalks on rented bicycles, and Brian kept especially vigilant for wild alligators, as the community had many ponds with flaring fountains, and invariably, one or two of the prehistoric reptiles could be seen basking freely on a rock at the water's edge. Marty's grandmother was all fired up to cook meals for the hungry boys and to chat endlessly about everything and she was keen to show her grandson around to friends. Marty's grandfather was forever joking and he was never without walnuts.

The vacation week was over very quickly and soon the boys were preparing for the return trip. Before leaving, two huge crates of Florida oranges and two more filled with grapefruits were loaded into the trunk space in the Toyota; these boxes of fruit were gifts from Marty's grandparents. The boys didn't have that much money left in reserve, just enough to get home, so Marty's grandparents made sandwiches and provided snacks and cereals and they also packed coolers full of soft drinks and so on. Before long, the teenagers were heading north across the state back towards the infamous Interstate 95.

Orangeburg, South Carolina is rarely visited by tourists unless an unwary driver misinterprets the left-exit ramp that swings west into the interior of the state. Brian was driving steadily for about three hours when the drone of the tires and the monotony of the roadway lulled him into an inattentive trance. The interstate split evenly and he veered the car left onto the wide lanes headed inland, and almost immediately he recognized his blunder. He had mistakenly exited Interstate 95 and he was driving on highway 17W headed toward Orangeburg. He cursed himself for having disconnected the GPS. There wouldn't be a ready turn-about for miles and he knew he would lose some time.

They were going the wrong way. Miles and miles out on route 17W they travelled, and each minute in the wrong direction was two minutes wasted, for the boys knew they would need to return the same distance back to the Interstate. Surrounded by flat marshland, there was nothing but roadway. Reinstalled, the GPS warned, "turn left …twenty-two miles" and that's when they knew the mistake would be a serious time-consumer. In light of the many hours of driving still ahead for them, Marty and Brian discussed a solution that appeared at that moment as a reasonable gamble. They needed simply to glide the wagon across the flat grassland of the median that divided the empty highway, and in seconds, they would be headed back in the proper direction. It would take only a few moments to accomplish, and as Brian slowed the car and breached the bumpy terrain of the median, a weighty breathlessness within the cocoon was palpable. Both boys exhaled when their speed returned on the other side, and travelling at last in the correct direction, they were grateful and they felt lucky.

"Glad that's over," remarked Brian.

He pulled a donut from the food stash.

"Hungry?"

From out of the clear blue sky, a highway patrol car appeared inches behind the Toyota wagon. The state trooper flipped on the dreaded rotating red and blue lights. No doubt about it, they were caught. They had crossed the median illegally, and despite their efforts to conceal the trespass, a well-camouflaged patrol car was hidden nearby and had seen it all. Either that, or a hidden highway camera detailed the escapade and notified the patrolman. No doubt at all. They were caught. Brian pulled over toward the shoulder and both boys made another terrible decision.

"I don't have my license!" Brian blurted to Marty as the officer approached the car. "What should we do?"

"Take mine," offered Marty. "Don't say much if you can help it."

It was four o'clock in the afternoon when the state trooper asked Brian for his license and registration. It took him but a few seconds to comprehend the ruse.

"Please step out of the car," he commanded as he scrutinized Brian and the details on Marty's driver's license. "Says here on this license that you are over six feet tall," continued the officer. "Where's your eyeglasses?" he enquired, confident then that the license identification was a deception.

Brian gave it all up first and he explained in near delirium that he was, in fact, a licensed driver, but his cautious mother insisted she keep his license on the kitchen shelf in New York. He explained that in a fleeting moment of anxiety and dread, he foolishly borrowed his friend Marty's license, claiming it was his own, hoping it would all be the same in the end. Marty chirped in next with an apology for stupidly giving his license to Brian, and he implored forgiveness, as he was only trying to help his friend Brian. He repeated that he was certain now that he had used poor judgment. The officer perceived most of this appeal as gibberish. He called for back-up and soon another police car arrived, and Marty and Brian were arrested right there on 17W in Orangeburg, South Carolina. The officer stated his name as State Trooper Wilkins and he was not particularly sympathetic to the young New Yorkers, and he seemed intent to razz the boys a bit before they moved to the courthouse.

"I can be a real pain in the rear..." he grunted at both of them as if speaking to trashy punks, "...a mean jackal. Don't you think?"

Marty figured correctly that Trooper Wilkins was setting them up for something worse than traffic infractions.

"No sir," Marty answered, "just doing your job, sir."

Brian remained quiet. The officer repeated the taunt, and then let it be. In a moment more, the two boys were handcuffed and seated in the back of the patrol car headed for jail.

Marty was more nervous than Brian, as he felt it was his idea to give Brian his license, and he felt responsible because he was older. He mustered the nerve to ask the trooper a few questions from the rear seat.

"What about my car? Where are you taking us?" he asked, and it was evident that Trooper Wilkins had softened a little.

Trooper Wilkins allowed that Marty and Brian were not punks, and no doubt he ran a background check that revealed the boys were without a criminal record. Nonetheless, he responded gruffly without looking directly at the worried teenagers.

"Your car will be brought over to the courthouse," he said. "Don't worry too much...after we see the judge to find out how much you owe, you can pay the traffic fines and be on your way."

Brian thought this response was reasonable, and it appeared things were going to work out after all. He was wrong. The judge was not at the courthouse; instead, he was at his farm. Trooper Wilkins veered south to the judge's dusty plantation to locate him to procure the necessary signatures so the boys could pay the fines and be released. The patrol car came to a stop outside an old farmhouse. All was quiet. Finally, an irritable old man wearing overalls ambled out into the open yard and he approached the officer. With a grin, he could be heard, asking:

"What do ya want me to do with them, Wilkie? Lock em up?"

State Trooper Wilkins knew better than to punish these kids too hard. Perhaps he had a few teenaged kids of his own at home.

"Naw! Just fine em up good, Judge. I think they can get the money...I don't want to put them in jail."

Brian was fined ninety dollars for driving without a license, sixty dollars for illegally crossing the median, and another one hundred dollars for presenting false testimony to an officer of the law. As an alternative, if unable to pay the two hundred and fifty dollars, Brian could satisfy each offense by serving fifteen days in the county jail; his incarceration not to exceed forty-five days. Marty was fined fifty dollars for giving his license to another person, and another one hundred dollars for presenting false testimony to an officer of the law. He owed one hundred and fifty dollars, and if unable to pay, each offense could be satisfied by fifteen days in the county jail; his incarceration not to exceed thirty days.

Together, because there would be an additional one hundred dollars owed to the county to pay for towing the Toyota from the highway to the jail, the fines totaled five hundred dollars. The boys could pay for only three hundred of it and still have money to get home. Marty and Brian pleaded guilty on the spot. There was a problem. Because the banks were closed, it would take time to arrange for the additional money to be sent from New York to the county clerk. Until the additional money arrived, Officer

Wilkins, with signed confessions in hand, drove the convicted youths to the jailhouse where they would wait in a cell until someone with resources in New York would wire cash through Western Union.

It was about six in the evening when Brian made the phone call to his mother. His mother was disappointed, but she agreed to rescue Brian with sufficient funds, and she promised to remain focused and calm throughout the ordeal before killing him with her bare hands when he got home. Brian was honest and forthright when responding to his mother's questions: Yes, he had been driving. No, he did not have enough money to pay the fines. Yes, he had illegally crossed the median on route 17W. No, he could not call her again later as they sequestered his cell phone. Yes, he had lied to the state trooper when attempting to use Marty's license as his own. No, he did not forget the promise he had made to her. Yes, he would be placed in a jail cell until the money arrived. No, he did not forget the promise he had made to her. Yes, it certainly would be a lesson-learned if he spent the ninety days in the lockup.

The jail itself was a drab adobe building with national and state flags flapping haplessly about its entry; there were several more police cars stationed about its perimeter. Inside, the bureaucratic office contained two desks and a nondescript clerk who took the boys' belongings to a closet-safe behind him. In due course, Officer Wilkins spoke and he explained to Brian and Marty that they would be released in a few hours at most, and that their car had already been towed to the station. He motioned to a steel door behind the desks and he opened it with a loud jolt. Trooper Wilkins appeared huge in his uniform when he escorted the boys down the narrow hallway leading to the jail cells.

Prisoners are like sea shells; once collected and placed into a box, each one loses its luster and the entire contents seem of little worth. The first cell along the noisy corridor was occupied by petty thieves, the features of each as dull as a drawer full of common spoons. They rattled a grunt at the State Trooper as he passed, and their protests ended flat; they were resigned to their indigence and to the days of incarceration determined by the farmer judge. The second cell was a true threat. Several sweaty inmates pressed their dangerous faces to the bars and yelled belligerently at the boys, and one of them, reaching through the bars with muscled arms, belched out a specific taunt:

"Whata we gotta heeya?" he heckled. "I like doz sneekas ...c'mon offissa troopah ...pud doze lams in heeya wid us...c'mon babeez...c'mon in heeya wid doz sneekas!"

Trooper Wilkins paused for a moment and he turned with a curious look to the pugnacious inmate. He mixed a cough with a short laugh, and he held still as if considering the request of the loud-mouthed troublemaker. Fortunately, the trooper decided this cell was unsafe and unsuitable for the vulnerable youths from Long Island. He continued down the corridor.

Further along, two lazy men circled away from the iron door to facilitate an easy entrance. The first inmate was an old, slow-moving grey-haired gentleman named Gregory who appeared listless from years of alcohol abuse. Worn thin by drudgery, Gregory was arrested for vagrancy and he was no threat to anyone. The second man was named Foster, and he was a teenager full of energy, slight of build, and a tireless talker. Something was odd about Foster though, first suspected when he greeted Brian and Marty with a sincerely wholesome shoulder embrace and a hearty "hallo!" when they entered. By contrast, Gregory grunted once and slouched over to the side.

Trooper Wilkins spoke succinctly to the inmates when he closed the cell door: "These boys will be here a few hours...take care to get along..." and then he was gone.

Items inside the concrete cubicle were arranged so that Brian and Marty could settle together one above the other on the narrow bunk beds should it become necessary for them to spend the night. Foster introduced himself as a South Carolina native and he talked with a thick accent for a few minutes, mainly about himself. Marty wasn't handling things well at all. He listened without interest to Foster and he was clearly depressed and defeated by the incarceration overall. Brian was more animated, and because he was physically stronger than Foster and Gregory, he perceived no real danger. In fact, he was grateful he still had his sneakers, which meant he was relieved not to be inside the aggressive cell up the hallway.

When Foster concluded his preamble, Brian took his turn to explain the circumstances that led them to this miserable state of affairs. When finished speaking, he took a chance and asked for details about Foster's crime. The air hung dead in the room. In that silent moment, Brian realized the impropriety of asking about another's criminal situation. Foster hesitated initially, but then he decided to be up-front with the facts concerning his incarceration.

"I was tryin to git home, ya undstand?" he began willingly, "cause my ma was sick an maybe dyin...as I tole the judge...an dat's why I borrow the bunglo bar truck in the firss place."

Marty leaned closer to hear every detail. Brian was sure that Marty was intrigued by the curious accent. Foster continued:

"An so I had to git home to my sick mama... lak I sed...an so I was widout money in the Handy Pantry, ya see, when I wocked out wid a crispy cream donut an sum samwich or utter...an I just forgit exackly... but I need to git home qwick...so ousside da Piggly Wiggly I see da man waving mad at me wid his fist an all, so I qwick hopped da ice cream truck an sped da wheels heddin home to my sick ma... jes lak I tole da judge."

Both boys were dumbfounded by the details of this man's story.

"Let me get this straight," repeated Brian, waving his open palm to forestall Marty's satire-laced response for the moment. "You were eating a crispy cream donut in the Handy Pantry when you ran to the Piggly Wiggly where you stole a Bungalow Bar ice cream truck to get home to your sick mother? You went from the Handy Pantry with the Crispy Cream to the Piggly Wiggly to the Bungalow Bar? Is that what happened?"

Marty spoke next, and he couldn't help himself: "Wuz da ice cream man sellin da ice cream to youngins on da street wen ya stole his truck? Didja leeve da chillen right der wid da ice cream man on da street?" Marty asked with utter disregard for Foster's dignity.

Fortunately, Foster was unaware of the mockery, and Marty regretted his comments immediately because Foster was slow-witted. Foster answered him without delay:

"Dey cawt me on da sam hiway as yoo all..." he confided unoffended, "...an I'd be waitin for my ma now...to sey she wuz sick an all...an dat shud hep me wid da judge so maybe I wone spen dat much time in heeya. I nowed it wuz wrong wad I dun an all."

A thick silence ensued. Everyone settled and Marty spoke a bit with Gregory, and before long, several trays of food were brought to everyone. It was dinnertime, and Brian was hungry. Marty took one look at the gruel and declared he would not eat his meal. Perhaps because he was feeling guilty for having made fun of poor Foster, he offered the platter of chopped beef and beans to him first, and Foster was grateful. Time slowed. What was the delay? Nervous and impatient, Marty managed to ask a guard about the status of the Western Union transfer.

The unfamiliar officer working the night shift appeared puzzled by Marty's enquiry. He explained curtly to Marty and Brian that they would be released in the morning, as the whereabouts of the paperwork necessary to satisfy the fines was unknown to him. Marty protested and explained that he had been assured by Trooper Wilkins that it would be only a few hours of detention at most.

"Have a good night," replied the officer, and he was gone.

There wasn't much to do, and so everyone rested quietly. Marty and Brian, worried but safe, whispered themselves to sleep. In the morning, they reasoned correctly, they would be released and back on the road on their way home.

Late into the darkness, Brian perceived a furtive movement, and with a shy glance, he saw that Foster was getting out of bed. Like a shadow, Foster slid silently toward Brian's folded shirt and he padded it such that he might determine any bulk inside a pocket without unfolding it. He did the same with the pants. Brian remained motionless, pretending sleep, but secretly he witnessed the thief doing the same thing to Marty's folded garments before returning to his bunk. Fortunately, wallets and other valuables were removed and secured in the front safe. What was he looking for?

The morning arrived and with sudden understanding, it was apparent that all four prisoners would be sharing the lone porcelain toilet that lay open and naked in the corner of the cell. Brian thought of Carson and the crabs and he forestalled using the facility. Marty was appalled at the lack of privacy.

Later on, someone brought green scrambled eggs and a white gruel of grits with toast to the cell, and this time Marty ate the little breakfast with enthusiasm. Brian was thinking about the sneaky escapade in the night.

"I saw you last night Foster..." he said, without threatening him in the least. "...looking through our clothes. What were you looking for?"

Foster was dumb with surprise, but he came straight with a suitable reply:

"I was hopin ya mite a had cigg-retts ... das all. I wuz gonna tak jes one cigg-rett... das all."

Trooper Wilkins arrived about 9:00 am and he was genuinely surprised to discover that the boys from Long Island had spent the night in his jail. He quickly arranged for their release and he escorted the boys back to the courthouse vestibule. Everyone waited patiently while the clerk returned all of the secured items to Brian and Marty. The fines had been paid and the discharge was finalized, and it wasn't until Trooper Wilkins stood beside the boys at the Toyota wagon that he spoke to them.

"I didn't figure you would be here this morning," he said. "You can be on your way now. Be safe and stay on the road."

The southern morning sun was warming the air when Marty gratefully accepted the keys from Trooper Wilkins.

"One more thing," said the state trooper before the boys entered their car. "My family likes grapefruits and oranges...they surely do."

Brian was confused, but Marty understood.

"Perhaps you would like a box of oranges and another with grapefruits?" offered Marty, figuring that he would be driving through South Carolina for hours and he did not wish to be detained with another traffic infraction.

Trooper Wilkins opened the trunk of his patrol car.

"I would be much obliged...indeed I would...thank you very kindly," he said at last.

After the citrus gift was deposited inside the trunk of the officer's patrol car, the trooper waved and conveyed a friendly gesture of departure.

"Drive safe now!" he said.

Indeed, Marty drove safely, and he dared not exceed the speed limit. Brian kept looking back for any sign of any trooper.

"I figured we would never get out of the state if I didn't give him a box of fruit," Marty explained. Brian nodded, and not much else was spoken inside the cocoon for quite a while. The boys didn't relax again until they entered the nation's capital, six hours later.

Marty and Brian approached the Goethals Bridge about ten o'clock that evening, and when crossing the Verrazano Bridge, celebratory fireworks could be seen erupting everywhere. It was New Year's Eve! The Manhattan Island skyline was ablaze with dazzling colors; festive explosions of triumphant illumination flashed above Lady Liberty from the South Seaport below. It was a spectacular nocturnal display. It was New Year's Eve, and the boys would be home in Babylon by midnight!

On Long Island at last! Both boys were a bit fidgety and Marty turned off the radio; navigating the Belt Parkway near the Verrazano Bridge is a challenge for experienced drivers, and maneuvering through this section of the drive for the boys was intense. The two worked in tandem as co-pilots and they were careful to remain alert in the slow lane as many other confident motorists making the same trek home sped recklessly on the congested highway. When they reached the Southern State Parkway, the white-knuckle driving was over and they could settle themselves and allow some excitement to return to them.

"Glad to be home," commented Brian, stating the obvious. "I wonder what kind of mood my mother will be in?" he asked rhetorically. "Do you think she will be glad I made it back safely, or is she going to kill me dead on the spot?"

He pulled a donut from the food stash.

"Hungry?"

Burnt Toast and Crispy Bacon

Sometimes at breakfast, a thin black smoke will rise up from between the red hot wires inside of a silver or black bread box and a distinctive scent will be readily discerned. Other times at breakfast, boiling grease will shrink fatty pork inside of a frying pan and an unmistakable aroma will be pleasantly detected. Burnt toast and crispy bacon, as everyone knows, permeates an entire house and alerts the senses; when either is amicably encountered, one simply must shout out the obvious source of the aroma: "Someone's toast is burning!" or "I smell bacon!" will then be broadcast about the home. In my house, these proclamations would occur most frequently on Saturday mornings, because plain cereal was the usual morning staple on schooldays, and on Sunday mornings after church, my family would gather in the kitchen for pancakes or waffles with eggs.

In retrospect, crispy bacon and burnt toast may have been the reason I woke up suddenly on that fateful Saturday morning. Specifically, it was the strong redolent air and the strange dryness within my throat that alerted me. Who could be burning toast or frying bacon at three o'clock in the morning?

Years ago, my sister Patricia kept her possessions and rested her twelve-year-old head on a pillow each night in a bedroom located upstairs in our small cape-cod home. That is, unless she extended an invitation to a girlfriend to sleep-over at the house. In that event, with her head full of intrigue, Pat would ask me if she and her friend could occupy my ground-floor bedroom for the night because my bedroom had a large flat-screen television that received all of the cable channels. It was not very often she asked for the favor. I didn't mind in the least. At fourteen years old, sometimes it feels good to help out your little sister with things that are

126

easy. Without much concern, I agreed to sleep upstairs in her room so she could entertain her sleep-over friend in mine. It wasn't the first time she had asked and it likely would not be the last. No big deal.

On that particular evening, after hanging around with my friend Joey Culver until about ten o'clock, I filled a glass of water from the kitchen sink, drank it, said goodnight to my mom, and made my way upstairs to my sister's room for the remainder of the evening. Previously, I had secured my laptop and my cell phone from my bedroom, and I brought them upstairs with me before I settled in. I didn't want my sister and her friend messing around on my computer.

Her room was considerably smaller than mine, and it was located directly at the top of the stairwell. With the bedroom door left ajar, I could hear familiar noises from the den area beneath me. I heard, for example, that my kid sister and her girlfriend were still awake, giggling and rummaging around the kitchen, looking for chips and cookies. Ignoring them, I clicked on the small television set and checked my Facebook page for a while. Soon, I felt drowsy enough to shut everything down for the night.

It was a humid evening in late summer and I guess I should have checked the thermostat because the air conditioning wasn't doing anything to cool the bedroom. It became uncomfortably warm after a while, and I was experiencing some difficulty sleeping. Hours passed, and in complete darkness, I realized I was perspiring. Tossing and heaving in bed, I remember feeling a strange heaviness in the room. It was two or three hours past midnight and I knew something was strange. I was exceedingly thirsty! My throat was choked and dry, and swallowing was difficult. I lay half-asleep for several moments more, rubbing my throat, when I asked myself in a hoarse whisper, "Why am I so thirsty?"

When finally I opened my eyes, a hazy film of dust stung at them. Blinking wildly, I could see nothing but an irritable bleached mist within the room. Tossing aside the bed sheet, it was my intent to get some drinking water from the washroom when a pungent smell halted my confusion. I gasped. Dropping to the floor, I saw above my head a thick loaf of smoke; it floated three feet from the ceiling of the room. On my knees I could discern the lower pegs of the nightstand; above me, cloaking the upper regions, there was an impenetrable cloud. The house was on fire! I fumbled and groped my way toward the stairwell. There were no visible flames. I perceived at the landing, however, an unrelenting plume of smoke surging up the narrow tunnel. Everywhere it gushed high against the ceiling and wallboards.

"Fire!" I cried over and over again. "Fire!"

I scrambled low, nearly on my chest, down the stairwell and I realized that my sister Pat with her friend and my mother were already on the move toward the front door to safety. I knew it was a poor decision, but from the hallway at the bottom of the stairwell, I realized for certain that the smoke was coming from the kitchen, and with some foolhardy confidence, I ducked inside to see what flames were there. Shocked, I saw at once that the abundance of smoke was originating from a relatively contained source. The wire plug from the toaster on the countertop had sparked, and a few simple flares had produced flames that lapped at the kitchen cabinets above the small appliance. Who would have thought so much smoke could result from such a small fire? I put it into my head that I could extinguish the blaze with a dash of sink water. Racing to a cabinet near the stove, I retrieved a large pasta bowl and placed it beneath the faucet. I waited for it to fill. A furtive movement dashed behind me then, and I saw it was my sister racing to the back door of the house. We exchanged glances and I followed her until she disappeared unharmed through a doorway to the backyard. I knew she was safe.

I could not have imagined how long it would take to fill the blasted pasta bowl with water! I tossed its contents once upon the flames and smoke billowed in protest. I was refilling it at the sink when I heard a shout from behind:

"Get out of the way!"

I looked back, and there in plain view, I saw my sister Pat with the outdoor garden hose in her hand, preparing to release a torrent of water from its nozzle.

"Get out of the way!" she repeated, as I let drop the futile pasta bowl into the sink.

With a single surge from the hose, she aimed the liquid skillfully, and within seconds, the flames were extinguished. Together we sprayed the charred cabinets until all was dowsed and thoroughly soaked. We blasted the toaster with water until it lay demolished upon the floor. The immediate danger was no more. When satisfied, we retreated to the yard. There, we were joined by my sister's girlfriend and my worried mother. Before long, our curious and concerned neighbors poured from their homes. The fire department was dispatched to the scene. Everyone had escaped without incident.

My sister had acted bravely. I was not embarrassed in the least by her superior response to the crisis, nor did I begrudge her gutsy action. She had assessed the danger and she had prevented the burning house from becoming an inferno. I chided her actions but briefly.

"You could have been harmed!" I said without much conviction.

She remained silent, and I could see she was shaken by the ordeal. Perhaps she had recognized all the while that the danger of the episode was not from the flames in the kitchen; she understood it was the *smoke* that had posed the lethal threat. Deadly fumes! The toxic enemy had attacked surreptitiously like an assassin late into the night. The hushed killer had infiltrated *her* upstairs bedroom while everyone was fast asleep.

It is curious. Was it by chance alone that I was destined to occupy her room? What if she, my young sister, had been asleep in her usual bed that ill-fated Saturday evening? Would she have been awakened at all?

The Baby Boom Experience - Famous Babies

By Diane Kennedy

It has taken nearly twenty-five years to respond to the frequent personal questions that people have asked me concerning my daughters' involvement in movies, commercial modeling and television production. Often young parents have the desire to showcase their own children, and so they are inquisitive about auditions, talent agents and so on. "How did you get started? What was it like overall? Why aren't you pursuing their careers anymore...or are you? Tell me! Tell me!"

Michelle and Kristina were famous little girls and it is because we deliberately chose to get out of the business that I feel compelled to relate this narrative. It was very evident from the start that enormous compromises would be necessary for us had we continued to seek fame and fortune. People have told me openly that I must have been crazy to have passed on such an opportunity. What were you thinking? How could you have dropped the golden egg? How bad could it have been to turn away from such riches and celebrity?

The simple truth is that it was a terrifying gamble. After all, if movie production was all roses, then every child-acting role would be taken by the children of directors, actors, producers and others directly connected to the movie industry. As it is, you won't find their young children auditioning for anything but a cameo appearance at most, and by the close of this narrative, it will be very clear why.

What about the money? This is likely the most important consideration that underlies our decision to leave the business altogether. It is also the reason many parents remain and continue to dream the dream. Because of the compromises inherent in the entertainment industry, it is self-evident to everyone that the only reason anyone would put their children through the arduous ordeal of television, feature film or commercial production would be for the money. How naïve I was in the beginning when I thought somehow that there was more to it than simply the money. I felt so proud and honored that Hollywood had chosen my twins to "star" in their movie, and if we hadn't done the film after all, I would still feel that way. After having been there, though, I know the business of producing successful films to be an adult-only enterprise. But you can decide for yourself. Read my narrative. Witness the absurdity of adults when children toddle into show biz, as told by parents who believe that they got away with something especially valuable by finding the exit just in time.

Early on.

The first audition for us was an instant success and a miserable failure. We made eighty-seven dollars after a full day in Manhattan. I did learn something important however. I realized that if some psycho murderers with the audacity to run an ad in the newspaper wanted unsuspecting young mothers to bring their children right to their doorstep, they need only advertise for child actors or models. In the beginning I admit that I had no idea what I was doing and I brought my children to a place that frightened me. Thank God nothing happened because I believe we were vulnerable, and possibly in some danger, and certainly we could have used better judgment overall.

Why dangerous? It was only a print audition being held by a freelance photographer on the lower west-side of Manhattan. Did I know who this person was? What company he was with? What magazine he represented? It happened this way.

One day in July, I received a call from a woman named Beverly who worked with a children's talent agency called "Star-Makers." Beverly knew where all the twins were on Long Island. She asked if I might be interested in starting an acting career for my twin babies. "Would I go to an audition at ten o'clock the next day for a trade publication? I took down the information. What did she mean by a trade magazine? I decided to give it a go.

Early that morning, we arrived at a building in Manhattan at a place that was confusing and disturbing. The building appeared to function primarily as a loading dock for trucks carrying vegetable produce and food.

In the rear was a small office somewhere on the third floor and I was told by a crusty dockhand that we should use the warehouse elevator, the one that has a chain-link fence with steel braces and metal teeth designed to haul bulky stock items. So there I found myself with two little babies in a twin stroller on a filthy platform of discarded lettuce and rotting vegetables hoping to get to the third floor. I felt nervous immediately. It occurred to me that this could be some kind of a set-up. This was not Park Avenue. It was raucous and seedy. How did I get here?

The office was probably rented by the day. A photographer was there, a man in his forties who appeared to be in a hurry, and he posed various backdrops for my children to sit with, and he must have snapped some seventy-five shots before we were through about an hour later. Thank you very much and I signed some papers and we were out of there. No money at this time. He told me he would contact Star-Makers if he could sell any of the photographs. I raced back through the steel gates to the street, very happy to be going home.

We would never do anything like that again. But who would have guessed it? Some weeks later, I opened my mail to find a trade magazine and I discovered a full-page picture of my daughter Michelle on the cover. It looked very professional. The guy sold one after all, and I thought…where is the pay? I called Star-Makers and they were unaware that a photograph was sold and published. At the time I thought it might be worth a thousand dollars or more. I asked Star-Makers what to expect. They told me then that the "print media" does not pay very well. It might be one hundred dollars. I was also informed that they would be taking 15% at any rate, as their management-agency fee, which I was told was standard in the industry. I was disappointed I guess, but only for a moment. I forgot about it straight away and got on with the business of caring for twin eleven- month old babies. Over the next few weeks however, I must say I admired the cover photo on the trade magazine. I had it framed, and I guess that was something after all. My parents and friends made a fuss over it as well.

We were through with the industry, until I heard on a local radio station Z100 that an open audition was to be held for a feature film yet untitled featuring twins as co-stars. This was some six weeks after the trade publication.

Three Instances of Fate: A Pleasant Beginning

It was an audition for identical twin babies between the ages of 12 – 16 months with MGM /United Artist for the feature film titled *Baby Boom* starring Diane Keaton. After the last fiasco, my husband really did not want to pursue it any further. I didn't either. I guess I kept looking at the cover page of the trade magazine though, for it kept the flame alive. This one would be different, and indeed, it was very different.

Once again we traveled to Manhattan, and upon entering the lobby, I knew we were certainly in the right place, for there were twin strollers parked everywhere. This was going to be crowded. The audition room was on the 30th floor and it was quite large and very plush, and it was loaded with toys and apple juice. There were diapers and plastic-wrap bottles and new teething rings and anything else one might need for the taking. Obviously, someone had been hired to make this audition-thing run smoothly, and it really was being handled with obvious consideration for the children. There were at least forty babies in the room. Of course we had never seen so many twins before, and I believe the feeling was rather uplifting for everyone. It was for me. I felt loose, so my husband Jim and I settled into a clearing near a make-shift play area where the toddlers were sitting on a carpet. It was pleasantly noisy without much crying.

Apparently, we were waiting for someone. I spoke with some of the parents and it was a funny atmosphere after all, no doubt because it was a quirky kind of competition, with an odd "whose baby is prettier" thing in the back of our heads. Before long, it became clear to everyone that it was altogether absurd that someone was going to arrive and actually "judge" these beautiful children, but here we were, all forty of us. No one knew what might happen next and so we waited and chatted for about twenty minutes. Meanwhile, I noticed that there were four fashionable young ladies, casting agents as it turned out, shrewdly ambling around the room asking questions and distributing application forms. I was filling in the blanks on the form when one of the casting agents signaled to me. Another was already by the window talking to my husband Jim. Something was definitely up.

Her name was Pam Dixon, Casting Director, and she seemed to be genuinely interested in our story. She began with congenial off-hand questions about our twin girls…name, weight, "Can they talk? Walk?" …etcetera. My husband meandered over and we waited another ten minutes or so more. We were informed that we were waiting for Charles Shyer and Nancy Meyers, the writers and directors of *Baby Boom*. I had not heard of them before, but I did recognize their previous films, *Private Benjamin* and *Irreconcilable Differences*. They would be here shortly.

A *Daily News* photographer arrived. A *New York Post* photographer was next. They took shots of all of the twins and their parents. The casting director came over again, for perhaps a third or fourth time. Another agent sat on the carpet with Kristina and they played with a plastic ball. My husband asked about the audition process. Rather suddenly, the producers arrived and they walked directly to an adjacent room reserved for them alone.

Charles Shyer was a thin, silver-haired enthusiastic man in his late thirties and Nancy Meyers was a pretty, petite and confident woman about the same age. Before I could form an opinion about the two based upon first impressions, I noticed that they were looking down at their feet. A stray toddler was crawling into the office chasing a rolling ball from the make-shift play area. It was my daughter Kristina, marching right in. This was a first instance of fate. Kristina was out of my reach for less than a second and before I could scoop her up and apologize, to my surprise, Nancy and Charles were genuinely delighted.

"Well show them in!" someone exclaimed, in mock ceremonial fashion. "Right this way!" and we were invited inside the small adjacent room.

We were the first to be auditioned. It was strange all right, but there you have it.

The audition itself was not very long and it was comfortable. At first I am sure we tried to maintain a composed seriousness to our demeanor, but with thirteen- month old babies crawling all over everything, this attempt broke down quickly. I plopped Kristina on the table and she bee-lined it over the paperwork straight toward the director Charles Shyer. Maybe it was his watch or his jewelry, but Kristina just mauled him. His wife and co-producer Nancy Myers continued asking questions, principally about whether or not the family, if selected, would be willing to relocate to California for six to nine months to make a movie. She asked me if we had done any other professional work with the children. I answered, "No, we hadn't," but my husband remembered the cover ad from the trade magazine. He showed it to them. It was left open-faced on the table. They asked if they could keep it for a while and we obliged.

Would we commit ourselves to a movie that might take up to a year to complete? We really hadn't thought it through; we needed more details, but we believed the timing to be pretty good. We told them "yes, we thought so."

Glancing over, Charles was in a real wrestling match with Kristina and he was losing. He appeared amused by it all, and he laughed a hearty laugh and before long we said our goodbyes. Upon leaving, I noticed the other parents were peering at us unabashed. Perhaps I didn't realize the fuss the casting agents had made during the preliminaries. We left feeling positively giddy. Our minds were reeling. This was, indeed, a pleasant beginning.

Meeting an Academy-Award Winning Actress

It was pretty incredible. When we arrived home that Sunday night from the audition for *Baby Boom*, the phone was ringing. A production assistant asked: "Would we meet Diane Keaton tomorrow morning at a Manhattan Hotel? We would like everyone to meet and see how it goes."

We were floored. This was definitely not an ordinary second audition.

"Diane Keaton!" I exclaimed.

Then I settled down. I told them I thought we could arrange things at home in order to meet with Diane Keaton at ten o'clock that Monday morning. As if there were any doubts about it.

Our appointment was for ten o'clock the next morning, and so we arrived around eight-thirty or some time ridiculously early. Meeting Diane Keaton was a very big deal of course, and my entire extended family was on Keaton alert. We contacted everyone we knew and so a small flock of friends and family waited to meet, if only vicariously, an academy award-winning actress.

My parents came along with us to Manhattan with Jim's sister Barbara and we strolled the twins outside the building until ten o'clock. We wondered if this might be Diane Keaton's apartment at first, but discovered later that it was a wardrobe room that was rented for the movie. Diane Keaton would be meeting my daughters Kristina and Michelle and she would also be fitted for wardrobe at the same time; two birds with one stone.

As we strolled, my father Ben, a retired baker from the Bronx, spotted someone getting out of a cab. It was Diane Keaton in classic Annie Hall garb from head to toe. In particular, she wore elbow-length, fingerless gloves and a distinctive hat. She walked to the corner, looked around a bit puzzled, and crossed the street toward the building entrance.

My husband Jim spoke to her first, calling:

"Hey Diane! Diane Keaton!"

She acknowledged us with a friendly "Hello" as she would to any New York passerby who might recognize her.

"Diane!" Jim continued, "these are the twins...the girls you are here to meet...the little girls for the movie."

Ms. Keaton's expression changed to one of a sudden surprise and then to amused interest. We introduced ourselves there on the sidewalk and Diane Keaton quickly returned her attention back to the twins. After all, she understood (more than we) that she would be spending enormous time over the next eight months with these babies, and she peered into the stroller and cooed and smiled. Generally, we got the feeling she was looking forward to it. She appeared genuinely delighted.

"Well. I'll see all of you upstairs!" she said as she made her way into the building.

We knew that this chance meeting was a tremendous stroke of luck, a second instance of fate, because all of the anxiety we harbored about "the big meeting" was gone. The ice was broken. Our first impression was that the famous actress was personable, friendly, and she evidently loved kids. We were right.

An Unusual Audition

Inside the building, a small fitting room was crammed with wardrobe. It felt no larger than a walk-in closet, especially with our entourage, the producers Charles Shyer and Nancy Meyers, of course Diane Keaton, and a wardrobe professional named Susan Becker. It was decided we should sit on the floor in a circle and wait. There was no set agenda. It was explained to us that everyone was present to simply see how the babies reacted to… everyone else. This was going to be interesting, I thought.

At thirteen months old, the girls were toddling walkers but expert at crawling. They began to swim around this fish tank of a room and all over everyone, sort of upsetting the ring of serenity. There was a bit of a circus mood really, when Kristina tumbled over to Diane Keaton and began clinging to her. She crawled all over her with an unusual display of affection. A third instance of fate.

I looked at my husband and eye-browed my astonishment. What is this? When Kristina was through wrestling, she settled gently and rested her head tenderly on Diane Keaton's shoulder. Kristina clung to her as if trying to crawl inside of her pouch. I know that Ms. Keaton was surprised. She exclaimed, "So this is what it's all about!" and she was right. While Kristina snuggled, Michelle kept active rolling on her back and reaching for her feet in the air. Susan Becker of wardrobe went to work holding up clothes and soon we realized that Ms. Keaton was needed elsewhere.

Everyone thanked everyone else and we were on our way home, but not until we were given scripts and some real encouragement. This was Monday. A decision would be made no later than Friday.

The script was engaging. If you have seen the movie *Baby Boom*, the finished version is edited from the original and many scenes were omitted completely. We could see plainly that the role of *Baby Elizabeth* was a large one indeed. We still had no idea what we were getting into, but doors were opening with hardly a nudge. It looked like we were going to go for this thing.

Things happened very quickly. It was, in fact, a mad scramble and we had no experience to compare with it. We received a phone call every day from *Baby Boom* affiliates and apparently we would get the part, however, nothing was officially confirmed. The reality of moving our considerable entourage began to sink in. My son Scott, age three, our twins Michelle and Kristina of course, and my mother and father, my mother-in-law, my sister-in-law Nancy who volunteered as "nanny" with perhaps others to help as well; this was going to be expensive. When my husband explained to production who we wanted to bring along with us on this adventure, we were told that "money could be saved" by choosing twins from California. "Don't push it" was the initial message overall, yet the calls kept coming in. We explained that we hadn't made a final decision yet and they countered that they hadn't either. All that week, however, the phone was wild with calls inquiring about the girls' dress size, shoe size, transportation needs and so on. Management and production seemed to have gotten the green light. When were we going to be notified? On Friday, as was their promise.

It will be a great adventure, right? Let's forget the whole thing. Sounds too good to be true and my instincts were holding me back. I began to feel awkward inside. The feature film would take six to eight months from November through April, if all went well. And this was already the second week in October! Only three weeks to get ready! Specifically, we would spend three weeks in Vermont, ten days in Manhattan, and three to five months in Los Angeles. Everyone we spoke with encouraged us to go for it. My family was eager to help out and to come along if possible. If we could put a package together that made sense, perhaps it wouldn't seem so implausible; perhaps it wouldn't be such a mad scramble after all.

Baby Boom: The Movie Experience: Vermont

It gets awfully cold in Vermont. Making movies can be an awfully cold business. The first three weeks in Peru, Vermont was our initiation to an industry and it felt like a northern blast...an arctic awakening. After our meeting with Diane Keaton in New York (sudden prominence) we were awarded the role of *Baby Elizabeth* and we settled into the Manchester Hotel, which is one of the finest hotels in Vermont. We were expected to be ready to roll on November 1st. We were handed a bundle of updated scripts with a daily manifest for the first week. These manifests were of various colors, some pink, then blue, and again green, and we were sure they could not pertain to us. Each one was an update of the previous one, and together they revealed an apparently indiscriminate schedule of scenes. Everyone was plainly bustling to be ready, but something else was happening; something subtle and ultimately very counter-productive. It caught us off-guard.

We were being treated extremely special. Wardrobe personnel arranged "fittings" for the girl's clothes and each session revealed dozens of outrageously expensive garments collected from all over the world. Everyone, it seemed, needed information of some kind, whether it was the head of transportation, make-up or hair artists, assistants to the director and so many others. It was a whirlwind initially. People, in fact, could not do enough for us. Anything we needed, just ask.

The head of MGM/United Artists sent the girls each a teddy bear with his best wishes. There was champagne and flowers on the table of our room. We had every reason to think that this was going to be alright after all. However, a protective flag was going up. What are they going to do if the babies do not cooperate? They are thirteen months old? How, exactly, are we going to be able to film with any kind of regular schedule? Does anyone know that the babies need to be on a schedule themselves? Who, we wanted to know, has worked with children before on a movie set?

His name was John Kretchmer, the Assistant Director, or 1st AD, as he was called by everyone. Our first meeting with him was short and obviously designed to reassure us that our mounting anxiety was unwarranted. Kretchmer, the 1st AD, would take care of the babies schedules.

"Have you worked with children before?" I asked.

He assured me that his experience with children was exceptional, and what's more, he explained with confidence that he had a recent daughter himself, and so he was sensitive to children's needs and their demanding schedules.

We discovered later that in Hollywood, if you want to work on a movie set, it is routine to say nearly anything at all that will get you hired, and if that means stretching the truth about one's experience, well, just do it. One has to get their foot in the door somehow, and so, if a movie production is looking for someone to work with a baby on a movie set, it is acceptable to step right up and fabricate any sort of gibberish if it will get you the job. What is the worst they can do, fire you? You might pull it off. In fact, you probably will, since production is so chaotic at first that no one is able to pay much attention to many of the details down the line. So novices will take advantage of any opening they can get, and no one can blame them; it is simply the way to survive and hopefully thrive in the most celebrated industry in the western world. Of course John Kretchmer had said he had experience with babies. He would be a fool to have said otherwise.

Kretchmer did his best to attend to our needs, but he was too busy. He was responsible not just for our schedule, but for arranging everyone's schedule; a task suited for perhaps three full-time workers. His plan for us was simple: one baby would arrive early in the morning and the other baby in the afternoon. A total thirteen hour day! God help us. The children were expected to nap twice a day, eat their meals and generally function "fully fresh and prepared" on an "on demand" basis, which meant that no one actually filming the movie knew when they might need the babies in a scene.

Also, I realized that this arrangement called for the twins to be separated, one at home while the other was on location, necessitating my husband and I to also separate for the same reason, decidedly splitting the family into fragments here and there, maybe for the next eight months! We were assured that this was a worst case scenario, and that adjustments would be made. This worst case might happen on occasion but it would not be a typical day.

On Location: Nuts and Bolts

An actor's base of operation when shooting "on location" is inside of a travel trailer or Winnebago-styled camper parked somewhere near the production. This was a bit of bad luck for us because the large motor home was comfortable for adults but very confining for children. Supplies we had requested were there; diapers, milk and cheese, and also there waiting for us were two young women from wardrobe. A pretty young woman from make-up arrived as well and she checked Kristina only for a blemish or a scratch; rarely did the babies need make up.

On this first day of filming, my three-year old son Scott remained sleeping at the hotel with his grandparents, and of course, with Michelle. Fortunately, my parents had come to help us during the Vermont stay. We had the necessary support for now.

We were sitting restlessly in a travel-trailer parked on a side road off Route 10 on a bitter cold November day, waiting. My husband headed outside and ascertained that the first shoot involving the girls would be of the baby sitting among baskets and baskets of apples. It should happen around ten-thirty. We waited all day. Michelle arrived at two o'clock that afternoon. I sent for John Kretchmer, the baby expert and 1st AD. It took some courage for me to speak up but I needed to let someone know what to expect.

"John," I began. "Babies are not like adults. If you wake them up prematurely, they will be cranky, maybe all day. When a thirteen-month old baby wakes up at seven-thirty in the morning, they are ready to go in ten minutes. Their batteries are fully-charged. They do not need coffee, showers, or anything else but a change of diapers…and when their batteries run down…it's over. No power…no play or laughter or giggles…only crying, cranky behavior until they are recharged…period."

I was getting anxious, indeed.

"Are we going to do anything today? What scene might we be shooting?" I demanded to know.

"Didn't you get the updated manifest?" he responded, rustling through his vest pockets like someone who had misplaced his keys. "Didn't you get a blue manifest?"

John Kretchmer, on the first day of shooting, suddenly appeared to be a man possessed by demons. He was having a very tough day indeed. If he had a dozen hands, each would be doing something necessary. Waves of thoughts and concerns were crashing through his head relentlessly to distraction. He was haunted by the walkie-talkie at his side. He had a duffle bag overflowing with different-colored scripts, each with an updated manifest, and he was fumbling through it all and talking at the same time. He might, at any moment, ask me to repeat my question, as he did already several times. Overwhelmed, he admitted:

"I can't do anything for you right now. Is everything all right? Good. It should be soon. I think it is an apple orchard scene. OK? OK?" he nodded.

He was gone. He was a typhoon of pressure and deadlines and he was running late. He ran away with the walkie-talkie squawking at his side. He was needed elsewhere on the double.

Around four o'clock the first scene involving the children was at hand. Eureka! An open field, an apple orchard in fact, where appeared many baskets of fruit filled to the brim. Diane Keaton was there and she had worked all morning on only one short scene, and she appeared genuinely happy to see us. She was always careful to take time with the babies and so she came over at the first available moment and she played with Michelle in a delightful manner and she held her and spent some time with her.

The scene called for Diane to be on a ladder in the orchard where she was picking apples from a tree. As she turns to the baby below, she says comically, "I think we have enough for a pie." The camera would then reveal my daughter sitting amongst dozens of baskets of apples. Easy enough we guessed. On sight, my husband was amused that many of the apples appearing on film were hand-tied to the tree limbs.

They did the brief shot perhaps eleven times. We were finished and we were back at the hotel around six o'clock. We needed to sign a testament sheet confirming the number of hours the girls worked that day. These were legal documents. It was dark by then. I felt drained and dismal. Our call time for Tuesday, and for the whole first week, was going to be a repeat of this early start and late finish routine. We had collected a stack of the colored scripts and manifest papers. I was happy to be at the hotel. This, we could see, was going to be hard work.

The second day went much as the first. We waited all day "on call" without a clear idea what might be forthcoming in the shooting sequence. We waited and waited inside the Winnebago.

On Wednesday of the first week, something happened. We arrived early and by noon Michelle needed a nap desperately. The scene called for her to appear happy and alert in a car seat. It was cold that morning and everyone was concerned that the baby was kept warm, which is fine of course, except it was maybe 90 degrees in the car. It was an autumn scene and Michelle was not to wear a winter coat, only a sweater, and so the responsible prop master made sure there was plenty of heat inside the car; full blast in fact. Well, Michelle was asleep as quick as that; out cold. This was not a comfortable predicament. You can sing, play games, whistle and dance all you want; this child was asleep. Wake her up and she will cry. Michelle was enjoying the solid, deep, pure sleep that we, as adults, get maybe once a year. It was an absurd dilemma. No one wanted to forcibly wake up a sleeping infant. This would be our first contest with production. What were we going to do? Wake the baby? Wait in the trailer until Michelle was rested? I realized this was the dilemma that defines someone as a "stage parent." The stage parent would not hesitate to rattle that child awake. Were we stage parents?

Our being treated special the previous four days did not prepare us for what happened next. Everyone was furious! Why didn't we notify! Didn't we know? Keep informed! You are costing this production a fortune with this delay! They were terribly upset and they were yelling openly and I was shaken by the tirade. "It takes hours to prepare for this scene...for nothing? What do we do now?" All hell broke loose, or so it seemed to me. "Inexperienced parents!" was bellowed to everyone within earshot. "Inexperienced parents!" rang out Kretchmer on the set. And he was right, but only in one sense. We were inexperienced making movies, but we were not inexperienced as parents! Didn't everyone know that delays like this were going to happen? A standoff was inevitable, since working on a movie set was really no place for children. Voices were raised and frustrations were finding outlets. A meeting would be held at week's end. The production team demanded performance from us and we demanded consideration!

No one wanted to hear it. It was, of course, no one's fault. Nonetheless, "timing" or scheduling, Jim insisted, was crucial with these babies. It was to be the beginning of input and feedback. How much would they give and how much would we take?

I overreacted and did, indeed, take the verbal onslaught personally. Our inexperience was going to be a problem. Their lack of sensitivity, at least initially, distanced us from the production. By the third day, I felt like we were doing battle in a war. What I didn't realize from the start was that making feature films was sometimes combative. It was a wildly intense environment because so much money was at stake. They would spend millions of dollars to make this film, and cost overruns were not to be taken lightly. Not on this production, anyway, and not on the third day of shooting.

We lifted Michelle from the car seat and she whined in my arms and she promptly fell back to sleep. The car scene was over for her that day. Kristina was brought in and the scene went fairly well. A few hours had been lost due to the circumstance. We retreated to the Winnebago like it was a bunker in order to regroup and to rethink what had just happened. It was a stormy day and the admonition by the director was a prolonged outburst in broad daylight and it hit me square on the chin. I was agitated and in no mood to cooperate. I felt angry and guilty at the same time.

Someone knocked on the trailer door. It was a young assistant to the director, or 2nd AD, nicknamed "Vee Bee," and it was his job to notify and to escort the actors to the set. I'm guessing he was twenty-five years old and he was quick-witted and funny by nature, doing a thoroughly comfortable job. He smiled and laughed often. Vee Bee was the son of the famous musical comedian Victor Borge.

We told Vee Bee we felt bitter that after three endless days of tortuous dawdle in this blasted prison of a Winnebago, we should be the objects of criticism.

"Don't take it personally," he said. "Do you think you are the only ones to be berated for causing delays? It is nothing...standard procedure. They have forgotten it already, as you will see."

We were beginning to see. When we returned to the production site, no one appeared upset with us, and certainly *not* upset with the babies.

"Well, this is insane," I commented, loudly, to which Vee Bee added: "Welcome to Hollywood!"

This was just the beginning. The baby scenes were increasing and masterminding the babies' schedules was running us haggard. I was nervous all of the time. Heretofore, the twins napped whenever they tired; ate when hungry and so on. But now, "Can you get her to smile? Can she pout? Can she crawl on cue? Can she eat apple sauce with a spoon?" We were attempting to predict and modify their behavior "on cue" and my precious daughters were completely unaware that they were acting in a movie. All the lights and sounds and all things else was reality for them! This craziness was taking a toll on the whole family. I could not justify any of it, not really. They are babies! They can realistically be counted on to do absolutely nothing on cue. They wanted us to try. Work with the situation. We would try.

Both sides got it together in a hurry though. Things the first week were frenzied for everyone, not just us, and we thought it best to address our concerns in writing so that we could go over them at the meeting on Sunday. I was losing sleep and only one week had passed. Jim and I wrote out what we thought were the ideal time slots and schedule for the girls to be on the set.

We were no longer drowning. As matters improved the second week, I had the free time to roam and to observe the everyday technique of feature film production. I began to feel more as an ally with production instead of as an adversary, and so I could look around and see more objectively than before. Having been identified by everyone, I discovered I had wonderful access to observe many areas of production. It was an interesting perch from whence I looked into the workings of these professional men and women of wardrobe and props, lighting and sound mechanics, of grips and cameramen, and so on. Since I was not a part of management, I was a threat to no one, and yet I was integral nonetheless, and so I could come and go unrestricted. I had clearance to be anywhere, within reason, wherever my walk-about might bring me, and it was very enjoyable.

Children and Acting

Too many people were coming over to smile and be playful with the babies. It is natural of course for babies and even young children to "cling" to their parents and this reality cannot be ignored. Not all babies want to be held by strangers, and already Michelle and Kristina were becoming overwhelmed by the frequent stops by well-intentioned personnel. Everyone was eager to smile and babble or coo with the babies. Consequently, they were beginning to cling to me and soon they would not leave my arms.

When I walked to the set and attempted to place Michelle or Kristina into the setting of the scene, even into Diane Keaton's arms, both girls began to turn inward for protection. Separation anxiety...and my husband and I did not have a solution. We began by asking Diane Keaton to spend more time in our trailer so that I could "transfer" the baby to her in those familiar surroundings. This strategy worked for a while. Diane would come to the trailer so that she and the baby could walk/play to the set together, while I kept under cover a few paces behind. Further, in order to offset the baby's association of the crowded set with Diane Keaton, I would spend time with them near the set as well. Soon however, the girls were making the connection. Whenever Diane came to the trailer, they deduced that it was time to go to "the crowded place" of the set. We even tried to mix up our places of transfer but with little success. They were reacting to nearly everyone by clinging to me and my husband, and who could blame them? Production didn't want to hear about separation anxiety; they were making a movie at enormous expense and time was always important. And we were causing delays. I was so stressed that I was losing weight. By the second week of shooting in Vermont, I was pallid and frail and felt jaded all the time I was on the set.

One shot was taking all morning inside a small country grocery store. It was uncomfortable for Michelle because it was very warm in there and crowded of course, and they were shooting a winter scene and so all the while Michelle was wearing a wool winter coat. As one take followed another and then another, it was apparent to me that Diane Keaton was holding Michelle for a very long time. The director would call, "We're ready!" and Diane might politely respond, "Well, we're not!" While there was clearly a job to do, Diane maintained a terrific balance of priorities and a wonderfully amusing way with the babies. This worked for a few days more, but other concerns surfaced.

Loud noises and blaring lights and the sea of strange faces all together made the situation volatile. For me, it was intolerable. Try as I might, I was feeling responsible for the progress of the scenes and the delays were torture. "One more time!" would be sounded and it was shrill to my ears. The children were expected to "work" their role like automatons, (or as adult actors would) and it was humiliating to restart a scene again and again as if these babies were machines. And yet no one intended anything mean-spirited or hurtful. "Didn't you know? What did you expect? This is the way it is!"

Yes, this is the way movies are made. Indeed, it can be exciting for adults…but this is no place for children.

And Then There Were Bubbles: An Important Insight

During the third week of shooting, a major breakthrough occurred. It was staring us in the face, but because feature films with young children were rarely being done at the time, we needed to rediscover the obvious, and it was a lifesaver for me.

Our schedule was manageable, the number of people in contact with the babies was limited to as few as was necessary, sudden noises were being effectively monitored and controlled. We were engineering a better environment for the children and there was some improvement; it was less chaotic and more predictable; but each scene was uphill all the way. Things should be getting better, right? Not one of these changes was worth a nickel to me. I was always stressed out whenever the scenes included the babies.

There were some amicable shots but there were few. One delay in a scene caused by the baby erased all of the previous good takes for me. I was definitely too sensitive at first, but now I could feel my skin thickening. I wonder if production could see it as well. I was becoming callous to the wants and the demands of the movie production. I stopped making excuses for my children's perfectly normal behavior, and when needed, I calmly rebuked them with silence. I was furious with the humiliating circumstances of repeated take after take after take. My mother and father could see what was expected of the babies and they saw it as absurd. My mother in law started to make pejorative comments aloud for all to hear:

"This is ridiculous! Another take? " she would blurt out. Our team was gaining confidence; "Are you all crazy?" she would ring out to the crew. My mother in law was in her sixties and she could care less about the needs of the production. I think some understood that she would shut the whole thing down if they pushed too hard.

The scene called for the baby to stand with Diane Keaton in a barn. The scene was supposed to capture a rural moment when mother and daughter would bring fresh milk from the barn to the kitchen. Michelle was having a terrible time. She wanted to be held and Diane Keaton could not put her down in order to carry the pale of milk to the kitchen. I was called in to help but nothing was working.

Also, the cow would not behave according to the script. I know this sounds crazy but there you have it. The script called for the cow to stand placidly inside the barn. Well, each time the barn door opened, the cow moved out into the yard. My mother-in-law seized upon the moment, took center stage, and shouted:

"What is wrong with that cow? Didn't the cow read the script?"

Mimicking everyone, she began demanding to know exactly when that cow could be expected to get it right. It was funny, really, witnessing adults scrambling across the field chasing a cow back into the scene. Few were laughing, though. Too bad, we thought. It is a pity when things are funny and no one dares to laugh.

Specifically concerning our problem with setting the baby into the scene, the directors asked, imploringly:

"What is the problem? Tell us what you need, you got it! Please hurry!"

But we were helpless; there was nothing we could do. I kept trying to put Michelle down playfully but it was useless. Anyone who has young children knows the routine well.

Things were becoming adversarial again. It was exasperating for everyone. Someone asked if we had brought her "very favorite toy?" We were groping for solutions. We would try again.

It was evident that we were unable to get anywhere because Michelle was clinging to me and she simply refused to stand next to Diane inside the barn. In the corner of the barn, there sat a concerned prop man silently observing the predicament. He had the good sense to try something new. He began blowing bubbles from a children's ring, one he had purchased for an upcoming scene with the baby. Michelle was instantly intrigued. I put her down and she stood and then playfully chased the translucent orbs around the barn. In twenty minutes, we had eight or ten takes and we were released for the day. I'm sure she had no idea we even put her down. It was a pivotal discovery and I wished it had occurred to us sooner.

His name was James Wagner, an experienced prop master who also held a degree in Special Education. Years ago, he had worked with autistic children. For the past twenty years or so, he worked props for the film industry. He was in his forties and he had a winning demeanor. He was clownish and playful by nature, and he enjoyed doing celebrity impressions and making fun of the directors. It was readily apparent that he was easy-going and very amusing with children. And he knew what he was doing. He was an industrious fellow as well, and he knew when to take his cue and run with it. Within a week, he had proved himself invaluable to us and to production as well. The very next day he went shopping; he wore a fly-fisherman's vest with many pockets that were filled with rattles and dolls, whirly-wind toys and always he had bubbles. There were flashlights and balloons, trinkets galore, and whenever we needed a little help, there he was, ready to entertain. Everyone started to call him "Bubbles." The name stuck. "Get Jimmy Bubbles! Hurry!" and without delay, James Wagner became Jimmy Bubbles, and to our knowledge, he invented and was the first "Baby Wrangler" on any movie set. And he was determined to be the best.

We knew what we were doing also. Jimmy Bubbles, we insisted, must be hired full-time for the remainder of the film. What we needed, or I needed desperately, was to be insulated from production and not to be held responsible for the "acting" of my babies on the set. After all, he knew the business very well and he could be objective and he acted as an ambassador for the babies and as a buffer from the stress. Soon, Bubbles became the point man and we knew he could handle things. Whatever "rehearsing" might be necessary was no longer on our shoulders, and if a scene didn't go too well, the prop master turned baby wrangler intercepted the negative feedback. It was perfect. We were a team, and Jimmy Bubbles was the spokesman. When things went wonderfully smooth on the set, the well-earned credit was his alone. He was sometimes heralded as "brilliant." And when the director would bark, "You said you could do this scene!" he took on the responsibility.

Jimmy Bubbles was a regular sort from Chicago and my family liked him immediately. He had no pretensions to stardom though he might mention the few times he managed to get a role on television or in a movie. He was around movies long enough to know how to take care of himself. He negotiated a contract with production for himself and we helped by insisting he get the wrangler job. Maybe he tripled his salary; we never asked, but he seemed pleased overall. We discovered that he had plenty of experience on such notable shows as Riptide, The Barbara Mandrell Show and many others. He was an invaluable source of information for us, easily explaining procedures, and most importantly, he was predicting potential hazards. He knew the business in and out and typically when one of the assistants asked us to be ready "soon" to go to the set, Bubbles would head out to evaluate the scene and return, saying, "Relax. We've got two hours at least." We were no longer running around haggard; he was taking on the pressure. The children liked him. He could and would exaggerate the clownishness he possessed, making ordinary things game-like and enjoyable. My husband liked him as well, and together they kept the pressure off me and the children. We had our ally and we achieved the distance we needed.

Other Things Going On

The first two weeks in Vermont was surprising in other ways. Meeting celebrities, for instance, like Jessica Lange and Sam Shepard, who recently had a baby together, was interesting and exciting. Sam wouldn't fly, he hated airplanes, and so he drove up in a new Chevy Suburban from his farm in Virginia. Jessica Lange's daughter with Mikhail Baryshnikov was there, and she and my son Scott bounced a ball around in the afternoons. Sam Shepard was primarily a writer as far as my husband was concerned, and they talked about plays and playwriting while I listened in. Sam's ease with children was readily apparent; he popped them on his hip with the grace of an experienced dad…nothing awkward there. He had a few scenes with the children and their stay was a brief one.

I was feeling better. Jimmy Bubbles was intercepting any torpedoes and a secretary was added to our team. She would keep us updated on the script changes making it unnecessary for me to forage through the multi-colored script papers. We refused to do it anyway. Jim and I always felt that it was not our responsibility to help production make their movie; our hands were full keeping our three children happy and alert and so on.

The pond scene was unforgettable. The cinematographer became concerned with losing daylight; they would need to hurry if they were going to complete it before darkness set in. The scene on the pond called for ducks to swim placidly near a rowboat, enhancing the pastoral setting as one of harmony and serenity. Curious, I watched the prop master unloaded a mother duck and her brood from a wooden crate. The idea was to set the ducks alongside the boat. It was a fiasco, of course, and I could not believe that anyone thought for a moment that these wild birds would cooperate by swimming lazily on cue. The prop assistants waded into the pond with the crate of ducks. The director called out something like,

"Get the ducks ready…We are ready for the ducks!" and to this day, I still cannot believe what happened next.

The prop master in waders was chest deep in the pond and he opened the crate full of ducks. Instantly, the water fowl shot out of the crates like bats from a cave, flying, swimming and scattering in all directions. Flustered and horrified at the scatter-brained plan, the prop master began scrambling to gather the chicks, lunging and slapping at the water like a drowning man. He was able to catch one of the chicks and I was astounded when he threw it at the boat! He was trying to scoop the elusive young chicks and then toss them into formation for the camera! Forget about the adult ducks; they were already on the other side of the lake. Did they really expect these ducks to swim uniformly toward the bow of the boat? I'm watching all of this chaos and I am thinking, "What is going on? They must be from another planet!"

"Forget the ducks! Forget the ducks!" the director screamed and he was flapping at the ridiculous on-goings of this absurd strategy.

The prop master continued throwing the chicks at the rowboat! Everyone present was absolutely stunned beyond words. This was embarrassing. The locals talked about it for a few days. Some were angry at the treatment of the animals though the chicks were unharmed. For me, there could be no mistaking it. These Hollywood people making movies were not some omnipotent group of professionals who were beyond reproach. Some of the things they planned in the film were cockamamie ideas made up as they went along. Now we knew. Now we knew for sure.

One of the final scenes we did in Vermont was one of the most difficult for us. It involved many extras from town. The scene called for an annual Vermont Harvest Dance at a local civic hall and it was at night. There were maybe seventy "extras" there and set-up for the scene took all day with many hands engaged in preparation. Baby Michelle and I were called in to work the dance scene at 6:00 PM that evening. In general, we had an understanding that the girls would not work beyond 8:00 PM so things would have to go pretty smoothly to get it done in two hours. Michelle had other ideas for the evening, however. She was teething badly and she was beyond cranky and clingy. Jimmy Bubble, Diane Keaton and I tried everything imaginable to comfort her. Unfortunately, Michelle had but one desire, and that desire was bedtime.

Inside the converted civic center, the *Harvest Moon Dance* held a packed house waiting for the arrival of the baby. The scene called for Sam Shepard, playing a hometown veterinarian, to arrive at the dance and to begin a romance with Diane Keaton. When Sam the Vet arrived and asked Diane to dance, baby Michelle needed to be handed to a matronly neighbor so that Diane and Sam could, in fact, dance together. Well, it went awry immediately. Michelle looked tired and she would not let go of Diane Keaton and she certainly was not going into the arms of the actor/ neighbor she had never met before. Just because the script says that the neighbor is Aunt Bee from Mayberry doesn't mean the baby will go to her. Sam joined in and he twisted a flower in his hand and played with Michelle to settle and playfully distract her and perhaps change her mood. It worked for a few minutes but Michelle was heading into a full-blown cry. Each time Michelle resisted going to Aunt Bee, it seemed absolutely obvious that the scene was in serious trouble.

Now I must admit that it was not reasonable to simply try again tomorrow. The whole town was there as extras and the enormous effort to create the set demanded that we continue until some solution was possible. We went back to the Winnebago and things were very tense as you might imagine. Production was wild because it started to really set in that they might not get this shot. We tried a fresh-start approach but Michelle was already nodding-out. Jim and I looked at each other. Inside the trailer, Kristina was bright-eyed and chipper. A quick wardrobe change and we returned to the scene with a well-rested Kristina. She went to Aunt Bee without missing a beat. In fact, I think she wanted to stay at the dance. I believe the director suspected that we had switched babies. At any rate, he never asked, but he nodded appreciatively that we bailed out the production. This time, common sense prevailed. We were home by 8:00 o'clock.

The very next day I could not believe my ears. A local townsperson approached me and she identified herself as an extra who was one of the dancers the previous evening. She marched right over and there was an air of indignation in her manner. She commented to me with some malevolence:

"It certainly was a terrific turn-around in moods with the baby last night. What did you do to change her mood? Whatever you gave her certainly was effective!"

What did she mean, "Whatever I gave her?" Did she mean drugs? It dawned on me then that she and many others at the dance scene were quite unaware that there were twins making the movie. She assumed that we were uncaring stage parents who might do unspeakable things to become "stars." I felt angry and humiliated. This business was not fun; it was not flexible; it was no place for children. I got over the comment. You can't linger on those things anyway. And if the director was appreciative of our caper the previous evening, it was soon overshadowed by the pressing business of the movie.

Before moving on to Manhattan for ten days, there was one last shot in Vermont that had us reeling. This scene had Diane Keaton and the baby selling home-made applesauce to local moms in an open-market setting on the village green. It was a beautiful day in Vermont and all of the moms were shopping with their children in strollers, and the peace on that village green that sunny afternoon was reminiscent of a Norman Rockwell painting. So all we had to do for the shot was to show Diane Keaton and the baby eating the applesauce she was selling. Diane was to announce for all to hear that the applesauce was "Delicious!" and she would then offer a spoonful of applesauce to the baby. The baby was expected to hungrily gulp down the delicious applesauce from a spoon, thereby eradicating any doubt the moms might have concerning the worthiness of their product. It was a good scene and we knew we could do this and we knew that Michelle was the baby to do it. Michelle was a voracious eater while Kristina preferred to play with her food, even to wear it like make-up. We knew that Diane Keaton would have difficulty feeding Kristina.

It would be a morning shot. We would have Michelle there, and having rehearsed it once with Jimmy Bubbles that went off perfectly, we awaited the call. As 10:00 AM turned to 100 PM, we sent for Vee Bee. In his usual cheery way, he would relay the message that it was important to do the shot right away, as Michelle would soon be off the clock and therefore unavailable. Vee Bee returned with the disappointing news that they had changed the shot to the afternoon.

"But it may not work with Kristina" we insisted.

This was typical of production to ignore our concerns about the baby's schedule. Diane Keaton stopped in.

"Don't worry about it," was her response overall.

We ate lunch together and talked. Three weeks into it and she could tell it was difficult for us. She was reassuring and she listened intently to our situation and predicament. She is a great listener. Holding Michelle on her lap, she was "Aunt Diane" now to the children. After the hours she spent in the general store and the many hours she spent with the babies between takes had paid off. It was clear that Diane liked children, in particular our children, and Kristina especially liked her. And now Michelle had come around to her as well, pulling on her earring, punching playfully at her nose and snuggling and so on.

The afternoon applesauce shot went exactly as we predicted. Happy and laughing, Kristina reached again and again for the spoon instead of allowing Diane to feed her.

"Cut!" bellowed the director for the fifth time.

They wanted Diane to feed the baby with the spoon and Kristina wanted to grab the spoon and feed herself. Kristina, we knew, wanted to play with her food. Diane spoke up:

"Why can't I simply give her the spoon and she can feed herself?"

Jim and I were amused. The director was not. Jimmy Bubbles was very concerned. Finally, Kristina was persuaded and the shot was going just fine. I think Kristina was beginning to get it, the whole movie thing I mean. She was getting used to the routine of having to do the same thing numerous times. At any rate, Diane Keaton and Kristina were having fun with the spoon. Diane was saying "Here comes the airplane" and she was telling the director:

"Lighten up! This is good stuff! Go with it for heaven's sake!"

Her mood was sing-song and cheerful and it was our last shot in Vermont and our spirits, relatively speaking, were excellent as well.

But the director was insecure with the subtle changes to the script. Suddenly, it was as if I had seen him for the first time. He looked thinner and drained white, even sickly. He appeared as a man who was being consumed in flames. While it was his third film project that we knew about, he was not handling this filming experience well at all. He appeared high-strung; a fever blister had emerged and was still visible on his lip; he looked ghoulish. He needed a break as much as I needed a break. I could not help thinking once again that this was no place for children.

New York: Seven Days at the Mayflower Hotel: The Interview

Our home in Oakdale was about an hour's drive from Manhattan yet it was decided that we would stay in the Mayflower Hotel instead of fighting the traffic each day for the shots. We were relieved to see "will notify" beside their names on the manifest. Jimmy Bubbles had carefully perused their upcoming schedule and he informed us about mostly simple, distance shots; things like the baby in a stroller or crossing the street, and there weren't very many of them. We would have plenty of down time.

With the recent revival of movies based in Manhattan, New Yorkers seemed pretty familiar and unfazed by production on the streets. Passer-bys looked in and inquired about the stars and then moved on with their business. The promotional end of the film was in full swing. Newspaper articles were springing up and friends were dropping by the hotel with snippets of press releases. *People Magazine* ran an article about the film. Most of the press releases featured Diane Keaton holding the baby. It was exciting.

Some of the filming locations were fun. The famed FAO Schwartz toy store, Rockefeller Center, a horse and buggy ride through Central Park were each on the agenda. Whoopi Goldberg meandered through the set saying hello to Diane Keaton and Susan Becker of wardrobe in particular. Mary Kay Place had a small part in the film as a girlfriend to Diane Keaton. Other notable celebrities came around.

We were approached by several reporters. Speaking with reporters was a skill all its own and we knew nothing about protocol in this area. Who would have dreamed they might want to talk with us?

I was answering questions with generalities. A New York Post columnist was inching toward my husband asking mundane questions about Diane Keaton and the children. She asked:

"How does Diane Keaton keep the children looking so happy? They seem to get along wonderfully?"

Jim responded openly and honestly:

"Sometimes," he explained, "Diane will playfully cover her face and say, 'peek-a-boo' or act kooky to spark their interest. She is very comfortable with the babies. She plays games with them and she will sing and play 'the itsy-bitsy spider.'"

Jim certainly did not expect what was printed in the paper the next day. It read; "...that Diane Keaton sure is a kook" says Mr. Kennedy, the father of the babies in the new film, *Baby Boom*! Can you imagine that? It is no wonder celebrities avoid the press. My husband explained to Diane Keaton what had happened with the reporter and how the slanderous scoundrel had invented the quote out of context. Ms. Keaton understood immediately how these things work. Jim never forgot the unfortunate misquote and he never did speak to the press or appear for interviews again after that incident.

It was Thanksgiving and we enjoyed a great day at home with family and friends before we set ourselves off for Los Angeles and the MGM Studio in Culver City. We made our own flight arrangements and my mother Sandy and my father Ben would be with us to help and hopefully to enjoy the rest of the adventure. We knew for sure that it would be no vacation, but we looked forward to the fine Southern California weather and reuniting with some old friends from high school who had relocated to the Los Angeles area years earlier.

California: Home Field Advantage

There were many really delightful moments in California. As concerns the movie production, everyone was back home and on familiar turf so to speak. The MGM studio where we would be working was a bustling place of fantastic historical interest to anyone interested in films. The studio itself is guard-gated, and of course a pass is necessary for entry. Inside, huge pavilions appeared where popular television shows and feature films are in production. We were in stage 10, and near our stage, they were filming the popular "Moonlighting" television show starring Bruce Willis and Cybil Shepard. Around the corner was the set-up for one of the *Ghostbuster* films, and on and on. It was altogether a friendly atmosphere, and I believe the people who worked at the studio felt pride and they exuded a sense of purpose that they were working on important things and that they were involved in a part of something historically significant. I could feel that there was a sense of well-being there, as everyone believed the studio itself to be a very credible place to be. Many believed the film studio to be one of the most meaningful and creative places on earth. The feature film *Baby Boom* was completed within six months from the time we had landed. We were glad when it was over.

Wouldn't you know it? After its release, a year had passed and the directors and production called us at home on Long Island and asked if we might audition for a television series with Kate Jackson and Joy Behar? We were out of the business for over a year and my daughters were two years old by then. Do you think we took the role of Baby Elizabeth in the television series? Yes, we did it after all...and that adventure was another fiasco. But then...that's another story entirely.

Waiting (one-act play)

Two professional housepainters, a master mechanic and an apprentice, are preparing to paint the interior of a Roman Catholic Church. The characters are in continual movement, sometimes climbing and descending the ladder, sometimes painting with a roller on a painter's pole, sometimes mixing paint in five gallon buckets, sometimes kneeling and circling…and so on. Their movements are sometimes exaggerated, as if in a blue-collar ballet. Enhanced with lighting, this "dance" that is their work sometimes is a pantomime and sometimes the dance is clownishly hazardous. Much effort is needed to choreograph their movements as in an Abbott and Costello – Charlie Chaplin - Three Stooges – Vladimir and Estragon routine.

Setting:
The interior of a Church with a fully-dressed altar. A stained glass window is at rear above and at each side of the altar. At rear, there is a door leading to the sacristy. Suspended at center, there is a life-sized statue of Christ on the cross. Forward, there is a middle row or aisle that divides several rows of pews representing the church interior. The action takes place mainly between the pews and the altar. There are rows of lit, deep blue candles, aside. *Of course, the play may be performed in an actual church.*

A painter's aluminum ladder leans against a side wall. The paint "supplies" are clustered at center consisting of drop cloths, five gallon paint containers, brushes and extension poles, rollers, a step ladder, and so on.

Characters:

Mechanic:
Early 60's, gray-haired painter appropriately dressed in stained whites. He has no discernible ethnicity except he is robust and loud at times suggesting an Italian or Spanish background. His faith in Catholicism is text book. He is a man of principle who believes firmly in traditional values. He is a proud man, an honest man, and a skilled professional.

Apprentice:
In his twenties, he is athletic, good-looking and a street-wise young man who is often irreverent. He is a survivor of social abuse who works hard at his craft and despite impertinence, he, too, is proud. His remarks are flippant and disrespectful but not very menacing. His interests are strictly secular, i.e., sports, money, sex and so on.

Father Mack:	Roman Catholic priest who has hired the painters
Homeless Man:	Enters the church.
Woman:	In her eighties.
Younger Woman:	In her twenties with two small children.

Waiting

Lights up on paint buckets and supplies, then gradual to interior. Softness like candles.

ENTER the Mechanic from behind a church column, appearing for a few moments wearing whites and painter's cap. He moves slowly, deep in thought, perhaps prayer. He genuflects when he crosses the center aisle. He makes the sign of the cross. He "circles" while examining the walls in 360 degree turns as he mumble into speech, musing…

Mechanic: So much to be done…too much for one man alone…and so little time. It will take some time to bring these faded walls back to life. Mustn't lose heart. But…(*musing*) …so much to be done…(*circles*)…it may be a struggle, of course, but it is reasonable…we must get started at any rate…

ENTER the helper carrying the extension ladder. He swings it wildly 360 degrees as he looks in all directions at the walls. He stops.

Helper:	I thought you said this job would be quick and easy? What is it then? Where shall we begin?
Mechanic:	Put the ladder beside the other one, over there. Come with me and listen to me. I want your opinion. It matters to me…your opinion. (*He spins a final 360 circle where he stands*) Where shall we begin? (*pause*) Where shall we begin our work in this holy place?
Helper:	(*Places ladder, comes over, looks at altar…loud*) Wow! This is one big job! Take us all God damn week!
Mechanic:	(*shocked as his knees buckle*) What are you saying? You are in a church for God's sake!
Helper:	(*upbeat*) Good morning, Yuno. Nice job. Very nice. Let me embrace you. (pause) And…I am not here for God's sake. That is for sure. For the money I am here and that is all… and so are you…Ha! Ha! and very likely the church too. Ha! Ha!
Mechanic:	I want you to behave yourself on this job! You must promise me…
Helper:	Not to worry. (*circles*) I will behave like I always do. We wouldn't want to upset the homeowner, eh? Ha! Ha! Hey, big bucks for this job, Yuno? I've got to hand it to you. How much? I ask you again…what did you crucify them for? six or seven thousand? Ha! Ha!
Mechanic:	Will you stop? You will behave yourself…yes? Never mind that. Let us begin. (*pointing*) Check along this wall here for scraping…and please be careful. And…you are feeling rested? I want you to work the ladder today.
Helper:	Why do you always ask me, "are you feeling rested?" I am a young man who is afraid of nothing. I can climb the ladder with ease. I am not in the least unsure of myself. I feel fine. (He gets busy near supplies)
Mechanic:	I will tell you again today as I do every day. Climbing the ladder is the most dangerous thing besides the fumes. Where is your mask? (*Hesitates, changes subject*) And that is the other thing. Why do you refuse to wear the mask? I insist that you wear the mask. We are inside all day and it

	will protect you. With all of the fumes from the paint… the mask will shield you from…the fumes, I say, the fumes! Anyway… the ladder. You take the ladder for granted and you fall from above…into the hospital or worse. (pause) But first…
Helper:	Yes, first…Where do we begin? (*He circles and drifts away behind the altar, to the rear/side sacristy door.*)
Mechanic:	(*mumbling and pointing, makes his way to the supplies and he prepares to mix the paint, arrange the drop-cloth, etc. Facing the audience…*) Yes, indeed. Where to begin?
Helper:	I suppose we are repainting?

(*He is at the altar, handling, examining everything. The Mechanic cannot see him and he does not turn around.*)

Mechanic:	(*busy with supplies*) We are repenting. We are repenting the original sin…Adam and Eve and the Garden of Eden… when Adam and Eve were tempted by the serpent, you know the story…
Helper:	Re-PAINT-ing, I said. I suppose we are rePAINTing!
Mechanic:	Repainting… yes of course…what?
Helper:	Oh… (*He reflects*) We wouldn't have to go into the details. (*pause*) What about the colors? Yuno, what colors are we going to paint? Earth green, perhaps? (*calling*) Yuno! Are we going with the same colors on the surface of these walls or are we changing the colors?

As the mechanic speaks, the helper disappears into the sacristy offstage. The mechanic, who has had his back to the helper and the altar, is squatting and he wears the breathing mask on his forehead. He stands and faces the audience…a soliloquy.

Mechanic:	The color indeed. We must not disturb things too much. (pause) It is important. Very significant…central…of the essence…fundamental! The colors must be soothing you know…harmony. (*resumes tasks, pours paint, mixing with five gallon buckets. He senses the helper is distant and he speaks louder*) How would it be if we selected say, the colors red and black, which are the very devil's colors… for God's home! We would surely be damned! No, no. We

must leave the colors as they are…we must not alter the church…we must respect the original choices and disturb them as little as possible. We must leave the colors as they are…a holy sky- blue base…The Virgin Mary blue…and the cloud white above…the sacred white…in accordance with Father Mack's wishes…the scheme…the ceremonious color scheme of the church!!!

The helper has re-emerged from the sacristy wearing the priest's robe. He stands behind the altar. Silent.

Mechanic:	(*continues*) So much to be done. (He *stands and stretches in crucifixion pose beneath the suspended Jesus. He resumes kneeling, and for a moment, he appears to genuflect…and then appears to kneel in prayer…he stirs the paint in the buckets, which was his intention after all.*) The trim we shall do last, of course. And there does not appear to need too much scraping…yet the big question remains… (*an absurd proclamation, standing*) I've got it! I have decided! We will start here. Right HERE! Get the drop cloth will you? Let us begin!
Helper:	(*play-acting as priest*) Syllabus! Omnibus! Carnivore! Crayola! Tu Tu Daaaay Y-oooooh!
Mechanic:	(*stunned and outraged, turns and charges toward helper*) What are you doing? Get Away! Get! (gestures) Get out! Where did you? Why did you! Get out!
Helper:	(*over his protests*) Today's reading from the Holy Gospel, according to Cashew…Please fill my cup with wine…and my basket with large bills…In the name of the Father…
Mechanic:	(*racing to altar, angry, waving his arms ad-lib protestations*) How dare you do this here! (He stops…stares at helper and turns…) I cannot even look at you! (*so angry, he begins to cough*) I choke on your insolence! (*coughs, choking, ad-lib protestations*)
Helper:	I am joking for God's sake! Take it easy Yuno! Are you all right? There is no one here! Relax, will you? It is a joke!

(*The helper has removed the robe quickly and he returns it to the sacristy while the Mechanic coughs and composes himself. Helper returns to the supplies beside Mechanic.)*

Helper:	Alright already. I will behave myself. Take it easy, Yuno.
Mechanic:	I cannot believe in you. I am losing my faith in you…that you can run this business one day. You are like a child, I know…But this! It is sinful what you do! Sacrilegious!
Helper:	O.K. I know. O.K.…I am heart-fully sorry for having offended thee! Ha. Ha. (pause) I'm sorry. I'll stop. (*picks up drop-cloths*) Where did you say we begin? (wanders to radio…turns on the radio…loud rock and roll)
Mechanic:	(*deep breath…looks at helper imploringly…Helper turns the radio off.*) *Must* you mock everything?
Helper:	I have decided also, Yuno. But I want to know the details! The specifics! You must tell me everything so I will know what to expect! Tell me what happens next so that I will succeed…I will be saved? Yes?
Mechanic:	Be careful! Let's stop talking for a minute. (*pause… movement of supplies and ladder and so on*) Let's get going. Let's work here. You do remember, of course, the first rule of painting?
Helper:	The first commandment of painting you mean? Ha! Ha!
Mechanic:	(mood is lifting) Let's go. There is no reason to wait! Waiting is absurd!

(The helper scampers up the extension ladder eagerly with scraping tool, spackle plate etc. he will repair a blemish on the wall. The Mechanic attaches a roller to an extension pole. We watch them work. They are very skilled and their movements…a balancing act…a dance.)

Helper:	No reason to hurry you know.
Mechanic:	The sooner the better.
Helper:	I will get paid the same regardless.
Mechanic:	True. But one mustn't dawdle without reason. Why?
Helper:	Why what?
Mechanic:	Why do nothing? The whole world cries out for action. Why wait? There is simply too much to be done. Waiting is absurd. We must embrace movement and take action, don't you agree?

Helper:	But if I get paid the same, why shouldn't I drag it out? What's the hurry? Why bother? If I should earn the same at the end, why shouldn't I drag it out?
Mechanic:	That is the stupidest idea yet.
Helper:	How do you mean?

(The helper descends the ladder; fills small hand-held bucket and selects a hand brush. He will trim out the wall.)

Mechanic:	Don't be careless there. Remember the first rule of painting…Using a Purdy Nylox Sprig two and a half?
Helper:	(*climbing*) No. A Purdy Elite Swan… three inch. (pause) You agree?
Mechanic:	An Elite Swan brush, yes. (*big smile*) Yes, of course…a good choice. You are already a fine mechanic. You are sometimes a fool but you have become an honest person and a reliable worker. How long have we been together my boy?
Helper:	You know very well how long…eight years…But answer my question. Why shouldn't I drag my feet for hours if I get paid by the hour? Explain it to me.
Mechanic:	You know that I want you to be a partner. When you join me, you will know. It is because…for six years you have worked for me very well, and at the end of every job, there was another job, and then another. I will tell you that when I was your age…in the beginning, when the business was just beginning and I worried… I lost sleep even…because I had little faith in myself and in the future. I didn't know what might happen from day to day and I wanted assurance…I wanted to know what I could never know. But with time, and God willing, I built a reputation for honesty and integrity…
Helper:	And luck and low bids! You work because you are cheaper to hire than the next guy.
Mechanic:	It is not so! Let me speak! Let me tell you the truth! It is true that I worried…perhaps that is the way with all young men…that we worry more than we admit to ourselves and to others. And when my family came along, I worried even then more…but with time, slowly I must say, I believed that one job would follow another just as night follows

day and that because of my skills...my REPUTATION! Integrity and hard work would provide for me. I was able, finally, to believe in others as well, though it did not always go smoothly, of course. How could it? (*pause*) Ha. Ha. My mother once said to me, "Yuno" she said. "Life is one damned thing after another!" Ha. Ha. She said it with a smile you know, and she was saying to me that no matter what, there will always be troubles.

Helper:	Yuno? I am tired of this. Let's change the subject, could we?
Mechanic:	Alright. I agree. What shall it be? You take the ball for once, will you?
Helper:	How about sports?
Mechanic:	O.K. Sports. Which sport?
Helper:	Sport cars.
Mechanic:	Sport cars then. Tell me about sport cars.
Helper:	I prefer horses. Horse racing...Gambling.
Mechanic:	O.K. O.K.
	(*pause*)
Mechanic:	How is your daughter? How old is she now?
Helper:	(*His face lights up... He is animated and sincere*) Eleven... months...Eleven months, one week and four days. I was holding her, Yuno, early this morning for an hour and I never felt so...so...emotional! She smiles all of the time! You remember how I was hoping for a boy? How important I thought it was that I would have a "son." How silly after all. My baby daughter and I were together this morning in the dark and I was having coffee and it was so quiet...and I realized something, you know... (*heart-felt*) I love her so much that the very idea that it mattered at all...whether I had a boy or a girl...what foolishness there. And we spent an hour together while the world was sleeping. "Where's the light?" I asked her. "Where's the light?" And she points to the light. Yuno, she is the greatest thing.
Mechanic:	She is an angel, yes? A miracle!
Helper:	And she is crawling about. (*mimic*) "Where's your nose?" I asked her. And she grins and she beams at me. "Where's your toe?" I can see her face now just bursting with

happiness. "Where's the light?" And she looks up at the light...you know?

(The helper has made his way toward the supplies and his lunch cooler. He retrieves a "Tall Boy" beer. The Helper stands tall and proud and he "pops open" his first beer of the day. He toasts...)

Helper:	She is the greatest!
Mechanic:	What in heaven's name? Is that a beer? Are you drinking beer? It is barely eleven o'clock! Don't drink that here!
Helper:	I told you. (*sipping*) I was up early. And I always have a beer before lunch.
Mechanic:	This is not a pool hall!!! You talk from your heart about your daughter and then you pop open a beer? Never mind... (*silence*) Go ahead...drink your beer...your holy water.
Helper:	Listen to you, all bent out of shape. Here, I should behave differently? I am working. I want to have my beer before lunch, like always. God knows there's enough wine going down around here.
Mechanic:	That is enough! (*pause*) It hurts me. Do you know that you are hurting me? I love you like a son and you spit in my face. Eighteen years old, a kid on probation comes running in to me... a snot-nosed punk comes in saying "Hey mister, can I have a job, mister?"...and I don't know you from Adam but I know that you are racing cars and chasing women and why would I hire this orphan trouble-maker...for what? (*pause*) And you have been with me for eight years and you will show me some respect! If you don't care about God...fine! But respect me then, can't you? Your whole generation...the same! Always joking... Big joke! Go ahead. Drink beer in a church! (*pause*) But it does matter! I tell you. It must!
Helper:	What matters?
Mechanic:	All of it! (*pause*) WAIT!
Helper:	I'm not going anywhere? Please, calm down. Don't get so bent out of shape. We're having a discussion, right?
Mechanic:	Your daughter. The last time I saw her was at the ceremony. She is christened?

Helper:	What are you talking about?
Mechanic:	Baptized. She has been baptized?
Helper:	Yes, of course. You were there? Why?
Mechanic:	Why? Exactly. Why …didn't you simply use the faucet at home? Or a garden hose?
Helper:	Hey now! You are going too far! Stop talking about my daughter that way. Watch what you are saying…a garden hose! Leave her out of it!
Mechanic:	I will not. Who is going to teach her about…values? How to behave? What to believe? How will she know? How can she find herself and know…?
Helper:	I will teach her!
Mechanic:	You cannot teach her anything worthwhile unless you believe it yourself. You know why? We don't really teach our children anything with our words. We just give them who we are. If you love something in front of a child, the child will see that. We must…all of us must… provide a worthy environment…with traditional values…about family and culture and…authentic beliefs.

(*Enter a woman with two small children. Mechanic stops working.*)

Woman:	Hello? Excuse me? Hello? Are you…open?
Mechanic:	(*ceremoniously bowing with sweeping arm*) The church, my dear lady, is always open. How can I help you?
Woman:	Oh! (*realizing*) I'm sorry to interrupt your work. I am looking for the rectory…Father Mack… (*beat*) …I heard there is a child care center here. And well, we are new in town. We just moved in and everything is up in the air. Anyway…What I mean is…Where is the rectory?

(*The children have been crawling around the pews. Twins, ages 3 or 4…one of them points at the helper on the ladder.*)

Child #1:	Mommy. Mommy! (*points at helper*) Is that man Jesus Christ?
Child #2:	Mommy. Mommy! (*points at Mechanic*) Is that man the priest?
Woman:	No dear… (*embarrassed*) Come girls…
Mechanic:	The Priest? Ha! Ha! My. My. (addressing everyone) Look at our clothes. Isn't it obvious? (*no response*) Let me show you

the way. The rectory is behind the church, facing South Street….and …Welcome to town!

(*Woman and children exit in a flourish. Mechanic returns to business at hand*)

Mechanic: *(to helper)* Do you see what the church is? How it helps people? It is not simply "going to Mass" you know. There is a very practical side. A very useful and helpful…

Helper: Yes. Yes. I agree with you there.

Mechanic: and God forbid, when you are sick or worse…some crisis and for so many people… the church is important… essential …central…fundamental…

Helper: Yes. Yes. I know. But…and I don't mean to be disagreeable Yuno, really…but…there is so much pain and suffering in the world…senseless murder and you know what else…

Mechanic: That is why you must admit…It is a mystery.

Helper: Some mystery! A mystery with very few clues! Yuno, I think about it sometimes and it's just that…I'm not sure at all, to tell you as I see it…these people who come here every Sunday and fill these seats…they don't know either. They are simply hedging their bets IN CASE there is a God. No! No! In case there is a Hell!

Mechanic: You are an imbecile…a bloody ignorant ape! Ha! Ha!

Helper: Take it easy! We're having a discussion, right? (*pause*) How do you explain all the misery? (*pause*) And the Bible… Noah's Ark? And the world was made in seven days? What is that? Adam and Eve and…the planets. Explain that! We are the only planet among the billions in the universe? Don't you think there are other planets with other people on them? What of that?

Mechanic: *(forceful but friendly still)* No! There is only one at this moment. I know the argument, but it is true! We, on earth, we are the only ones! (beat) Just as for you… your baby daughter, among the multitudes of people on earth, she is the only one. (*pause*) As for the rest, I already told you. It is a mystery.

Helper: We can't even agree on a name? Buddha…Allah…Christ… Wah Wah or whatever that…

Mechanic:	Yahweh. It is pronounced "Ya-way."
Helper:	Yes. Yes. O.K. Now can we change the subject?
	(pause)
Mechanic:	There are some very great stories in the Bible. Can I tell you one?
Helper:	No! (*frustrated pause*) Do I have a choice? You are going to tell me a Bible story?
Mechanic:	I will tell you a story that happened right here in town. It is not a Bible story but instead a story *like* a Bible story that is a true story about Lake Rescue. Do you know the story of Lake Rescue? How the lake got its name?
Helper:	Lake Rescue? I'm not sure. I remain in the dark. Can I assume that someone was drowning and was…rescued?
Mechanic:	Everyone assumes that. But no…no one was drowning.
Helper:	You are my only hope. Tell me the story of Lake Rescue. It will pass the time.
Mechanic:	It happened…some ninety years ago when all of the acreage near this town was woodlands and potato farms, with some dairy farms and dirt roads only…when only eight or nine families lived in a three mile area. It happened that one very cold January afternoon…a little girl and I don't know her name but it doesn't matter, she was only two or three years old, barely more than a toddler…well she wandered out from her yard and she became lost in the woods.
Helper:	Near the lake?
Mechanic:	Yes, near the lake. And the families, they searched and word traveled quickly that the baby is lost and the business of the world that day was to find this lost child…because the temperature would fall below zero at night and the entire village knew she would not survive the bitter cold. Everyone searched and it seemed that she may have been lost to the lake, but there was no sign of her at all and all of the lake was frozen solid enough to hold her weight. Along the edges where the ice was weakest, there were no signs that she fell into the icy water. None whatsoever.
Helper:	I don't like this story. Remember, I have a daughter…but go on. What happened?
Mechanic:	And so through the night they searched and in the morning, some of the men decided that she must have walked away

from the lake and over the ridge. It would be difficult for her but there was nowhere else for her to have gone. Time passed and there was anguish and pain in everyone's heart. It was sometime the next morning that they found her. Alone, crying and very cold…but she was alive and it was a miracle because it was simply too cold to survive the night. But here's the story. The little girl was babbling and her words were puzzling. She seemed to be saying that she managed to stay warm that night by huddling up against "the black sheep." She was hysterical and she was repeating, "The black sheep! The black sheep!" telling everyone that she nestled into the sheep and the sheep's fur kept her warm.

Helper: Oh! She wandered into a neighbor's barn perhaps, and there…she slept.

Mechanic: Yes. That is what must have happened, of course, except… the neighbors knew the farms…they knew it was impossible yet they checked all of the farms, all of them for miles around. There were no sheep, not white, not black. Not anywhere. (pause) Can you guess? It was settled by one of the neighbors at last. It seemed reasonable after all. It was determined that the sheep were black…bears. Bear cubs. It was decided by everyone that she had to have crawled into the den of hibernating bears and that she slept with the bear cubs. And for that one night, she was accepted there. It was the only way.

Helper: (*stunned*) Bears! Bear cubs? A true story?

Mechanic: I believe it. Lake Rescue. A miracle.

Helper: Hmmpff. Good story Yuno. It is curious after all. Now I have one for you.

Mechanic: I shudder to think…Is it a virtuous story? Remember, you are in a church…

Helper: A true story. Do you know old man Gregory? His story?

Mechanic: Old man Gregory, yes. I know of him. His old farmhouse is over near the river. His story? I don't think so. Tell me his story. It will pass the time.

Helper: Old man Gregory is about 90 years old now…and if you hang around for a while you can see him still…working around that old farmhouse…but the story is that when he was eleven years old, some 79 years ago when around this town there were only woodlands and potato farms… (*smile*)…Well he was working with his father in the barn. And I don't know the season or the reason, but his father was very drunk. People say that he was a mean-spirited man who was a bully and angry more often than not…and anyway, this one afternoon…he was working with his son in the barn and he started beating the boy and he couldn't control his rage. He beat the boy and he kept beating him and he beat him into unconsciousness. It appeared he had killed him…he killed his only son… and as he sobered and he saw the lifeless body of his boy, he cried out…but it was too late. His pain and his anguish were nothing to the truth of what he had done. It drove him out of the barn and into the farmhouse. They say he "swallowed the end of his shotgun" when he pulled the trigger. He put his rifle into his mouth and he blew his brains out. But here is the story. The boy survived! He wasn't dead! He awoke…and bruised and beaten as he was, he dragged himself into the house to discover the suicide-corpse of his father in there. Can you imagine that? Is there an end to the horror and the living hell of that day? (*beat*) And that boy who was beaten and left for dead by his own father…he is old man Gregory, who is 90 years old now and living on that *same* farm. That is no miracle.

Mechanic: I admit I cannot explain it. It is a mystery and that is all. Look!

ENTER an old woman, 80's, who moves slowly with bowed head. She is wearing a full-length dark, winter coat; a black kerchief covers her head. She makes her way to the blue candles left of the altar. She lights a candle and she puts money into the cashbox there. She sits first pew and prays with Rosary beads. They wait. The scene takes a few moments, it is solemn, yet it must not take too long. She exits.

Mechanic: So, are you going to be my partner? (*big smile*) I am anxious to put your name in grand style beside mine on the trucks.

Helper: Let's talk about it. There are a few questions I need to ask

	you. Now let's take this job for example. How much you pay me I know, but, these are personal questions...How much do you earn here? How much did you earn this year?
Mechanic:	You will be pleasantly surprised. (*gestures grandly*) "Argo Painting." It makes money, you have no idea. I told you I will show you the books. You will make a nice living.
Helper:	But a painter? I always thought I would do more with my life...you know...play music or ...I don't know what else.
Mechanic:	Yes, I am a painter...an ordinary painter. But I am not an ordinary man. I have a wife, my children are grown and happy, my grandchildren and...my home and all of this because I worked at it. I paint, yes, but I am much more than a housepainter.
Helper:	You are not. You are a house painter, for God's sake. Look. Haven't you ever had a dream that gnaws at you? You know I play the bass guitar... and ever since I was a kid, I was crazy about being in a band.
Mechanic:	Ever since I was a small boy I was crazy about lighthouses.
Helper:	Seriously?
Mechanic:	Not all lighthouses, of course, but they have always meant something to me that I can't quite define. It is curious. Perhaps it is the rotating lights?
Helper:	Rotating lights? That means police cars. I am not crazy about police cars.
Mechanic:	I mean the height of lighthouses...there's just something...I don't know...majestic about a lighthouse...something noble. Do you know what is curious? For many years I thought lighthouses called to sailors and promised to the ships a safe passage if they come closer to the light. But I had it exactly wrong. A mariner explained that the purpose of the light was to keep ships *away* from the shore... *away* from dangerous rocks and so on. I had it exactly opposite.

(Both painters are up on ladders at the moment)

Helper:	We're talking about painting, I mean, every working day,

maybe for the rest of my life. You have done well, I'm sure, but I have dreams still...and the world is a different place for me. You have no computer, no fax machine, and no business cards even! I know your reputation has done very well for you and...don't get upset and take this personally, but...the days of the "fair-shake" are over. I want to expand this business...grow...maybe have seven or ten trucks... and here...look at this...

The helper reaches around for his wallet and stops suddenly. In his hand is a business card that he intended to show when a homeless man enters. The Mechanic does not see the card. He puts the card into his shirt pocket. Enter a homeless man. He walks about and he checks the pews for loose change. He goes to the same candles as before and he rattles the donations box, stealing little more than a glance at the painters.

Helper: (*whispering*) Look at this. He is trying to steal the money. (He calls to him) Hey you! We're closed. Get out of here! (*to himself*) Bum!

The homeless man sits down suddenly and begins to pull at his boot. He pulls at it with both hands...panting...rests...tries again. Mechanic watches for a moment and descends from ladder...approaches.

Mechanic: Ssshhhhh. Old man. You must leave now. Come, let me help you.

The homeless man accepts the help and then suddenly scurries grotesquely away down the center aisle, picking up his pace. As he passes the painting supplies, he steals the mechanics lunch and attempts to get away. The helper sees this and leaps from his ladder.

Helper: He just stole your lunch!
Mechanic: What!
Helper: Give me that! (*He pounces on the scoundrel and retrieves the lunch*) Get out of here...now! Do you believe this? Get away!
Mechanic: Now easy does it. Ha! Ha! (*taking his lunch from the helper,*

calling) Hey old man! Wait! Come here. (*He gives to him from his lunch*) Take this…here. Now you must leave.

The tramp exits. The Mechanic turns to look at the helper.

Helper:	What did you give him, an apple?
Mechanic:	No, a turnip…
Helper:	(*disbelief*) A turnip! Ha! Ha!
Mechanic:	I mean a carrot…whatever.
Helper:	He's not going to eat that! It is poison to him. He will die! He lives on rubbish and alcohol. A carrot! A turnip! Ha! Ha!
Mechanic:	Did you see he tried to steal my lunch!
Helper:	They are parasites. These homeless ones, they are good for nothing. (*pause*)
Mechanic:	I am beginning to come around to that opinion. All my life I tried to be reasonable, to forgive all transgressions, but it is a struggle. I will admit, sometimes, when I see them, I turn cold.
Helper:	Cuff them by the collar and give them the boot is what I say.
Mechanic:	What are we able to do for them? There are so many of them *waiting* … doing nothing…and their numbers are increasing. They have given up the struggle. Certainly, no one can envy their idleness.
Helper:	They are bloody ignorant apes!
Mechanic:	Then again, perhaps they are unable to take part…to do anything worthwhile because they put their faith in themselves and the world and it has failed them. It is hopeless. If you lose all faith, there is nothing to be done.
Helper:	Don't make excuses for them. It is a level playing field.
Mechanic:	C'mon. Let's break for lunch. (*shaking his head*) He tried to steal my lunch! Ha! Ha! Ha!

The Mechanic and the Helper put the supplies together with the ladders secured in a central spot as they would every day at lunch…a familiar ritual. They sit on the five gallon paint buckets and face the audience. They eat.

Mechanic: What were we talking about...yes...the business. You asked about this job, for example. I tell Father Mack that he needs Ox-line paint. He comes to me and he says that someone else has bid lower for the job. But I told him my price is fair and that my work is the best and we will get the job done on time. Next week, you will see, we will begin the outside of the church...and not THAT is a big job. In fact, remind me to look around outside before we leave today. We need to estimate how much paint we need to buy. And again, we will buy good paint...that will last. Father Mack should be coming here any minute with some money...

Helper: We are waiting, then. We are...waiting for the dough!

Mechanic: Yes, we are...waiting for the dough. (*pause*) Do you remember the first week we worked together? What happened that one day?

Helper: You will never let me forget, will you? It hasn't happened since.

Mechanic: You broke the first rule of painting!

Helper: (*by way of explanation*) I remember I was painting the ceiling, using the roller and the extension pole, and I was looking up all the while painting, when...it happened.

Mechanic: So what is the first rule of painting? Shall we say it together?

The Mechanic and Helper look directly at audience and shout together absurdly.

Mechanic: The first rule of painting! (*together*) DON'T SPILL THE PAINT!

Helper: (*re-enacting*) I'm looking up at the ceiling, like this and ka-plunk...I knocked over five gallons of paint.

Mechanic: An expensive lesson as well...Ha! Ha! (*enter Father Mack*) Here he is...right on time.

Enter Father Mack, middle-aged priest. With him is another painter, Mr. DeCarlo, 40's, slicked—black, jet black hair. He wears a thick gold chain... rings...and touches of black and red paint splatters about his painter's cloths.

Priest: (*tentative smile*) Hello my friend. (handshake with Mechanic) How are you? How is it going? (*nods to helper*) Yuno, the work is quite good. Is there anything you need?

Mechanic: (heartfelt) It is good to see you again, Father. (*He is puzzled by the other painter's presence*) We are fine here…Going very well, in fact….

Priest: This is Mr. DeCarlo. (awkward) I need to speak with you for a moment… (*Priest escorts Mechanic away to stage left*) …over here.

The Priest and the Mechanic express their conversation in pantomime. Father Mack hands to the Mechanic an envelope (money) for the work and supplies thus far. As they "speak," the Priest is informing him that he has awarded the contract for the exterior of the church to DeCarlo. The Mechanic, affable at first, becomes visibly shaken and animated and agitated. Mumbled bits of speech become audible as the disagreement escalates.

DeCarlo, with a cocky attitude, approaches the helper who is finishing lunch.

DeCarlo: Hey kid…The name's DeCarlo…everyone calls me D.C. (*handshake*) nice work…very nice work. (*pause-musing*) Listen! (stealing glances) Are you interested in a little work on the side? You know, when the old man is sleeping. I just landed some big accounts and some big numbers, especially this exterior job, and I could use a good man like you… You don't look like some rookie, greenhorn mechanic. What do you say? Here's my card. (*hands one*) "Cadillac Construction." Remember it. Send me a text when you come to your senses.

Helper: Thanks D.C. Did you say that *you* have the exterior job on *this* church?

DeCarlo: Why so surprised? C'mon, you play the game. We bid nice and low…and maybe there are a few cost over-runs later… you call me and I will show you how to climb the ladder, kid because we are *growing*, man…not just painting either. Hey, what's your name?

(*Mechanic is arguing /upset with the priest. Bits are heard*)

Mechanic: I don't understand? You come to me? We've been on this... (*mumble ad/lib*)... Why should I...

DeCarlo: It's getting hot in here. (*gestures to priest and mechanic*) I'm going outside to look around...place gives me the shivers...

DeCarlo exits. Helper crumbles the card in disgust. He watches the mechanic keeping his distance.)

Priest: Calm down! Don't take it so personally.

Mechanic: How could you do this? I am so disappointed...I was counting on you! I thought ...you promised me...

Priest: (*loud*) It was not my decision! (*silence*) The council controls the finances! The council has financial obligations that have nothing to do with you. They decided to go with the lowest bid! I'm sorry.

Mechanic: (*begins to cough, choke*) I am...Why didn't you speak to me? (*cough*) We had an understanding... (*choking*) excuse me, I need some air...

The mechanic exits to side. Silence. Finally, the helper approaches the priest.

Helper: (*respectfully*) Father, can I have a word with you please? (*gestures*) He will be all right...he chokes like that when he gets upset. Father?

Priest: Yes. What is it?

Helper: The man you hired today is a thief. You cannot trust him. He is a dishonest man. Let me show you...come over here a minute. (*They walk to the five gallon paint buckets.*) My partner is upset because you may as well hang yourself... Let me explain. See these buckets? They read "Ox-line Paints." A very high-quality and expensive paint. Do you know anything about paint?

Priest: No, Not really.

Helper: In fact, how do we know that this is Ox-line paint? With all due respect, Father. How do you know that we didn't buy cheap paint and pour it into Ox-line buckets? (*whispers*) Cheap paint in expensive buckets!

Priest: I see what you mean. I trust Yuno. He would never do that.

Helper: That's right. He would never cheat you…keep you waiting…not show up. You made a mistake Father…you and the council are about to hang yourselves.

Priest: You know that this is true? About switching the paint?

Helper: Switching materials is nothing…quite routine with thieves. Have you checked DeCarlo's insurance? Is he licensed? This guy you hired is a snake. Let's say he climbs a ladder and he goes down when no one is around and he claims an injury. He sues the church for a big settlement.

Priest: What? Sue the church?

Helper: Why not? Father. Why don't you go and speak with Yuno. He is feeling humiliated. Go and straighten this thing out. One more thing…Is there any way we can still bid on the job? The exterior?

Priest: Why yes. I suppose if you would change your bid? To tell you the truth, it's a matter of dollars and cents…the lowest bid. Church finances are struggling and…that is how it is right now.

Helper: How far off are we? How much lower must we bid?

Priest: Five hundred dollars.

Helper: Okay. Consider it done. Tell the council and tell Yuno. Tell him that his *partner* has decided to lower the bid and that he needs to speak with him right away. Thank you.

The priest exits. The Helper takes an empty five gallon bucket and disappears into the sacristy. He re-emerges with the bucket full of water. It is heavy and awkward. The Mechanic re-enters and walks directly to the helper.

Mechanic: Why did you tell him that we could work for less money? There is no way! (*sees bucket with water*) What is that? What are you doing? Water? You are thinning out the paint! You did not learn this from me!

Helper: Don't look at me that way…you know as well as anyone that this is the reason we are losing bids. We tried it your way. They are all of them outbidding us. Nobody is interested

	in quality anymore…they won't pay for it anymore Yuno! It's a matter of dollars and cents…to compete…
Mechanic:	It is stealing! You did not learn this from me!
Helper:	It is not stealing! It is business! It is not stealing for God's sake. No one cares…its business…and we really have no choice anymore.

The helper kneels at the buckets preparing to pour the water into the paint bucket to thin it out, resuming his intentions. He is embarrassed by his actions but believes it is necessary. He stirs the thinned paint with a paint stick)

Helper:	What are you waiting for? Give me a hand here…You must act! Don't wait. Waiting is absurd.

The mechanic comes out of his stupor and dramatically pushes the helper aside and he dramatically spills the five gallon paint bucket, tipping with his foot the tainted, water-thinned bucket of paint on the ground.

Mechanic:	You will not do this in front of me! You will show me respect! You did not learn this from me!

At this moment, DeCarlo and the priest re-enter in a panic. DeCarlo is furious and he is bulldozing his way through the priest who is attempting to block him. He shoves the priest aside violently and advances to physically attack the helper. At first the helper is unprepared for the onslaught. The scene should be as violent as possible.)

DeCarlo:	(*menacing*) What did you say to him? You son of a…!

(He slams the helper with both hands a very powerful jolt to the chest and shoulders as the first blow of a fist fight.)

DeCarlo:	(*violent*) I am going to murder you. Damn you, kid. (*They are literally fist-fighting and scrambling through and over the pews*) What did you call me! A cheat! Damn you kid!

(There is violent mayhem …ad lib)

Priest:	Get Out! Get Away! Stop!

Mechanic:	Stop him!
Priest:	I will call the police…Get out of here!
DeCarlo:	(*realizing the futility of chasing the helper*) I will not forget this! Watch your back, kid!

Still furious, DeCarlo kicks over the ladder (crash) and storms out of the church. Priest…mechanic…helper…stunned silence.

Priest:	(*still frantic*) I will call the police…My God…I am shaking…My God!
Mechanic:	(*soothing him*) Calm down. I know his type, Father. He won't be back.
Helper:	He was going to kill me. (*strained laugh*) Do you believe what just happened? He tried to kill me.
Mechanic:	It is over…he is gone. All he wanted was the money for the job and he knows he has lost it. He is gone and he won't be coming back.
Priest:	Did you see how he exploded? (*to both*) I am sorry about all of this. (pause) About the money…the five hundred dollars. I am sorry…please forget the money. I will explain it all to the council. We should never have hired that man! (*priest exits, still dazed*) I'm sorry.
Helper:	Maniac! Lunatic! (*goes over to pick up the ladder*)
Mechanic:	(*regrouping*) What now? I guess…we work!

The mechanic and the helper join each other at the spilled paint buckets in the center of the stage. They both look down at the spilled paint! They begin to laugh as a release of tension…an absurd hearty laugh, pointing at the spilled paint and buckets. They laugh hysterically and uncontrollably as they pantomime comically the spill scene and the fight scene and the coughing and so on. They have tears in their eyes from laughter.

Mechanic:	(*recovering*) Well, let's get this cleaned up. You realize what we did here, of course.
Helper:	Yes, of course. We broke the first rule of painting! Shall we say it together?
Mechanic:	Yes, of course! And what is the first rule of painting? (*together…inviting the audience to respond with them…all*

together…players with audience…) DON'T SPILL THE PAINT!

(Lights dim slowly and the two painters stand together motionless, as statues, side by side. Slowly they slip soundlessly behind a church column. Light illuminates the cross and the altar and candles and all things sacred. Without fuss, the old woman returns and ignores the painters…they are not there. As before, she kneels to pray on her rosary beads and we watch a moment…)

Lights Out

The short stories and one-act play presented in The Baywood Tales were written for those who seek classic mainstream literature. Dr. Kennedy is a master storyteller whose spirited writing is poignant and delightfully accessible. His narratives will enliven within you the warmth that endures forever within your heart.